I'LL REMEMBER YOU

Hell YEAH! Book Eleven

Aron's Homecoming

SABLE HUNTER

"I'll Remember You - Hell Yeah! Book Eleven is not meant to be a stand-alone book. It ties loose ends together from previous books and brings Aron McCoy home. There will be references to earlier events."

Continuing the Hell Yeah! Series with Book Eleven – Aron's Homecoming!

Aron and Libby McCoy became husband and wife. No woman could desire a more perfect love. But tragedy struck... while diving on their honeymoon, Aron does not come up from beneath the blue waters off the Cayman Islands. A massive rescue mission is launched, but the only clues found were his wedding ring and later a shredded wet suit covered in blood. The McCoy family is devastated. Libby is heartbroken - but none of them are willing to give up.

At the end of Skye Blue, Noah McCoy receives a phone call from his cousin, Jaxson, that he has spotted a man who is the mirror image of Aron working at a ranch in Northern Mexico. Noah, determined to make his family whole again, takes off with Skye to see for himself. But on the way, he calls their PI, Roscoe, and finds out that there is more at stake - Aron may be alive, but he may be in more danger than the family ever thought possible.

'I'll Remember You' will give the reader a chance to see the whole McCoy clan and friends come together to right a wrong that is tearing apart a family. There is action, adventure, a wedding, babies being born, a Christmas family reunion and enough love and tenderness to make you grab your heart and wish you could be a McCoy.

*Content Warning: This version of the Hell Yeah! Series contains Explicit Content.

Six brothers. One Dynasty—

TEBOW RANCH.

Meet the McCoy brothers and their friends— men who love as hard as they play.

Texas Cowboys – nothing hotter.

HELL YEAH!

Take a moment to check out Sable's current and upcoming projects.

Visit her on:
Website: http://www.sablehunter.com
Facebook: https://www.facebook.com/authorsablehunter
Email: sablehunter@rocketmail.com

Check out all of Sable's books on Amazon
http://www.amazon.com/author/sablehunter

Cover and Technical Advising by Added Touches
http://www.addedtouches.com

CONTENTS

Chapter One

Aron and Libby's Wedding Night

"Come back here, Libby, you're wiggling all over the place." Aron tried in vain to pin her to the bed, but she was scooting around beneath the sheets like a little gopher. "What are you doing down there?"

"I'm on an undercover mission." He heard her mumble about the time he felt his underwear being tugged on.

"Ah, now I know what you're up to. You're prowling around down there after my manly business." He teased as a muffled giggle met his ears. Soft breaths fanned against his swelling cock. Every time Aron heard Libby laugh, it was as if he were seeing a rainbow for the first time.

"We're married now, Mr. McCoy." Her tongue twirled around the tip end of his rod. "This is community property."

In spite of the mind-boggling pleasure, Aron laughed. An overpowering wave of love swept over him. He flung the sheet back and exposed his gorgeous wife.

His wife.

"God, I'm going to love being married to you."

She looked up at him, all the love in the world shining in her eyes, and he thought his heart would burst. "Mrs. Aron McCoy." Libby beamed. "Who would've ever thought it?"

Biting her lower lip, she concentrated on the task at hand, intrigued by the thick thrust of his cock pushing into her palm. Rubbing her lips across the wide crest, she purred to find it was hot to the touch, slightly damp with his excitement. A waterfall of tingling sensations cascaded down her body. She became wet, the intimate muscles of her sex opening and closing, longing to be filled.

Libby ached, lord, she ached. Loving Aron was more than a want; it was a necessity.

"Always and forever, Libby." His next breath caught in his throat as she slid her tongue over the thick head with one slow, luscious lick. "Mercy!" Incredible heat flamed through his loins as she took him into the honeyed recesses of her mouth. Her kisses captivated him, they were pure magic. Aron wove his fingers through her silken hair. Watching her love him, seeing his cock disappear between her lips was amazing.

This was his woman. The knowledge of what they'd been through and the miracle of their love only made the experience sweeter. This was more than sex; this was a celebration of their commitment. Aron had to bite his lip to keep from moaning. He didn't know what was better, the ecstasy of the act or the wonder on her face as she brought him pleasure.
"I never thought this day would come. You're mine, Libby. Mine." She didn't speak, but she was listening. He could tell because she petted him, caressing his thigh, his sac, holding the base of his dick as she sucked him deep – that hot, pink tongue laving the sensitive underside of his shaft.

"Uh-hmmmmm," she agreed, making him gasp anew. His Libby had been innocent, he was her first and he'd have it no other way. But she sure as hell knew how to drive him crazy. With lips and tongue, she stroked and sucked hungrily, hollowing her cheeks and taking as much of him into the wet velvet of her mouth as she could.

"Hell yeah," Aron couldn't contain the growl. "Perfect." And she was – perfect for him. She came into his life when he'd given up on love and showed him what it really meant. Words weren't sufficient to describe the exquisite pleasure sizzling from his balls, to his shaft, and right up his spine. It was like being bathed in ecstasy, a euphoria which intensified, building – filling him with desperation to claim her body as surely as he'd claimed her heart. When he'd given her his name, he'd also given her his devotion, his future – his life.

Aron's thighs tightened, straining to hold back his release. It felt too good to let go so quickly. Beads of sweat were popping out on his forehead, his shoulders. He was awash in heat, trying to stem the rapture, to give her time to play all she wanted. "Fuck…" he groaned when she let his cock slip from her lips, as she moved down to lick and suck at his balls. Aron was quaking, his control was slipping. Staccato bursts of sensation flowed through his body, making his dick throb as he strained to relish a few more moments.

One more kiss. One more lick from that velvety tongue.

Aron was holding Libby, his fingers tangled in her hair, the other hand rubbing her shoulder. His hips were flexing upward, pushing his cock into her mouth in short, sweet strokes. Barely hanging onto the precipice, Aron sought to stem his release. It was torture, but he didn't want their first sexual act as man and wife to end by his cumming between her sexy lips. He needed to be inside of her when he came, driving deep and hard. Her mouth was amazing, but her pussy was tight, sweet – and it was home.

But he had priorities, the first orgasm of the night belonged to Libby.

"Up here, baby." She whimpered her objection when he pulled out of her tender grip. "It's my turn." Guiding her to lie beside him, he stole a kiss. "I want to push my tongue deep inside of you, suck that cherry clit and make you cum all over my face."

The smile she gave him was worth a million dollars. A rosy blush stained her cheeks. "You're determined to make this honeymoon perfect. Aren't you?"

"I'm determined to make your life perfect." Taking one of her hands in each of his, he held them next to her head while he straddled her small body – kissing her lips, sucking her neck – licking those luscious tits before making a place for his shoulders between her thighs. "Beautiful," he whispered as he gazed at the pretty pink flesh before him. She was hot, glistening with arousal, and the noises she made as he kissed the tender folds gave him as much satisfaction as when she'd been pleasuring him with her tongue. Sucking her clit into his mouth, he licked it, twirled it – worshiping her in the most intimate way he knew how.

Libby closed her eyes, drowning in the attention her husband was giving her. He knew exactly what to do, the man was a master. Waves of bliss were swamping her. She couldn't be still. Opening her legs wider, she invited him to do anything he desired. Threading her fingers in his hair, she raised her head – hypnotized by the sight of the wide shouldered cowboy whose every intention was to bring her joy.

This was heaven. Every kiss, suckle, lick or nibble made her hips buck. "Aron. I love you so." The admission was wrung from her lips as ecstasy commanded the attention of every cell in her body. He didn't speak, he didn't have to – he showed her he loved her with every kiss, ever lick, pushing his tongue deep inside of her as she lifted her hips wanting more.

The pleasure was more than she could process. An amazing heat built within her, a firestorm which flared red-hot as she flew apart. "Aron!" With grasping hands, she held on to his shoulders, trying to pull him up. "I need you. Please." Her sheath was still fluttering amid her orgasm when he thrust inside her with one sure, powerful stroke. "Yes!"

This was not their first time to make love, but every time was rapture. He filled her so completely, stretching her perfectly as he pushed in and pulled back. The pleasure did not abate as he possessed her; rather it continued and multiplied, making her writhe and scream. Her fingernails marked him as she clung to the man she loved.

Aron was losing his mind. Holding himself up on his arms, he looked down into her face and then down to where they were joined. God, she was beautiful. He'd worked his way in and now his balls were slapping her pussy with every stroke. She was still cumming, one climax had flowed into another and his cock was being milked with every spasm. He was losing control, no matter how much he wanted to postpone the inevitable. Throwing his head back, he drove deep. His balls were so tight they hurt and his cock was near to bursting. He knew he was either going to cum hard or die. Bending to suck at her nipple, he gave himself over to the mindless sensual pleasure, losing himself in the love he had for this woman – his bride. Undulating his hips in a sensual figure eight, he let his cock drag in and out, watching her face as she surrendered to him – giving herself up to one more sweet release. Closing his eyes he let go, fucking her with pounding, hammering strokes. Burying himself to the hilt, he groaned as hot jets of his semen filled her. "Libby! God, I adore you." As she tossed her head from side to side, she held on to him – not only with her hands, but with her pussy – gripping, rippling, milking him of every drop. Aron shook, collapsing onto her, careful not to crush, but needing to feel her all the way up and down his body. "I love you so much."

Libby wrapped her arms around him, cradling Aron to her. "I know. I can feel it. And I love you more than anything."

4

"We're going to be together forever, Libby. Nothing will ever tear us apart. I promise." He was thinking of her remission, the battle she'd fought and won against leukemia. What would he do without her? Easing off to one side, he pulled her against him, placing his hand between them and over her tummy. "I will cherish you and our family all the days of my life."

Libby didn't doubt him. This was her Aron. "Thank you for marrying me."

"Let me rest up, and we'll do it all over again."

"Get married?" She teased.

"No, silly." He kissed her. "I did that wedding thing right this time, no need for do-overs."

Cupping the side of his face, she looked deep into his eyes. "As long as you do me over and over again, we won't have any trouble."

"I called 'Tag' baby, you're mine forever, you demanding little minx."

***

Honeymooning in the Caymans

"You owe me one, Libby Pearl." Aron waded into the water. "And I expect to collect - tonight."

She ran her fingers down his back, dipping into the waistband of his wetsuit. "What if I promise to pay you back with interest." Libby playfully pinched his hip.

"Hey!" Catching her to him, he held her close, loving the feel of the small bump between them. Their babies. "Ah, a sexual incentive program. I can live with that." The tide lapped up to their waist. Aron put his chin on her head and stared out at the ocean.

"You really don't like the water very much, do you?" Taking his hand, she gazed at her husband. To her he was invincible; a superhero who conquered both on the football field and in the rodeo arena. But his greatest accomplishment was holding his family together after they'd lost their parents. He was strong, solid, and compassionate – the best man she'd ever known. The idea that anything gave him pause was unfathomable to her.

"Nope." Aron squinted toward the horizon, noting cruise ships in the distance and a beautiful yacht, the Isabella, anchored not too far off shore. "The truth is, I almost drowned as a child on a summer vacation trip to Galveston Island." He could still remember the clutching horror as he'd slipped beneath the waves. "My folks rented an inner-tube for me to float in just off shore." We'd gone to the Gulf of Mexico often, until this incident. "Jacob was just a baby, so I was bobbing around out there all alone."

"Aron…" She could tell the memory bothered him.

"But something happened, Mom and Dad were visiting with another couple and I wasn't paying attention, just splashing and staring down into the water, looking for fish. The tide was going out and I drifted too far. When I looked up, I could barely make out my parents on shore." Aron's voice got distant with the memory. "I panicked, slipping down into the tube and under the water." He laughed wryly. "Swimming was a skill I hadn't perfected. You should have seen me. I must have been a sight. Swallowing water, clasping at the rubber, fighting and kicking to get a hand-hold, I screamed every time I surfaced." The truth was, Aron had almost given up. "But a hand reached down, caught me, and pulled me up and into his arms. My father saved me."

"All right, that's it. We're not doing this." Libby was adamant. "We'll go shopping instead."

She turned, starting to tromp out of the water with fins on her feet. Aron thought she looked like a tropical penguin. "Shopping!" He grabbed her arm to halt her exit. "Stop it." Disappointing her was not an option. "I'd rather dog-paddle to Cuba than go look at girly giggle-gaggles." That wasn't exactly true, but he was trying to use his considerable charm, here. "Come on, I want to do this."

Libby moved closer to him, close enough she could kiss his chest, licking a few of the tiny water droplets from his skin. "Are you sure?"

"Positive."

"It's safe, I promise."

"I believe you."

"Great!" She bounced in the water. "Come on! Let's go." She grabbed him by the forearm and began towing him deeper. "This will be so much fun. I've always wanted to snorkel. We're going to have such a wonderful life Aron. Adventure after adventure."

"I'd rather have orgasm after orgasm." He muttered, envisioning a lifetime of rescuing Libby from one perilous situation after another. Visions of the bar fight where she walloped Sabrina came to mind. And the terror he'd felt when Molly had thrown her after being spooked by the chicken snake. Both times she'd been fine, but every small bruise and scrape he found on her body just made him weak in the knees.

"How about both? I want to do it all, Aron." She held her arms up like she wanted to hug the sky. "I've been given a second chance at life; and not just any kind of life…" She turned and wrapped her arms around his neck, hugging him hard. "I have a chance to live and love with you and that's more than I ever dreamed."

He enclosed her in his arms, loving the way she cuddled up to him. Closing his eyes, he vowed he would never disappoint her or let her down. Making Libby happy was his aim in life. "You know I can't resist you, you have me in the palm of your hand. Let's go check out the fish, I'm getting pruney already."

"Okay!" She perked up, pulled down her mask and dove in, swimming out a few feet. "Come on, slow poke!"

Aron grunted and followed suit. As soon as he was beneath the waves, he was fascinated. Maybe this wouldn't be too bad. True, he probably went up for air too often, but he had to get his nerves settled. Watching Libby, he smiled around his breathing tube, swallowing a bit of water. Immediately he went up, so he could cough without choking. What he'd said was true; he would do anything for Libby Fontaine McCoy.

Even drown.

He smiled at the thought. Taking a deep breath, he dipped beneath the surface again, searching for her. She'd been right. It was another world beneath the waves. He'd never seen a bluer blue than the color of these waters. And the fish were beyond anything he'd ever seen before - all hues and shapes, darting here and there. But the most beautiful sight was Libby, cavorting and dancing about, obviously thrilled by what she was seeing. She motioned him over and he went to her, watching a school of parrot fish glide by. The look of absolute wonder on her face was worth any discomfort he could ever experience.

He had to go up for air more often than she did, but they finally got a rhythm and a routine going. She led the way and he followed. Amused, Aron wondered if it would always be like that. Oh, he knew he was the man and he was alpha enough to have no doubts on his masculinity, but where Libby was concerned, he was weak. He loved her beyond reason. As long as he had breath in his body, he would turn heaven on its side to make all of her wishes come true.

Laughing, he watched her pick up a starfish, point at a seahorse and wave at him frantically when a dolphin came close enough for her to touch. That was a dang big fish – mammal – hell, whatever. Reluctantly, he had to admit; this had been a good idea. He bet he would hear her talking about this for years to come.

Going up for another gulp of air, he looked around at the island. The Westin resort, where they were staying, was a five star hotel with every amenity a honeymooning couple could desire. All in all, the Caymans were a beautiful place with crystal clear waters and pristine white sand beaches. Aron was glad he'd brought Libby. True, if he'd had his druthers, they'd have gone camping in Wyoming. But pleasing her was pleasing him.

Taking another dive, he glanced around for his wife, always trying to be conscious of where she was. She reminded him more of a mermaid than he could have imagined, with long dark hair flowing behind her, that gorgeous body glimmering in the sunlight. The almost imperceptible swell of her stomach only made her more attractive to him, the evidence of their love. Okay, there she was and she was safe and happy – he raised a hand in her direction and she waved back.

So, what could he examine to amuse himself? Swimming just below the surface, so his snorkel tube stuck up for air, Aron paddled farther out, looking for his own brand of adventure. Noticing a small cave in the distance, he swam closer. This was intriguing, more his style than brightly colored fish and seaweed. Staring at the dark opening, he noticed something glimmering just inside, right where the sun-dappled sand gave way to shadow. Could it be gold? He grinned. Now this was more like it. If Aron McCoy was going to be messing around in the ocean, at least he needed to find some sunken treasure. 'Arg! Matey!' he thought as he drifted down to investigate.

Taking one last look in the distance toward Libby, who was nose to nose with some big orange fish, he ducked into the rocky opening and bent to retrieve the shiny object. Damn. Picking it up, it was obvious to him he'd stumbled upon something of value. Holding his breath past the point it was comfortable, he studied his find - a gold coin with the face of a beautiful girl. Gazing at the image from long ago, he smiled, realizing the woman could have been Libby. There was a distinct resemblance. He couldn't wait to show it to her. Despite his burning lungs, he went a few feet farther, just to see if there were more gold coins on the floor of the cave. Hmmmm, there was none that he saw, but there was very little light filtering into the darkness. Maybe he'd come back with a lamp. Grasping the coin in his hand and needing air, he started to turn and swim out of the cave when the waters seemed to shimmer around him. Movement, like the world vibrated for a second. A muffled sound reached his ears. Aron looked up and saw a dark shape coming toward him. Rocks. It was a cave-in! Desperately, he started backing out. But he didn't make it. A crushing blow to the back of his head made his gasp, losing his last bit of air. He swallowed water as he lost consciousness.

The last image Aron had in his mind was of Libby...

***

Libby had never had so much fun in her life. Since she entered Aron's world, everything had changed. The idea that she could look forward to many years with the man of her dreams was flippin' amazing. A blue spotted fish was playing peek-a-boo with her around some seaweed. The sun-dappled water looked like someone was spinning a huge disco ball overhead and a small sea turtle came right up to her and stared. Libby noticed while meeting his gaze that her eyes had crossed and she giggled. The giggle made her choke a bit, so she glided upward, kicking her feet as she broke the surface.

Where was Aron? She hadn't seen him near her. Honestly, she halfway expected to glance up on shore and see him lounged out in all of his manly glory, half-naked girls in bikinis tempting him with grapes or something. But no, he wouldn't go to shore without her, nor would he accept any bits of fruit from the fingers of sexy women. She would bet her life on the faithfulness of Aron McCoy. He would never leave her nor forsake her.

Dipping back down, she looked around for him. Why, that rascal. He had swum away from their area. She paddled out farther from shore, looking for him. Nothing. Hmmmmm. Surfacing again, she took another few breaths, then dove back and traveled parallel to Seven Mile beach. He had to be here somewhere.

Several times she saw something out of the corner of her eye, and would whirl around, expecting to find him right behind her. But he wasn't. Libby began to panic – she swam to the left and to the right. She went up to the surface, countless times. She went to shore and ran up and down the sand, looking, calling, "Aron! Aron!" People stared at her. They started coming to her and she cried. Several helped her look. She went back into the water, searching and searching.

Libby didn't give up looking, not until two men came and urged her to sit while they began looking in her stead. One of them called the authorities. "Help me, please." She began to cry. "Help, Aron. I can't find him." Big hiccupping sobs racked her body.

"You need water." Somebody urged her to drink. "You're too hot."

Libby felt sick, but she couldn't stop. She pulled away from them and ran back into the water, not even putting on her gear. The people who were helping her, caught her – pulling her back and she literally collapsed, screaming Aron's name at the top of her lungs. "Aron!"

A concerned couple called emergency services and a doctor from the hotel came down to see to Libby. A whole crowd of people hovered around her. After he'd learned she was pregnant and under such stress, the doctor wanted to call for an ambulance. But Libby adamantly refused to leave.

"Who can we contact for you?"

"Jacob McCoy." She gave them Tebow's main number. "I want Aron!" She wailed as her heart broke.

***

ON THE NAUTA YACHT - ISABELLA

"Senorita, come quickly. Paco has pulled a man from the water."

Martina Delgado slammed her drink down and stood; fire in her brown eyes "No! Is he insane? We can trust no one!"

"We assumed he was dead, Senorita." The man held his arms out. "He was floating face-down."

"Assumptions kill. Why would he bring a dead body on board?" Slinging a towel over her shoulders, she started walking across the top-deck of the Isabella where she'd been sunning. "The Toro Cartel will do anything to hurt me, even planting a bomb on a body to blow us sky-high." Hurrying down the stairs, closely followed by her first-mate, she flung her long dark hair over her shoulder in frustration. "Did anyone search it? Where is this body? Perhaps he's just a Cuban refugee."

"Sanchez put him in your office on the couch."

"My office? In God's name, why?" Huffing her anger, she rushed down the hall. Pulling open the door, she found two men standing over a body laid out along a sectional sofa. "Stand back! Let me see."

Most young women would feel uncomfortable surrounded by men carrying AK47s, but Martina didn't even notice it. She was the Diosa de la Guerra, the Goddess of War, queenpin of the El Duro Cartel. Her reach was wide; her word was law and anyone who got in Martina's way paid for the indiscretion with their life. "Is he breathing?"

"Yes, Senorita." Paco cleaned up the puddles off the shiny hardwood floors, before his mistress could slip and fall.

"There is bleeding from his skull. I fear he is injured internally. He needs x-rays and an MRI." Juan Carlos, her personal physician, glanced at her for direction. "Shall we help him or let him die?"

From what Martina could see, the stranger was broad, tall, muscled-up, in other words – ripped. Paco had removed his mask, but the victim's head was turned, facing the back cushions. "Let me see his face." They rolled him toward her. She moved closer to get a better look. And when she did...

'Ay Dios mio!' she thought with wonder. No matter how long she lived, she would never forget this man. The Texan, Aron

McCoy. "Any identification?" Her voice did not betray her recognition or the emotion she felt.

"No, Senorita."

Aron had visited Los Banos twice to inspect the prize Criollo-Corriente bulls her father's family had bred for generations. She placed a hand on Aron's chest. The hand trembled. How many times had she dreamed of touching him? But he'd never more than acknowledged her existence with a polite greeting, even when she had blatantly come on to him. "Do not let him die." As much as she tried, Martina could not keep the concern from her voice.

"Shall we take him back to shore? I can make some calls." The doctor took his stethoscope and listened to the patient's heartbeat.

"Can't you help him? We have the necessary equipment on board."

Dr. Carlos started to speak, but he was interrupted by Captain Fernandez. "Diosa, I have been alerted of earthquakes. There is no tsunami alert, but I would feel better if we headed out to open sea." The elegant older gentleman, intensely loyal, spoke from the doorway.

Martina tore her eyes from Aron. "Is Alessandra back?" Her sister and her bodyguard had taken the banana boat to the island so Alessandra could do some shopping. The younger Delgado sister lived a different life from the elder – less worry. And that was the way it should be.

"No, Diosa, shall I phone Ruiz?" The captain asked, taking his cell from his pocket.

"Yes, she needs to return quickly." Martina walked to the porthole. Already she could see trucks and cars on the beach. A search was being launched, of that she was certain. "Leave me. I must think." Her words weren't harsh, but she was instantly obeyed. Displeasing Rodrigo Espinoza's granddaughter could be hazardous to your health. For decades the cartel had ruled the Sonora region with an iron fist, transporting cocaine and heroin from Columbia across the border to America.

Going to her dressing room, she wet a washcloth with warm water. Pulling up a chair beside the sofa, she began to clean his face. "You are safe," she whispered. "I will help you." As she stroked his brow, Martina remembered the first time he'd visited Los Banos.

She had been home from university on spring break, arguing with Tomas over the fact her new Maserati had a bent front bumper. As far as she was concerned, a new one was in order. Her father disagreed. Refusing to take 'no' for an answer, she followed him to the barn where he was meeting two American cowboys. From the moment her gaze fell on Aron McCoy her panties had been wet. The whole weekend he'd visited, Martina had shadowed him, coming on to him in every way she knew how. She'd touched him, brushed against him, even tried to play footsie under the dining table, but he seemed to be totally immune to her seductive moves. His second visit had been different. He'd handled all of the paperwork from the barn, staying only a couple of hours. Although the handsome Texan had never given her an ounce of encouragement, she had still fallen for him completely – lock, stock and barrel.

If only….Martina smiled. Now, he lay on her yacht at her mercy. She knew an opportunity when it reared up and bit her in the ass. She pondered her options; she could send someone ashore with him or she could keep him for herself.

Beneath her touch, Aron shrugged his massive shoulders and groaned. "Where am…what happened?"

"Be still. You must take it easy. How do you feel?"

"Like shit." He threw the sheet from his body – his magnificent body. His right hand was tightly clutched around something. She wondered what… until she glimpsed the left hand and then the previous thought vanished from her mind like a poof of smoke. There was a wedding band on his ring finger. Dios!

"You need to rest." She touched his knee, attempting to comfort him.

"What's going on?" He had a stunned, confused look on his face. "Who are you?"

"You were injured." She grabbed her phone and pressed the number to call Juan Carlos back. "Do you remember how?"

"No." Shaking his head, Aron closed his eyes as if in great pain. "No, I don't remember." Another groan slipped through his lips. "Head hurts."

"Can you tell me your name? Is there someone I can call?"

Silence. Another groan. "No. I don't know my name, I can't remember…" His voice trailed off and he went limp. Aron had lost consciousness once more, and his breathing was shallow and erratic.

When the doctor returned, Martina hurriedly told him what she'd observed. He checked Aron's vitals. "I'm going to give him morphine, 5 milligrams. While he's resting, I'll prepare to run the necessary tests to ascertain the extent of his injuries."

Martina watched him give Aron a shot, standing by until his breathing evened out and he went back to sleep. "I'll sit with him until you're ready."

"That isn't necessary, Senorita."

"It's what I want. Call Paco and check to see if my sister is back on board and report to me." She didn't even look at him. Martina knew she would not be challenged.

Chapter Two

BACK AT TEBOW

"What do you want for your birthday, Badass?" Joseph asked with a twinkle in his eye. "It's less than two weeks away."

"I want a black cayenne Harley Street Glide with a batwing fairing and a split-stream vent." A look of pure lust glazed Isaac's eyes. He was sitting in a big leather chair in front of the fireplace.

"Are you gonna get a side car for Avery?" Cady asked with a grin.

"Foot." Avery said her favorite fake-cuss word as she came up behind Isaac and kissed him on top of the head. "I want a matching bike. With speaker helmets equipped with Bluetooth, so I can whisper sweet nothings in his ear." He wrapped an arm around her neck and pulled her headfirst over the back of the chair into his lap. She was giggling all the way.

The telephone on the desk began to ring. For a moment everybody ignored it, until Joseph got up to get it. When he picked it up, it was obvious Jacob had picked up the line in the kitchen because his voice could be heard trying to calm Libby down. Joseph put the phone on speaker, motioning the others over.

"Calm down, Libby. I can't understand you, Sweetheart." Jacob urged.

"I can't find him, Jacob."

"What? I don't know what you're talking about."

"Aron. I can't find him." She was crying so hard, her voice was shrill.

"What do you mean?" Joseph asked. "Where are you?"

"We went snorkeling off Seven Mile Beach, not far out and he didn't want to do it..." her voice faded.

"Is he okay?" Isaac demanded.

"I can't find him." She repeated, screaming. "He didn't come up."

Joseph, Isaac, Cady and Avery looked at one another in shock. Joseph disconnected and they all went into the kitchen where Jacob, Jessie and Noah were standing around the table. Jacob was still on the phone. "God, Libby. Try not to worry. We'll be there as soon as we can get a flight. You just sit tight." He hung up

and looked at his family. "We've got to get down there." He looked to Joseph. "You go see Lance and get everything squared away here. Isaac, you call Roscoe and let him know and I'll call Bowie Travis." He pointed at Noah. "You get ahold of Kane and Zane. We've got to get to the bottom of this. I just pray by the time we get there, Aron will have shown up."

Nobody moved right away, it was as if time stood still. "I can't believe this." Jessie wiped tears from her eyes. "They're on their honeymoon, for God's sake. What about Nathan?"

Jacob braced himself on the table, his hands visibly shaking. "I don't want to take him with us, he has school. Besides, we don't know anything yet one way or the other. There's no use upsetting him."

"I'll stay with him." Cady offered. Looking at Joseph, she spoke. "Call Beau and Harley, they would want to know."

"You're right." He grabbed his cell phone to place the call.

The family began to prepare to fly to the Caymans, a trip they never thought they'd make. One of their own was in serious trouble, so they all rallied to stand by Libby, to give her strength. All the time, Jacob and Noah were on the phone, calling authorities and authorizing searches. Rescue teams were notified and Joseph alerted as much media coverage on the islands as he could, knowing it would go a long way in insuring that everything that could be done would be done on the rescue mission. Not being able to reach Zane on the phone, Noah drove out to his ranch, knowing they would need him on the trip. The shock sent everyone reeling.

When they were on their way, the trip to the airport was quiet. Jacob was driving, staring at the gleam of the headlights on the highway. "All I can think about was how much he disliked the water. What was he doing snorkeling?" Just the idea that something could've happened to Aron scared him to death. "What are we going to do?"

"We're going to find him, Jacob." Isaac was adamant. "Nothing else is acceptable."

***

BANDERA, TX – LONGHORN BAR with BOWIE TRAVIS MALONE

The drive into Bandera from Vega Verde was only about forty minutes, but Bowie had been on the road so much in the past few weeks, he resented the time it took. If it hadn't been for Tanner, he wouldn't have bothered. But his friend was determined Bowie come meet Micah Wolfe and Tyson Pate who'd recently formed a company with other members of their former SEAL team. Tanner thought they would have a lot in common with Bowie, so he'd made arrangements for them all to have a drink together at Arkey Blue's.

Bowie ran his hand through his heavy mane of hair. "Damn, I need a haircut." His lifestyle was so haphazard, he neglected little things like visiting the barber shop. Finding a parking spot on Main Street wasn't easy this time of night. Arkey Blue's Silver Dollar Saloon pulled in the crowd, much more than the neighboring shops did during the day. He noticed there was at least thirty Harley's parked close, also. Biker clubs loved to ride the scenic hill country roads and camp alongside the Guadalupe. With a grin, he wondered if Isaac McCoy were here. It had been a while since he'd seen him. Giving the biker/cowboy a hard time was one of his favorite sports.

Snatches of Luke Bryan's *My Kind of Night* came floating out of the door every time it opened and closed. Laughter and the sound of pool balls striking together made him smile. Maybe this wouldn't be so bad after all. Walking in, he scanned the crowd for Tanner. He was early, so he would just get a drink and wait. Stepping up the bar, he asked Red for a Shiner beer. The old bartender had been passing out drinks at Arkey Blues for well over a decade. "Where you been, Malone?"

Accepting the longneck after Red had popped the top, he smiled sadly. "I spent the last ten days hunting an inmate who escaped from High Desert Prison and fled into the Mojave Desert."

"Find him?"

"Yea, he had sought shelter in a cave where a den of green rattlesnakes were holed up. When we found him, he'd been bitten a hundred and forty-five times."

"Yuck."

Taking his mind off the unfortunate outcome, Bowie turned to watch a lucky cowboy on the dance floor with a redhead whose bottom end seemed to be attached by a swivel screw – lord, the girl could shimmy. She could move her hips up to her fingertips as the old Elvis song went – she had all the hula dancer's moves with no grass skirt or lei in sight.

Two college age girls who were holding court with about a dozen cowpokes surrounding them, left their charmed circle to come ask him to dance, but Bowie was content to sit and watch. But as he did, he let his eyes wander around the room and that was when he saw her.

She sat at the back, at one of those extra-long tables, all alone. There were empty glasses around her, so it was obvious she'd had company, but they had abandoned her. He took a couple of swigs and watched. After a bit, a girl joined her, drained her glass, laughed and said a word or two, then let herself be pulled back onto the dance floor by an overzealous cowboy.
The doll who'd caught his eye just smiled serenely and continued to watch everyone else.

Bowie hadn't meant to stare, but he couldn't help it. She was beautiful. Strawberry blonde hair, a light tan, freckles if he wasn't badly mistaken, and the biggest pair of green eyes he'd ever seen. He couldn't see much of her body beyond a graceful neck, smooth shoulders and full breasts which looked to just fit his big, hungry hands. But that was enough. A groan of need escaped his lips as he watched – and waited. She didn't look unhappy, singing along with the music, even moving her shoulders and wiggling a little in her seat. He never saw anyone who wanted to dance more than she did. Yet, she sat all alone.

Why wasn't anyone asking her to dance?

Well, he was damn sure the man for the job. Bowie only hesitated a minute or two, making sure she wasn't waiting on a boyfriend who'd stepped out for some reason. And if he had, the man ought to be hog-tied and whipped for leaving her alone for so long. As the last song ended, people made their way from the dance floor. Several girls joined her, leading men by the hand. They took sips of drinks, regrouped, spoke to Angel Face, and then all went back out as soon as the band began the next number.

Except her.

He watched her look at them longingly, sigh and smile as if she'd decided to be happy anyway. Bowie stood, adjusted his slightly swollen package and decided to make his move. When he walked into her line of vision, he caught her eye. She gave him a sweet smile, but didn't try to hold his gaze, looking away almost immediately. Her shyness didn't deter him; he was a man on a mission.

Cassie patted her knee in time to the music, all the while wishing she'd stayed home and finished that second batch of candles. Nothing would do Felicity but she join them in celebrating Cordelia's birthday, but the truth was – they didn't even realize she was here and just sitting and watching everyone else dance made Cassie uncomfortable. The place had been jam packed when they'd entered, so most everyone had seen her arrive. Their taking note of her entrance assured her she wouldn't be inundated with male admirers. It was okay, she was used to it.

Setting her drink aside, she decided to slow down her consumption of liquid. Already she needed to go to the restroom and making that journey was about as pleasant as walking over a bed of hot coals. When she looked up, she saw him. Gracious, all he needed was a horse and a bow and arrow. She had seen men who looked like him on the fronts of those romance novels written about old west maidens who fall for the sons of chiefs. For about five seconds, she drank him in, then forced herself to look away. No use trying to lure him over, she had no bait to fish with.

But oh, how her eyes wanted to stray back and stare. His image was indelibly branded on her mind – long black hair, wide shoulders and eyes which were warm, dark and seemed to see right through her.

Was he walking toward her? Why? A shiver of awareness and nerves made her quiver; she wrapped her arms around herself, wishing she could throw an afghan over her head and hide.

Bowie had to sidestep several dancing couples who were moving to Eric Paslay's *Friday Night*. Once more, she locked eyes with him, a hopeful, inquisitive expression on her face. God, she was adorable. "Could I join you?"

Her eyes widened in surprise, her gaze moving past him, then to the right, as if she expected someone else to join him. "Uh, yes, of course." She motioned to a chair. "Please."
Motioning for a waitress, he held her eye, "What are you drinking?"

With a mischievous glint in her eyes, she answered. "Just lemonade."

Bowie chuckled. "Lemonade it is." He gave a gum-chewing pixie their order and she scampered off. Leaning over toward her, he held out his hand, "Bowie Travis Malone."

"Cassandra Cartwright, Cassie for short." Her voice was soft, but not high-pitched. She had a smooth Southern accent, like a warm breeze blowing through the delta.

"Hello, Cassie for short." The waitress showed back up about that time and as he paid their tab, he stole glances at her, wanting to say just the right thing. Pushing her drink near her hand, he made his move. "I've never seen you here before." Dang, that sounded like he lived in the bar. "My job keeps me on the road, I'm a tracker. But when I'm home, I sometimes come here to unwind."

She pushed aside her watered down drink and replaced it with the fresh one. "No, this is my first time. I don't go out much." Please, she prayed, don't ask me to dance. Don't ask me to dance.

"I don't believe that, a girl like you should be treated to nights out on the town all the time." A warm blush crept up her cheeks; he was so tempted to see how soft her skin was to the touch.

"I keep pretty busy," she offered. "Three afternoons a week, I volunteer at the animal shelter." After she'd said it, she realized how stupid that sounded. People didn't avoid social situations just because they changed cat litter boxes and walked dogs. Led dogs, she corrected herself. And she did pretty well. When she and about six canines, of varying sizes, took off down the street, they looked just like a parade.

"I have a menagerie at my house," he stated as he studied her face. She was nervous of him. He didn't like that. "People who love animals can be trusted, you know."

Cassie nodded her head. "I agree. What do you have?"

Bowie chuckled. "I live out near Camp Verde, which used to house the camels ole' Jefferson Davis commissioned to serve in the U. S. Military. So to preserve the tradition, I built a big log cabin and some outbuildings and filled them with three dogs, five cats, a rabbit, a pot-bellied pig, a horse, a donkey and two camels."

By the time he finished, she was laughing and the sound warmed his heart. "I love it." She clapped her hands. "All I have is a cat and a dachshund at home, but I'd love to have more if I ever get a bigger place."

Something to the right of her kept drawing her attention, but he didn't see anything in particular to look at besides a chair or two. "Where do you live?"

"Not too far from you, actually" She pushed her hair behind one ear. "I know where the Camp Verde site is, I live in the old Sever's place."

Bowie searched his memory, "Oh, yea. I know where you are." And he did. She lived in a small farm house set off by itself on a dirt road. "You're pretty isolated out there. Do you have a far commute to your job?"

"Luckily, I work from home. I make candles to sell." Why was she telling him more than he was asking? She knew why. Cassie was prolonging the conversation and trying to steer it away from him asking her to dance.

"Do they smell as sweet as you?" He was serious, but when she blushed furiously, he wondered if she was unused to being teased.

"Oh, I think they smell much better," she confided. "My favorites smell like the outdoors, especially the ocean one." With a serious nod, she added. "I'm going to see the ocean one day, I've promised myself."

This confused him. They weren't that far from the Gulf. "You've never been to Galveston?" Her small, delicate hands were on the table, cupping her drink. Bowie wanted to reach out and touch her, but it was too soon.

"No," she shook her head. "I stay pretty close. My grandmother lived with me up until a month ago, when she passed. I took care of her, she was bedridden." Chewing on her bottom lip, as if gathering courage, she raised her eyes to his. "Tell me about tracking? That sounds fascinating."

Another song was ending, now was his chance. "Okay, I'll do that, if you'll dance with me." Bowie was happy to ask her, and he expected her to respond with a smile. Instead, he saw her face drop. He'd never seen anyone's demeanor change faster.

Again, she focused on something to her right and answered. "No, thank you."

He didn't want to take 'no' for an answer. Holding her in his arms was too tempting to pass up. "Just one spin around the room. I promise not to wear you out." He stood and offered her his hand. "I'll take care of you."

He didn't understand her reaction. Hanging her head, she looked funny – almost embarrassed.

"I can't." Cassie felt her throat closing up. How stupid was she? For a few glorious minutes she'd been enjoying their talk, pretending she was a normal girl sharing a drink with a guy. But now she'd have to tell him the truth and she'd see that look of pity come over his face.

"You can't dance?" Still holding out his hand like an offering, he sweetened the pot. "I'd love to teach you. I won't step on your toes."

"I can't," she repeated. "I'm so sorry." Dismay colored her words.

"Well, if you don't want to. I understand." He'd been turned down before.

"No, you don't." This time she touched the chair over in the corner, easing it away from the wall. He saw what it was – and her actions made sense. It had been put over to one side because the arms wouldn't go under the table. "I can't walk, much less dance." It was a wheelchair.

Bowie sat back down, feeling like he'd been kicked in the stomach. "I apologize, Cassie. I didn't know."

"Hey, it's okay." She covered her hand with his, squeezing his fingers. He'd been aching to touch her. And now she'd taken the first move. "It was wonderful to be asked."

"Hey, Malone, we're here."

Bowie realized Tanner had come up behind him. Piss poor timing. "Tanner, there's someone I'd like you to meet first." He introduced them. Glancing over his friend's shoulder, he saw the two men waiting near the bar. Damn.

"Go, talk with them. Please." Cassie urged. "I'm fine."
Maybe this was a face-saving opportunity.

He didn't want to, but Tanner seemed to think it was
important. "Don't move. I'll be back," he told Cassie.

She gave him a warm smile and he left her, reluctantly. After
he'd been introduced to Micah and Tyson, Bowie had been glad to
make their acquaintance. They did share interests. Micah had a
spread over near Johnson City and after they'd compared notes, he
realized they had friends in common – the McCoys. Aron and Jacob
had played football with them at Texas.

After they'd agreed to get together again soon, Bowie had
risen to return to Cassie. The whole time he'd been trying to talk
business, all he'd wanted to do was stare into her eyes.

But she was gone.

Bowie ran outside, but there was no sign of her in the
parking lot. Damn. Sighing, he headed toward his truck. That was
okay. He knew where she lived, and all of a sudden, he had a
hankering for candles.

As he climbed behind the wheel, his cell phone buzzed.
"Malone."

"Bowie, it's Jacob. We need you. Aron is missing."

Bowie's heart lurched in his chest. "Where? When? How?"
After he'd been told, he started his truck and put it into gear. "I'll
catch a flight and meet you there."

***

Off the coast of the Caymans – Nauta Yacht Isabella

Waiting for Dr. Carlos to leave, she gave Aron time to settle
into a deep sleep. When his breathing evened out, Martina rose
and came to his side. Taking his left hand between her own, she
worked on the simple gold band until it slipped from his finger. She
put it in the pocket of her silk robe. Next, she walked around to the
other side of the bed and tried to open his fist, curious to see what
he was holding on to for dear life. But she couldn't force open his
hand, Aron was strong.

Standing by him for a few more seconds, she considered her
actions.

He was married.

Someone, somewhere waited on him.

Did she care?

No.

Moving hurriedly from the room, Martina went up on the top deck of the Isabella, staring out toward the shore where increased activity was obvious. Undoubtedly, Aron's absence had been discovered. Without remorse or a second thought, Martina drew back her arm and tossed his wedding band as far into the waves as she could throw it.

"Oh, there you are."

Despite her resolve, Martina jumped at the sound of her sister's voice. "When did you return?"

"Just now." Alessandra leaned over the railing, staring down into the waves. "What's going on?"

"We picked up a passenger." Sometimes a simple explanation is best.

"Care to elaborate?" The younger girl leaned her chin on the top rail, wiggling her bottom in time to the music coming from the outside speakers.

Martina smiled. "Christmas has come early this year. A present I've always wanted has fallen in my lap – finders keepers, losers weeper."

* * *

Seven Mile Beach – Caymans

"You need to go inside, Ms. McCoy. It's getting dark." A female deputy sat by Libby.

She had been questioned over and over and despite their urgings, Libby had not left the beach. How could she? "I can't," she protested. "Aron will be back soon. He'll look for me. I have to stay."

"When will your family arrive?"

Libby had to pause, it was hard to think. "Tomorrow, soon as they can." Calling Aron's family had been so hard.

"Fine. It's not good for you to be alone."

"It's my fault." She whispered.

"How?" The deputy asked, realizing this wasn't a confession.

"He didn't want to go snorkeling. Aron doesn't like the water." She hugged herself tightly. "He did it for me."

"Don't think that way." They deputy patted her arm. She didn't offer any false hopes, having seen incidents like this before. Each year they lost between six and twelve people in these waters due to drowning or diving accidents. "Nothing is your fault."

"I just can't believe it." Libby never took her eyes off the water "He's not dead." A chill settled on her skin. "If he was dead, I'd know. I'd know."

***

Onboard the Isabella

Within the hour, Dr. Carlos informed Martina that Aron was indeed badly injured. "He needs surgery." With a somber expression, he looked at his employer. "Either we get the man help, or he will die. I am certain there's internal bleeding in his brain and it may be swelling. You have to make some decisions. We either take him by boat back to the island to get him to a hospital or call for a helicopter to transport him elsewhere. There is no time for delay. Not if you want him to live."

Martina paced. She had a choice. Fate had played a hand in her life before, this was nothing new. Who was she to argue? Going to the bridge, she used the satellite phone to summon help. Conferring with the captain, she ordered the Isabella to pick up anchor and set sail. Their vessel was large enough that the helicopter could land on the top deck. "When the copter arrives, we will transport Aron to ABC Hospital in Mexico City."

The captain and the doctor went along with her wishes. Both had been with her family for years. However the captain was more outspoken. "Senorita, may I ask you a question?"

Martina respected Ferdinand. "Yes you may."

"I have heard the reports. The authorities radioed and asked us if we'd seen anything and I said 'no'. This man," he motioned toward the lower deck. "This man is a rich, important American. Are you planning on holding him for ransom?"

Martina was not offended by the question. Such dealings were not uncommon in her world. "No, I do not. I know this man. I wish him no harm."

The captain nodded. "I only wanted to know what to expect."

"Getting him help is my highest priority." Now that she had him in her clutches, Martina wasn't about to let him die. "My bodyguards can accompany us to Mexico City. You must escort Alessandra to the port in Cancun. She can join me at the hospital if she wishes, or return to Los Banos."

After they were underway, Martina checked on Aron and found him still sleeping. "Join me, I'd like to discuss his condition." Before she led the doctor out, Martina lovingly pushed Aron's hair from his forehead. "His skin is clammy."

Following her to a table by the swimming pool, he sat down and folded his hands on the table. "His pupils are dilated. I think he has a serious skull fracture." Even though she was clad in a skimpy bikini; her employee's eye never looked lower than her chin. "Find me the best specialist and have him meet us at the hospital in Mexico City."

"I have already placed a couple of calls. We have to be careful. Not everyone can be trusted."

"Money can buy silence."

He nodded, agreeing. Money could buy a lot of things, but some people could not be bought. Taking a sip of a mimosa, Juan seemed to contemplate his next question. "And what will you do if he remembers?"

Martina smiled. No one would ever accuse the good doctor of being a fool. "I don't know. I guess I'll do everything in my power to make him forget."

***

Westin Resort, Grand Cayman, the next day

When the plane touched down on the island, Noah had a driver pick them up and carry them to the hotel. Zane and Presley were on their way also. Soon a whole contingency of McCoy's and their friends would descend on Grand Cayman. They were about to turn heaven and earth upside down to find Aron.

Noah dreaded seeing Libby. Knowing how much she loved him, her heartbreak was going to be hard to witness. All of them were worried, but he was feeling numb. None of this seemed real.

When they pulled into the Westin, a group of emergency workers were standing by, waiting to brief the family on what had transpired.

As Libby had informed them, Aron had last been seen by his wife while snorkeling off Seven Mile Beach. No one had witnessed him returning to shore. But more importantly, no body had been found.

Jacob made his way to Libby, first. They found her on the beach. When Jacob saw her standing there gazing out to sea, it just paralyzed him. "Libby."

At the sound of his voice, she jerked around. "Aron!" When her eyes finally registered it was Jacob, she stumbled, nearly falling. "Your voice sounds so much like his. I thought it was him." He came to her and she went into his arms, allowing her brother-in-law to comfort her. "Why did this happen, Jacob?" She began to cry. "I don't understand."

He hugged her, trying to absorb her grief and fear. "We'll find him, Libby."

Relieved to have someone with her, Libby began pouring out the story, telling Jacob about their dive and what they had done. "We'd only been out there about an hour when I noticed he was no longer with me." She buried her face in her hands. "I had swum off to one side, looking at fish. If I'd only stayed near him, never taken my eyes off of him, he'd still be here."

"You can't blame yourself, Libby. Aron is a grown man." Jacob did know Aron hated the water, that he'd agreed to go snorkeling at all was a surprise. "Let's go up to the hotel and get you something to eat. We're all here to be with you, and we've already put a lot of things into motion." He began to tell her about the search and rescue efforts and who all they had contacted. "I can promise you we'll search high and low for Aron. None of us are ready to give him up."

* * *

Onboard the Isabella

Proficient at tying up loose ends of potential problems, Martina used the time before the helicopter came wisely. After she dressed, she made sure Aron had clothes. There was one crewman about the same size, so she gathered jeans and shirts for him to wear. As incapacitated as he was, she didn't foresee him needing them until they were out of the hospital and on their way to Los Banos, but she wanted to have the appearance of his being a passenger on board the yacht, just in case he roused enough to notice.

Her plan was to make it appear as if he'd been living with her for quite some time. She'd gone online and did some research on cases of amnesia caused by head injury. There was no guideline or guarantee of how long his memories would elude him. His amnesia could last from hours to years. By the time his hospital stay was over, she would have her act together. But right now, she decided to take out a little insurance policy. Retrieving Aron's dive suit and mask from the trash, she went to the kitchen and smeared beef blood on it, tossing them both overboard, wrapped around the largest mackerel in the refrigerator. No one questioned. No one stopped her. No one even dared make eye contact with the Diosa. What Martina Delgado wanted, Martina got. And right now, she wanted Aron McCoy.

***

Waves of agony crashed against his skull. He felt like his eyes were going to explode out of his head. This was no headache, this was torture. Throwing up seemed imminent, but it would kill him – the pain was just too excruciating. God, he needed to take a piss. Going on himself was humiliating, but there was no way he could move. He could barely open his eyes. The light coming through the window speared through his brain like knives. Through the haze of pain, he could make out a man standing over a table set for two. "Where am I?"

"At sea, Senor." The information was offered with an easy nonchalance as the waiter folded a napkin and laid it next to a place setting of gleaming crystal and china.

"What's wrong with me?"

"You almost drowned." The man was impeccably dressed in a black and white uniform.

"I don't remember." He started to rub his hand over his face, then realized he was clasping something hard in the palm of his hand. In fact he'd held onto it so tightly, the edges had cut into his palm. There was blood. Aron turned the coin over and over, looking at it through pain glazed eyes. It was old, looked to be made of gold with a woman's face on it. A beautiful face. He stared at it. A longing for something or someone rose up inside of him. He was lonely. "Do I have someone here with me?"

"Our Diosa will take care of you."

The waiter moved toward him. Quickly, he closed his hand, lest the stranger see what he was holding. This coin meant something to him. Was he a treasure hunter? That didn't sound right. But what the hell did he know? He didn't even know his own name. "Who the hell is Diosa?"

"I am." A cultured voice with the same Latin lilt as the waiter caused him to jerk his head around. Damn! That hurt. "We are on our way to Mexico City to get you some help, Amor."

Amor? He raised his eyes to take in the image of the woman standing next to him. She was beautiful – stacked, elegant, with perfect make-up, perfect features and a wide smile. An expectant look was in her eyes. She placed a hand on his arm.

"I need to use the bathroom."

She looked disappointed. "Very well. I'll get you some help."

In a few seconds, she returned with a man who worked to help him stand. But as soon as he was on his feet, a blinding shaft of pain caused him to groan and sink to his knees.

"Help him!" She urged.

Blackness rolled toward him as bile rose in his throat. With horrid heaves, he emptied his stomach all over the pristine floor. He remembered nothing, but this was not his finest hour – that much he knew.

Chapter Three

Westin Resort – Grand Cayman – a few days later

"The bay has been searched. The reef has been searched. No remains have been found." Roscoe reported to Jacob. "I suggest we move our focus on shore." Representatives from the family, hired search teams, volunteer efforts and island authorities were all meeting in a conference room at the Westin hotel.

"How's Libby?" Bowie Travis asked. He'd arrived, not too long after the family, and had been busy directing a team of local divers called Blue Hope.

"She's in our room. The physician was concerned the stress might cause problems with her pregnancy. He gave her something to make her rest." By way of explanation, Jacob offered. "We couldn't get her to return to the honeymoon suite. I've had her things moved in with me and Jessie."

"Understandable." Roscoe nodded.

"What do you think happened?" Jacob couldn't help but ask. Aron was young, strong – he just couldn't make sense of it.

"Right now, we just don't know." Roscoe looked out the window at the blue Caribbean Sea. "Believe me, I'm struggling with it, too. But we can't assume anything."

"I agree. Something about this doesn't seem right." As Jacob watched the wave's crash on the shore, a chill passed over him. "Aron," he whispered. "Don't give up. We'll find you."

***

At ABC Hospital – Mexico City

The Diosa paced in the waiting room. Two of her bodyguards stood at the door. They were armed to the teeth, but no one would know by looking at them. Alessandra sat by the window, leafing through a magazine. She looked more like a model than anyone Martina knew – she was willowy, delicate and graceful beyond compare. At four years younger, she was the pet of the family, yet her personality remained unspoiled and giving. There was nothing Martina would not do for her sister. Nothing.

Her uncle, Esteban, had been notified of Martina's decision to take a risk by bringing a true outsider into their midst. He had strong opinions, most of them negative, and Martina knew he was correct. Their whole operation was, in many ways, a house of cards. They depended on loyalty, luck and courage. Not only were the competing cartels out to take them down, now there was a renegade politician, the new Mexican District Attorney who was making loud noises about eradicating narco land. It was getting harder and harder to make a decent, illegal living anymore. Her thought made her smile. Sometimes Martina wished she led a normal life – home, husband, family – fixing meals and changing diapers. But the notion didn't last long. She was different. She was her grandfather's daughter. Her only weaknesses were Alessandra and Aron. And now was her chance to bring Aron into her life – an unexpected opportunity. Of course, much of her plan depended on the outcome of this operation and what Aron remembered when he awoke.

"You're going to wear a hole in the tile." Her sister commented quietly.

Martina glanced up. "He is undergoing a serious operation. There was a lot of swelling and his skull was fractured. Whatever blow to the head he received, almost killed him."

Alessandra threw down the magazine and stared out at the lights of the city. "I love this place, but I could never live here. Can you imagine? A population of twenty million and an area of five hundred square miles, just the idea of it all makes me shiver. I prefer living in the country. Brock says Wyoming is beautiful, I want to go there someday."

Martina didn't answer. Brock was beneath her notice.

"You're counting on Aron having permanent amnesia, aren't you?"

Ignoring her implication, Martina continued speaking in generalities. "Juan conferred with Dr. Connery. He is the best. All of this is being done in secret. After he has recuperated sufficiently, we will return to Los Banos. Until then, Esteban can handle things for me." And by handle things, she meant continue to make deliveries across the border, keep their customers happy, and kill as many of the Toro Cartel as they could find.

"Supervising your drug kingdom is not your biggest worry. This is." Alessandra flung a newspaper down on the table in front of her. The headlines were huge and disturbing. ***Texas Millionaire Rancher Goes Missing On Honeymoon.***

Martina stared at the paper as if it were a rattlesnake. "He is with me, now."

"He was on his honeymoon." The accusatory tone was loud and clear.

"I can make him happy." She had no doubt she could. Aron McCoy was what her life had been lacking. She possessed money, talent and ultimate power. What she did not have was someone to share it with. Her father, sister and uncle were family – but they weren't enough. She wanted excitement and passion. "The paperwork is being prepared. By the time we leave the hospital, Aron will be Austin Wade. All of his history will be manufactured, clothes will be bought, his room at Los Banos prepared and furnished as if he's been living there for some time."

"How do you propose to pull this off? This man is well known. He is the head of a powerful family. I've seen the news coverage. I've read the reports. They are going to turn the world upside down looking for him."

Martina raised her head – her chin stubborn. She looked down her nose at her sister. "I will make him happy. This man was meant to belong to me." Raising her hand into the air, she gestured with passion. "The Deity gave him to me. I did not go looking for him. He came to me!"

Alessandra narrowed her eyes at her powerful sister. "You are spoiled to having your own way, about everything. But these McCoy's will not give up." She rose and looked Martina in the eye. "I fear you will regret this day. And Aron will hate you when he realizes you took him away from his wife."

"Damn his wife." Martina whispered. "He's mine, now."

"I worry about you," Alessandra threw her arms around her sister. "Don't you know I stay scared to death someone is going to blow you up or assassinate you? I don't want you to die. And this is just crazy; you can't force a man to love you."

She held her sister, reassuring her with a pat on the back. "I have to try. He is my ideal, I have wanted him forever."

Stepping back, Alessandra sighed. "We don't always get what we want, Martina – no matter how many guns we have."

The double doors at the end of the hall swung open and Martina's heart surged up into her throat. She hadn't really considered the possibility that Aron wouldn't live through surgery. But now, the solemn look on the doctor's face scared her. She walked to meet him, leaving her sister standing in the door watching.

"Will he be okay?" She knew the doctor knew was aware of her identity, or rather what she was. It had crossed her mind that he might take out his prejudice against her by letting Aron die. That would be a mistake.

"Ms. Delgado." The doctor approached her. "Mr., uh, Wade had intracranial hemorrhaging. We will have to keep him in a comatose state to allow the swelling to subside and to calm his system."

"Will he recover?" Her voice sounded weak, even to herself.

"I see no problems at this point. We'll monitor his condition."

"Will he get his memory back?"

He crossed his arms. "An injury to the brain isn't like a broken arm or a burn. When the brain swells and compresses itself against the skull, the pressure can cause impairment. The type of impairment is unpredictable. There could be memory loss, confusion, erratic mood swings – all of this is quite normal."

"So, he could wake up and not know who he is?"

"Absolutely." He looked her directly in the eye, a half smile on his face. "I make no guarantees. I suggest you be ready for anything."

***

Weeks later – Tebow Ranch

Libby stood in their bedroom. She was lost. Aron had been missing for over a month and there was no word on his whereabouts or even if he were still alive. Picking up a photograph of him, she held it to her chest and bit her bottom lip. All she wanted to do was keen, to wail in mourning like a banshee, but all the crying in the world did no good. There were things to be done; life went on, no matter how grief stricken she was. The nursery had to be prepared. Ready or not, she and Aron were going to be parents. Twin boys were on the way. One of the things she'd hoped to do on their honeymoon was name the babies. "What am I going to do without you?" She kissed his face in the photo. "I was supposed to be the one with the uncertain future, not you."

Sitting on the side of the bed, she thought about her boys. Her choice of names was Colt and Case. She had never asked Aron if he had favorites. One of them should have his father's name, Sebastian. Libby grimaced. Such a big name. Colt Sebastian. Sebastian Colt. Case Sebastian. No, the names just didn't go well together. Maybe next time. "Next time. Oh, Aron. I want a next time. Please."

Jacob and the others insisted she return to Texas. If she'd had her way, she would have camped out on that beach where she'd last seen him. Over and over again, Libby had relived their last few hours. Mountains of guilt burdened her soul. Why had she insisted they go in the water? Why couldn't she have been satisfied just being with him? No, she'd been dead-set on doing everything on her stupid list. Heck, she'd made other plans – zip-lining, para-sailing. Now, she realized how stupid they had been. She was pregnant, for God's sake.

And she was no longer living on borrowed time. After she'd come back from the Cayman's, Doc Gibbs had checked her over. Her remission was holding. She was healthy. Her world could be perfect, if their daddy was home. Libby hadn't let her mind even contemplate a life without Aron. She ran her hand over the bedspread. Oh, how she loved him. Her body ached for him and her heart felt like it was breaking in two. "I love you, Aron. I'll love you forever."

***

Los Banos Ranch

Slowly, he opened his eyes. Something wasn't right. He looked around the elegantly appointed room. Rich colors of gold and burgundy complimented heavy dark furniture. Running his fingers over the bed linens, he could tell they were sumptuous and fresh. Why did nothing look familiar? Raising a hand, he encountered bandages on his head. Pressing down, he realized there was pain. He was sore. What had happened to him? Where was he?

Clouds of confusion muddled his brain. A faint recollection of bad dreams crept into his head. Dammit! He had no idea what was going on. All he knew was that he hadn't been sleeping well – moments of lucidity warred with bouts of night terrors and dark shadows – visions which haunted him, making him want to reach out and grab at some unknown life preserver, anything that would make him feel tethered to this world and not adrift in the unknown.

"Hello!" He called out. Kicking back the cover, he started to try and stand. Hell, he couldn't. He was as weak as a newborn calf. With that thought, came images of cattle, a barn, faint shapes of men riding horses.

"You're awake." The door to his bedroom opened and in walked a beautiful woman. She was smiling at him, but she walked slowly as if gauging his reaction to her – almost cautiously. Her shoulder length hair was dark and her eyes were brown. "I've been so worried about you."

"You have?" She was a sexy woman. As a man, he could not help but appreciate her. He struggled to place her, to place this room – anything, but he couldn't. "Do I know you?"

Martina swallowed. "Yes, you do." Searching his face she asked. "What do you remember?"

He looked at her blankly. "I'm not sure." A part of him wanted to escape, to hunt something or someone familiar, but he didn't know which way to turn. "I need my pants." Yea, pants. He didn't want to get out of bed in front of strangers with just his underwear to cover him. "And I'm hungry." Was she a nurse? She wasn't dressed like a nurse.

"Hungry? That's a good sign. What would you like to eat?" She looked a bit more relaxed.

Considering her question for a moment, he answered. "Scrambled eggs and toast."

"Of course. Good choice. It would be best to not eat anything too heavy just yet." She stepped over to the wall and pressed a button, giving directions for his meal. "Let me get Dr.

Carlos. He will be so pleased." Stepping out, she was gone only a few moments before she returned with a man who wore all white. He was Hispanic also.

"Nuestro paciente esta despierto." He'd just said 'our patient is awake'. English was his first language, of that he was certain, but he could understand Spanish.

"Patient?" This was no hospital. "Tell me what's going on? Why am I here?"

"Do you remember your name?" The doctor shined a light in his eyes. He jerked his head. "Does that hurt?"

"It didn't feel good." Name? He thought, a feeling of panic sweeping over him. He needed answers and damn soon. "No. I don't think I do."

The beautiful woman let out a sigh, came over and sat down beside him while the doctor did his examination. She took his hand in hers. He fought the urge to pull it out of her grasp.

"I'm so sorry you don't remember." Squeezing his fingers, she looked him in the eyes. "This is Los Banos, my family's ranch. We were vacationing on my yacht when you had your diving accident. You struck your head on something, that's all we know. After your operation, I brought you here."

He felt of his head. That explained the bandages. "How long ago was this?"

"Over a month ago. You remained comatose for a long while. Recuperating from brain surgery takes some time."

A feeling of uneasiness swept over him. "Is that why I can't remember anything?"

She stared at him for a moment before replying. A shadow seemed to pass over her face. "The surgery may be part of it, but you had no memory when you were pulled from the ocean."

"Why did I have to have an operation?"

The doctor answered the question this time. "You had a skull fracture and a cerebral hemorrhage. We must watch you carefully, you are not out of the woods yet."

"Great." The pain he was feeling was normal, he supposed. But he had to get his bearings; he had to make sense of what was going on. Right now, he felt as if was adrift — floundering in a sea of uncertainty. "Who are you?" He looked at the pretty woman who was still holding on to his hand.

She smiled a tight, patient smile. "I am Martina Delgado."

He hated the next question. "And who am I?"

The doctor stood up straight. The woman met the doctor's eyes, then looked back down to him. "You are Austin Wade. My fiancé."

"Fiance?" He repeated the word as if it were a foreign concept. "None of this makes sense to me. None of it seems right." He felt nothing for this woman. There was no drawing, no attraction. Nothing.

A tap on the door drew their attention. Another uniformed man came in with a tray. "Food, Senorita."

She stood up and made room for him to sit further up in the bed. "I have to go to the bathroom before I can eat, Martina." Vague memories of a damn catheter came to mind. He hated being an invalid. Waving the hands away which tried to help him, Austin stood, pulling on the soft lounge pants she handed him. Austin – the name didn't sound like him. Like trying to jam his foot into too small of a boot, it just didn't fit. But for now, it was the only name he had.

Seeing a door on the other side of the room, he began walking toward it, hoping it held a commode. The doctor came to assist him. "I've got this, Doc." The man stepped back. Glancing behind him, he saw his 'fiancé' standing, just watching him. Her actions puzzled Austin. She didn't seem comfortable around him, not like she would have been if they had been making love the way engaged people do. Not that he wanted her to hover over him. So, he wasn't about to complain.

Going into the adjacent room, he shut the door. God, in heaven! He felt as if he'd stepped into some sultan's palace. The bedroom was huge and comfortable, but the bath was crazy. A shower covered one wall, big enough to hold a basketball team. It had twenty heads, if it had one, and a bench covered an entire wall. There was a hot tub, deep and wide – big enough for a dozen people. The floor was heated. There was a skylight and a sauna. Two commodes sat to one side, and that was where he headed. Which one should he use? Then, he realized one was a bidet. He almost smiled. That answered one question. He wasn't very cultured and wherever his original home was, he didn't have a damn bidet.

Taking his cock out, he relieved himself, shook it and tucked himself back in the boxers he wore. He didn't normally wear boxers. A sense of weirdness struck him. How could he remember a foreign language, know he didn't own a bidet and didn't wear boxers – yet he couldn't recall anything else? Stepping over to the mirror, Austin looked at himself. Damn, he was a handsome fella. He chuckled and his attempt at self-humor backfired as a sharp pain pierced his skull. He touched the gauze and tape on the back of his head. Dark hair. Blue eyes. A scruff of beard. His face looked familiar, like he was gazing at an acquaintance whose identity had slipped his mind.

Leaning in, he stared at himself – eye to eye. "Who the hell are you?" Events from the last few weeks filtered through his mind. He remembered feeling helpless and hurting. He remembered having nightmares which were filled with rage and pain. He could remember a sense of drowning, of water closing over his head as he fought for air. Austin shook off a shiver.

But most of all, he remembered love. He loved someone more than life itself. Was it Martina?

"Austin? Are you all right?" It was his fiancé. Funny, she wasn't his usual type. She was too damn skinny. He wondered when his tastes had changed.

"Be right out." He washed his hands and opened the cabinet, looking for something for his headache. Finding a bottle labeled asperina, he took four. With a sigh, he braced himself to go back in the room filled with strangers. With a self-deprecating smile, he admitted he was one of them. Austin Wade was just as much of a stranger to him as they were.

***

Tebow Ranch
A few days later

The bed was warm. Libby cuddled down under the covers, and reached for Aron. She needed to be held. Her hand connected with warm skin. Oh, he felt so good. She traced the hard muscles of his arms, feeling them flex beneath her fingertips. Edging closer, she moved from his bicep to his pecs. "I love touching you."

As always, he welcomed her. "Why were you way over there? You're supposed to sleep in my arms." He drew her to him and she snuggled close.

"I don't know. I guess I just got away from you." Teasing him was one of her favorite past times.

One moment she was lying on the bed, the next she was lifted in the air and settled right on top of him. His arms came around her like comforting bands of steel, anchoring her body to his. "Don't you dare try to get away from me, I can't live without you."

Her breasts were pressing into his chest. She could feel her nipples dragging in the soft fur as she kissed her way up his throat to his lips. "I don't want to live without you, Aron. I need you too much."

"I need you..." Libby kissed him again, but she felt dampness and realized it was only her pillow; she was hugging it in her sleep. It was wet with tears.

Los Banos Ranch

Her hair smelled good. He buried his head in the softness and just inhaled. She was all woman. So soft. When his lips trailed down her cheek, he moaned at the thought of kissing her again. God, he'd missed her. She was so much a part of him. Loving her was the sweetest thing he'd ever known. His cock was pulsing. It had been so long. He needed her so...Lib...

"Austin, make love to me." A voice in his ear jerked him from his slumber.

"What?" He opened his eyes expecting to see – someone else. "Martina." She was not who he'd been dreaming about. Desperately he tried to hold on to the woman in his dreams – any image, a name – her touch. But the sensations were fleeting, drifting away like smoke in the evening breeze.

Austin pushed his head back firmly into the pillow, trying to escape the woman who was hovering over him. This stranger who said she was his fiancé ran her hand down his naked chest – lower – lower. Soon, she would encounter the evidence of his desire. But it wasn't for her. He caught her wrist.

What was wrong with him? He was a red-blooded male. Apparently he needed sex. But something was holding him back... "I can't."

She drew back, her dark Latin eyes burning with flames of desire and impatience. "Why not?"

At last, a good thing was coming from his accident. "I'm still weak." Weak – maybe. Horny and able to have sex – yes. But not with her.

"Would you at least touch me?" She grabbed his hand and tried to force it down between her legs. A tingle of interest sparked in his mind, but then he saw big blue eyes, heard a soft voice and he knew he couldn't.

"Sorry, I'm feeling nauseated." He got up and headed for the bathroom. "Maybe you'd better go back to your room." With that, he shut the door. Damn, he needed to start wearing pajamas to bed. It was normal for two engaged people to sleep together, to have sex – but this didn't feel right.

Austin stood in front of the mirror, waiting to hear her leave the room and shut the door. Here he was – gazing into this glass darkly again. A dull ache caused his head to pound. Headaches were common the first month or so after surgery, or so the doctor said. But Austin welcomed the discomfort. It reminded him he was alive. The memories he'd lost seemed to be closer at that time as well. He could almost remember. Detached, he gazed into the same stranger's face – unfamiliar, yet at the same time, familiar.

Finally, he heard the door shut. Keeping her at arm's length was becoming an uncomfortable struggle. He had no idea if he'd ever remember Martina and their life together or not. Could he accept that this was his world? Or would he hold out for the dream? Pulling himself together, he decided to venture downstairs. Getting dressed, he opened the door and headed into the hall.

Austin was a bit shocked. He hadn't known what to expect. Of course the suite he'd been given was extremely comfortable. But the rest of the house was very impressive - and familiar to a degree. Yes, he didn't recall anything about the upstairs, but he seemed to recognize the lower floor. He definitely got the feeling he'd been here before.

Slowly, holding on to the bannister, Austin stood in the foyer. The whole place was framed by grand arches and the floors were of white marble. A fireplace big enough to roast a hog was off in the room to the right, and to the left was a dining table big enough to seat all of the Dallas Cowboys plus the cheerleading squad. "Hello? Is anyone home?" He'd stayed in that damn bedroom, till he couldn't stomach it any longer. It was time he got up and took the lay of the land.

Hell, he didn't even know where he was. For some reason, he hesitated to ask Martina a lot of questions. First off, because he dreaded what her answers might be and, secondly, she appeared reticent to talk. In fact, she was a bit evasive. The whole predicament was driving him insane.

Stepping toward the seating area in front of the fireplace, he was surprised to see an older man entering from the right. "Saludos A...Austin." A hand was raised in greeting and a genuine smile was on his face. For the first time, Austin felt a sense of rightness.

"Hello, Sir." Who was this? He and Martina had barely talked, but she had mentioned a sister and an uncle, but he'd been under the impression Estaban was a much younger man. This gentleman had to be in his seventies.

"I am glad to see you walking around and looking healthy." He came up and clapped Austin on the shoulder. "How about some brandy?"

"Sounds good to me." He sat down where the gentleman indicated. Although he hated to ask, he didn't see any way around it. "I know I'm supposed to know who you are, but could you remind me?"

A kind smile creased the man's face. "I am Tomas Santiago Delgado, Martina and Allesandra's father." Tomas extended his hand in greeting.

Austin took it. "I'm so sorry." He started to rise.

"Sit. Sit." He handed Austin a snifter of brandy. "You were injured. I do not expect you to remember me."

A fire was lit in the fireplace, although the air conditioner was running if he wasn't mistaken. "I don't remember much, unfortunately." Taking a swallow, he decided to find out what he could. "Can you tell me exactly where I am?"

Tomas shook his head. "I'm so sorry this has happened to you. Sorrier than you can imagine." A look of guilt crossed his features. Austin didn't understand it.

"Hey, I'm alive. And from what little I've heard about what happened to me, I'm one lucky bastard."

"True." Tomas stared into the fire. "But to answer your question," he gestured broadly, "this is the Los Banos Ranch in Sonora, Mexico. My family has lived here for ten generations. I can trace my bloodline back to the conquistadors." He raised a frail fist in the air. "And that is my passion." He pointed to a painting on the wall.

Austin rose to look at what the old man was pointing to. He was still weak, but he needed to move around. "A Criollo-Corriente. Very nice."

"Ah, you do remember." Tomas seemed pleased. "You are a cattleman, like me."

"Really?" Austin was interested. This didn't surprise him, not like the information he was now in Mexico. America was his country of birth, of that he was certain.

"Padre, what are you telling Austin?"

Martina breezed into the room, closely followed by two men. The first time he'd seen the bodyguards stationed outside his bedroom door, he had been afraid he was a prisoner. But then he realized they accompanied Martina wherever she went. Why, he didn't know. Of course he realized this part of the world had its dangers, and a woman traveling alone always could use protection. But this seemed a little extreme. "Your father," he put a little emphasis on the word, "has been telling me things."

"Really?" Concern colored her face. "What kind of things?" She looked pointedly at her father, censure clearly in her voice.

"Is there something he shouldn't tell me?" Austin wondered at her attitude.

A smile came upon her aristocratic face. "No, of course not." Martina poured herself a drink.

"We were discussing cattle." Tomas volunteered. "I was telling Austin how much we had in common."

Her shoulders seemed to stiffen, but when she turned, she gave them both an indulgent look. "My two men. Of course, you have cattle in common." Martina came to sit next to Austin on the couch.

"Refresh my memory." He couldn't help but enquire. "Tell me about my past."

Tomas fidgeted, much to Austin's surprise. But his daughter was as cool and calm as a rock. "What would you like to know?" she asked.

"Where am I from?" He gestured broadly with his hands. "Do I have a home? Do I have any family? Am I broke?" Those all seemed like legitimate questions to him.

With a small half-smile, Martina began to speak. "You are from northern Wyoming." She took a sip of the brandy and locked eyes with his, as if she was gauging his reaction to her revelations. "You sold your ranch after it fell on hard times. Los Banos is your home, now. You have no family, but me." She flashed a huge ring in his face. "And you are by no means broke. Your fortune is in good hands. In our bank."

They had a bank? And why hadn't he noticed that ring before. Why had he given up his home to move in with this woman? Even though he didn't know himself well, this sure as hell didn't sound like something he would do.

"Would you like the see the ranch?" Tomas offered. But he seemed to look at Martina for permission. This action further confused him. What father looked to his daughter for permission for something so simple?

"Yes, I would." For no other reason than he needed to get out of the house. But ranches and cattle seemed to intrigue him. Austin wanted to investigate the matter further.

"Do you feel up to a walk or perhaps a ride?"

"I'm not sure if Austin feels like…"

He held up his hand. "I do and I want to get out. I'm going stir-crazy in here." Without waiting for permission of any kind, Austin Wade rose from the couch and retreated upstairs.

***

As soon as he was out of earshot, Martina wheeled around to Tomas. Her face was a mask of fury. "How dare you interfere?"

The older gentleman rose to his full height. "This is my home. He was my friend. And whatever power you may wield, and however corrupt you are – you will not tell your Father how to run his life nor how to hold his tongue. I am no imbecile and this whole mess is a travesty. How can you steal a man away from his family?"

Martina walked to the hall and looked up the staircase, then she quietly shut the door. When she came back into the room, she got right in her father's face. "He does not remember his family."

"But you know who they are, you could tell him. Set the man free before he becomes embroiled in this nightmare you call a life." He spat out the words, clearly not afraid of the young woman. "Don't you realize I know what you're doing?" He shook his fist at her. "Why you even have the servants monitoring the cable channels. Everything we watch is pre-recorded, edited to make sure no mention of Aron McCoy comes across on our television. Your secretary screens every newspaper and magazine which comes into the house to make sure he does not see the uproar his absence has caused or the search for him that continues until this day. How long do you expect to get away with this? His memory will return." Anger made his face blood red. "And I'll be glad when it does!"

"This topic is not up for discussion." Martina spoke through clenched teeth.

Tomas's face crumpled, but he did not cry out. "What happened to you, Martina? How have you become such a monster? How many deaths have you been responsible for? How much blood is on your hands?"

"Enough!" She slammed down her glass on the table and stalked toward the door. "Just remember this, old man." She said the words with disdain. "If you spoil this for me... you will regret it."

Her eyes were serpent like, and Tomas Delgado did not doubt her threat for a moment.

***

Tebow Ranch

The dream had knocked Libby off kilter. It had seemed so real. She'd actually felt him in her arms. She had tasted his kiss. Reaching down between her breasts, she picked up a gold chain. On the end of the chain was a gold band. Aron's wedding ring. Bowie Travis had brought it to her. One of the divers had found it, a miracle in itself. One small ring on a seabed – like a piece of gold tossed from a sinking ship. Yea, she knew she might be grasping at straws. But Libby needed something, anything, to hold on to.

"Come back to me, Aron," she whispered. Reverently, she kissed the ring, as if it were a magic talisman.

Harley, Beau's wife, had held the ring in her hand. She was said to have some psychic powers. Beau had told Libby those powers had kept Harley alive many times when she diffused bombs, letting her know which wire to cut or which switch to flip.

Harley had clutched Aron's ring and let her mind touch whatever power revealed hidden secrets, and she'd told Libby Aron was not dead. She had felt the continuation of his life force. And Libby believed her. She, too, felt Aron was still on this earth – somewhere. And he still loved her. That was her hope and her prayer. Libby was holding on to that dream with both hands.

Life at Tebow was continuing. Nathan was taking Aron's absence as hard as she was, but the family had rallied around them. Jessie was in the last trimester of her pregnancy and Jacob continued to work on their house. But he and his wife refused to move out of Tebow main house right now. They were afraid Libby would need them. And she appreciated that fact. She did need them. She needed the whole family.

Cady and Joseph stayed close to home. Joseph was competing again, but Cady was like his lodestar, she drew him home far more frequently than before. Isaac and Avery were together now and peace seemed to have descended on the family. Even Noah was getting a long better with everyone. Sighing, she stood and walked to the window, gazing out over McCoy country.

Aron's home. Aron's legacy.

She molded her tummy, feeling the slight kick of little feet. "We have to hold on. We have to believe. Daddy will come home, I just know he will."

Chapter Four

La Dura Headquarters – Cananea, Sonora, Mexico

Martina stormed out of the house, checking her watch. She was late. "Car!" She snapped and one of her bodyguards summoned the driver. In moments, the dark sedan drove up. The windows were so tinted they were black. She missed her sports cars, but these days an armored vehicle was the only thing that made sense. There had been two attempts on her life already, and she knew there would be more. Living to a ripe old age was doubtful, that was why Martina was determined to live well while she could.

"To the hacienda." She directed, looking out the window at Los Banos. Her father insisted the ranch be kept 'clean', none of her business could be conducted on the property. She didn't know why she put up with so much grief from her old man. He was senile and weak.

Martina sighed. She knew why. Because Alessandra loved him and she loved Alessandra. Family – they could easily become your downfall. Her uncle Esteban was trouble enough. He resented the fact that the power had passed through her mother, Iliana, rather than straight to him. But her grandfather, Rodrigo, had been able to gauge who could be trusted the most and Esteban had one fatal flaw – he was somewhat soft-hearted. He was brilliant, but with a conscience. So, they shared the power, divided the duties. To the world, she was the leader. But Esteban was the power behind the throne. Martina cut the deals. She made the tough decisions. She sentenced people to death. And Esteban used his magnificent brain to come up with new ideas for them to make more money, control more territory and sell more drugs.

It was Esteban who'd originated the idea of building their own submarines under the jungle canopies of the Amazon and using them to bring drugs in along the coast of California. He also thought of bypassing the fence in Southern California by catapulting bales of marijuana over the high-tech structure. He beat the authorities' game with twenty-five hundred year old technology. In Wisconsin, he contracted growers to plant fields of marijuana on national forest land to supply the demand in Chicago. He dug tunnels under the border, some of them air-conditioned with trolley systems. He vacuumed-sealed some of his drugs in tin cans and slapped pepper labels on them, shipping directly to Mexican owned grocery stores. Hell, he'd even shipped some drugs by FedEx. There was no end to Esteban's creativity or to Martina's ambition.

Today, they were negotiating a new deal with a Peruvian supplier. He was from the highlands, Alvara Vilca. If she had her way, the deal would be two thousand dollars for a kilo of cocaine. In Mexico, that same two thousand would translate to ten thousand. Across the border in the U. S. the kilo was worth thirty thousand. After it was broken up into grams for retail distribution, the value of that same two thousand dollars' worth of cocaine was one hundred thousand dollars. Martina smiled. She knew how to make a profit. And he knew how to transport – they were a good team.

The drive to town took over an hour. To pass the time, she thought about Aron and what their future held. Her greatest fear was that his memory would come back. So to alleviate her concern, Martina had contacted the smartest chemist she knew – a woman by the name of Emily Gadwah. Mrs. Gadwah was not a criminal, but she did owe Martina some allegiance. When her son had needed money for high priced medicine, she had received it from the Delgado's. But for that boon, she gave the Duro Cartel invaluable advice when they needed it. And this time, Martina needed a miracle. What she wanted might not even exist. But if it did, or if it could be manufactured – Emily would know.

Upon arriving at the gates of the estate, the driver paused while the electronic eye verified their identity. When the heavy doors parted, four armed guards stood on the other side. Their headquarters was a fortress. A small army of mercenaries protected their operations. Some didn't realize it, but this was no fly-by-night operation. Their attention to detail and high-tech procedures would rival corporations such as Amazon or QVC - except they were dealing in methamphetamine, heroin and cocaine, instead of books, jewelry or electronics.

When the car came to a standstill in front of the palatial stone building, she was immediately met, her door opened and she was escorted through the entrance and into a richly paneled office where Esteban and Alvara were awaiting her arrival. They both stood as she entered.

Immediately, she could tell something was wrong. Alvara was sweating and the temperature in the room was in the sixties. Esteban looked nervous. "Sobrina," he held out his hand. Calling her his 'niece', he kissed her on both cheeks. Looking down at Alvara, he spoke softly. "If you would wait outside for a moment, I will discuss this problem with Diosa."

She nodded her head, giving her permission. The man wouldn't meet her eye. What was going on? Esteban walked him to the door and stood there while he was escorted by one of the guards to another room where he would wait the outcome of their discussion. "Okay. What's going on?" She sat down and put her hands together, forming a point with her forefingers.

Going back to his chair, Esteban pulled out a notepad and looked at something he'd written. "Alvara needs to go up on his price, twenty-five percent over what he quoted us."

"No."

He held up his hand. "Wait. There are extenuating circumstances."

"His problems are his problems."

Esteban ignored her and kept on talking. "FARC has demanded he pay a 'tax' to protect them from abuse by intermediaries and drug traffickers."

"The Fuerzas Armadas Revolucionarias are mercenaries. We can't be responsible if they strong- arm the Columbians. Here in Mexico, we fight our own battles."

Keeping calm, making his point, Esteban leaned back in his chair. "Bribery is part and parcel of our business. You are not as aware of this as I am, but we pay off everyone. One of the reasons the government tolerates us is that we pay a higher rate in bribes than we would in taxes. We own the police force, we pay fees to every branch of the military to turn a blind eye – it's a fact of life for us. Many of the, so-called, hits you put out on our enemies are carried out either by our men dressed in police uniforms or actual cops providing paid assistance. It's so prevalent that when the government scores a big arrest which makes the papers, the police and military officials pose for the camera in ski masks to protect their identity. In our society, the cops dress like bandits and the bandits dress like cops."

Martina was bored. "We could find another source. Alvara is not the only game in town."

"We know him. We trust him." Esteban paused. "He has a family."

Martina sat up straighter. "There is no room for sentimentality."

"I want to do this. We are talking a twenty percent increase." He jotted down some numbers. "You will make up the difference in other ways." A frown came over his face. "I am aware of your little side-line business, Martina."

She knew exactly what he meant. Extortion, kidnapping and human trafficking were the next steps for most operations. "Those girls were rescued off the street. They'll be well taken care of, with protection, food and a safe place to sleep."

"While you sell their bodies to the highest bidder."

Was the look in his eye a warning? She locked gazes with him. "All right, Tio. Give him his twenty-percent." She rose from her chair. "You can bring him in. I want to talk to him first." Martina intended to demand faster delivery and the highest quality in exchange for the money.

"One more thing." Esteban sighed, shaking his head. Martina realized whatever he was about to say was the real reason for the meeting. She waited. He cleared his throat and spoke. "The war with the Toro Cartel is costing many lives – both ours and theirs. Four hundred people were killed in the last two weeks, thirty-four were slain yesterday."

She knew this. The six charred bodies found along the roadside near Ascension was her doing. "So, what's your point?"

Setting his mouth in a thin flat line, Esteban persisted in his argument. "We need to find a solution – stop the bloodshed. There has been an offer."

"What kind of offer?" Where was this coming from? She did not like to be last to receive information.

"Javiar Rios wishes to join our two families in analianza de sangre."

Alliance of blood? He was speaking of a dynastic marriage, a marriage to make peace. Fury flashed over her. "You wish me to marry Joaquin Rios? To sacrifice myself for the sake of sparing unrest?" She was the Diosa. He was second-in-command. The audacity of his request almost caused Martina to attack her uncle with claws unsheathed. It was out of the question. She would not lower herself to marry that sniveling weakling to procure any kind of peace with the enemy. Her priority was Aron McCoy. Already she was planning their marriage and no one – no one would get in her way. "Never!" She threw the word at her uncle like a grenade.

"Not you, Diosa." The words were quiet amid her turmoil.

"What?" She whirled around to stare at her uncle.

"Alessandra."

***

Los Banos Ranch

"Hello, my name is Alessandra."

"My pleasure." Austin tipped his hat to the pretty senorita. "They tell me my name is Austin Wade." Talk about night and day. Where Martina was aristocratic, elegant and self-assured – her little sister was easy-going, sweet and soft-spoken. They were both beautiful, but Alessandra was warm and made him smile.

"Oh, we've met." She led her horse out of the stall. No elaboration.

Tomas led two other mounts to the rear of the barn. "Here you go, Austin. Let's check out my herd." The horses were magnificent. He could tell they were pure bred Arabians, sleek and eager to be given free rein. They wanted to run. Just being near the animals made him feel good. Placing one booted foot in the stirrup, he lifted himself into the saddle. Yes, this was familiar. He knew horses. The clothes he wore didn't feel exactly right – everything was stiff and new. He wondered where his old clothes were. Austin had a sense that he preferred broke-in boots, well-worn jeans and cotton t-shirts. Soon, he and Miss Martina were going to have to have a long talk. He could smell manure in this situation.

"Coming with us, querido?"

His daughter smiled at the endearment. "No, Padre." She drained a bottle of water and pushed her hair over her shoulder. "I..." She looked around her. "I just wanted to take a walk."

Hmmm, Austin thought. A walk. Right. That girl was doing more than walking. He'd bet his left nut she was meeting somebody. Oh, well. It was none of his affair.

Riding high in an exquisite Mexican saddle covered in fine silver, Austin wondered at his life. For all extents and purposes, he appeared to be a kept man. And that wasn't his style. He didn't have to have a memory to know that much about himself. Austin Wade was used to earning his keep, paying his own way and staying busy. From what he could gather, his fiancé expected him to earn his keep by becoming Mr. Martina Delgado and he had news for her, that shit wasn't gonna fly.

"Tell me about your daughter." Austin surveyed his surroundings. The land really was beautiful. The Sierra Madre Mountains rose high in the distance.

Tomas chuckled as he led them away from the barn and out into the open pasture. "She's a gentle flower."

Austin snorted. Obviously he wasn't talking about Martina. "The other one."

This time Tomas laughed. "Ah, my iron maiden, doncella de hierro, she was such a headstrong little girl. And a much more headstrong woman."

"Tell me about our relationship." Austin knew he was pushing the envelope, but he needed to know.

"That I cannot do, mi amigo."

Tomas was choosing to stay out of the situation and Austin couldn't really blame him, so he changed the subject. "How many acres do you have?"

A look of relief passed over the old man's face. "There are twenty-four thousand acres, although if the rough terrain were flattened out, the amount of land would increase three fold." Austin could hear the pride in his voice.

They rode across the grazing pastures and he admired the cattle, a breed descended from the original Spanish animals brought to the Americas in the fifteenth century. "They're closely related to the Longhorn, you know. I raise Longhorns." As soon as he spoke the words, he reined the horse in. He bred Longhorn cattle. He had remembered something! Tomas met his gaze and he gave him a small, mysterious smile.

Ssssss Ssssss

Austin's horse reared. He clasped his knees, holding on to the reins, striving to stay in the saddle. The stallion bucked backwards and then danced sideways.

"Rattlesnake!" Tomas yelled.

Austin looked down in time to see the large snake strike out at the legs of the horse.

Pop! Pop!

Tomas had pulled out a pistol and shot the snake. "I detest those things!"

Austin calmed his horse and looked at the dead serpent. "Yea, so does..." Another name danced on his lips, but he couldn't quite find it in his memory.

"What did you say?" Tomas asked. "You're remembering, aren't you?"

Austin didn't say anything else. He couldn't see her face, and he didn't know her name, but there was definitely a woman in his life – somewhere. And it wasn't Martina Delgado.

Over the next few days, Austin struggled with his identity. He was striving to make sense of the world he was a part of and the past he had lost. Giving up wasn't an option, he was still game to figure out the answers. Over and over again he had questioned Martina – about their past, how they met, about the day he was injured. Her answers didn't change, but he could tell she was becoming frustrated with him. He didn't care. Shadows tangled and twisted together in his brain. Sometimes he felt like he was watching an old film in his head and the images were running through his mind on fast-forward, they raced too fast for him to see them clearly.

And the dreams.

Deep in the night, he would dream of her. A clear image of her eluded him. But he could feel her in his arms and she was heaven to hold. When he would awaken, his arms were so empty and he longed for her with every fiber of his being.

Martina had come to his bed twice more, and twice he had turned her away. The last time they had argued. She demanded to share his bed, saying she wore his ring. He wanted to ask her to remove it, but something told him to play it slow. Until he had answers, he needed to keep things status quo. But he was running out of excuses – first he'd told her he was weak and now the excuse he was using was that he wanted to remember her – he needed to remember loving her. This request just seemed to make her more furious.

Now here he was, seated at the table. While eating with Martina, her father and her sister, he could almost see and hear another family. He had brothers, a large family of brothers – one that laughed and shared and roughhoused good-naturedly. Somewhere there were people who missed him, who cared for him. He could feel it.

"Austin?"

"Austin?"

He jerked his head up. "I'm sorry. I was lost in thought. What did you say?" He looked at the face of each one of the Delgado's. They were dressed for dinner, a handsome Hispanic family, eating classic dishes, served by impeccably dressed help, and living in a mansion without a want or care of any kind.

And he, he didn't belong here. This was not his home. Home was...

"Did you remember something?"

Everyone at the table tensed. Austin paused, considering his answer. He hadn't remembered anything specific, nothing concrete. All of it was more feeling than anything else. And dreams. "No, I didn't remember anything." At least nothing he was willing to admit to her.

"Are you sure?" Everyone was so quiet. All eyes were focused on him.

"I'm sure." Especially considering the fact she was looking at him with the coldest eyes he'd ever seen. Austin realized he was being warned. Without words, Martina was warning him.

"Diosa! Diosa!" A man came running in.

"What is it?" Martina rose. It still confused Austin why everyone answered to Martina instead of Tomas.

"They have captured people, men who were crossing over Los Banos. Come quickly!"

"Toro?" She asked. Tomas groaned and threw his napkin down.

What was Toro? Austin wondered.

"I do not know." Her employee was panting with exertion.

Martina walked calmly to the buffet, opened a drawer and took out a pistol, a 9mm Beretta. "Let's go."

Austin jumped up to accompany her. He didn't feel possessive of her, as he should. But she was a female in a house in which he was a guest. And he was not a man who sat back and let the females in his household defend him.

When they made their way outside to the front of the house, there were six armed guards standing in a half moon shape. All of them were brandishing AK47's. Where had they come from? He was used to seeing a couple of bodyguards, but this looked more like a SWAT team. And why in the world were they carrying automatic weapons. Back in Texas everyone had a deer rifle. But a machine gun?

Texas... well, hell. He was from Texas! Not damn Wyoming.

Another seed of distrust planted itself in Austin's mind as he watched Martina march out to confront the trespassers. She was lying to him. Why?

Tomas and Alessandra came to stand alongside he and Martina. When one of the bodyguards herded eight men into their midst, all with their hands over their head, Austin couldn't help but react. He grabbed Martina's arm. "What's going on?"

"It will be all right." She reassured him. "This happens frequently."

The scene was surreal. He felt like he was watching an old spaghetti western or something. The men were like captured bandits, headed for the gallows. Austin could tell they were tired, thirsty and hungry. Two of them looked ready to collapse. After a few seconds though, he understood. He could pick up a smattering of their conversation. These men had been headed for the border when they had, unluckily, crossed Delgado land.

"We're sorry, Senorita. We were just meeting our coyote."

"Stupid! You should have checked a map." She sauntered out toward them. "How dare you come onto Los Banos?"

One hung his head. "El Duro. Diosa."

"Are you Toro?" Martina poked the pistol in one man's check.

"No, Senorita." He whispered. "We are not Toro."

"Did you check them for weapons or explosives?" She addressed her employee.

"Yes, Diosa." Another man spoke up. "They were clean."

"What should I do with you?" Her question was soft, but he watched the men who heard her speak, visibly shudder.

Austin frowned. "Martina." He called her name, softly. She ignored him.

"Where are you headed?" She asked, instead.

"America." One was brave enough to say.

"Where in America? Who are you working for?"

"No one. We go to meet our families." The younger one spoke, pleading with his eyes. "My wife and young son are in Texas. We will work for you, if you give us a chance."

"Who sent you?" She demanded again, ignoring the man's question.

"No one sent us. No one." Another wailed. "We would not cross you."

"Get rid of them!" She waved her weapon in the air.

"Martina!" Tomas shouted. There was true fear in his voice and Austin realized it was fear for the lives of those men, and not for himself.

She nodded her head as she passed a silent message to her guards. They took their assault weapons and pushed the men around to the side of the house. Austin braced himself, almost expecting to hear gunfire. Instead in a few moments, he saw a truck pass by with all the men loaded in the back, accompanied by two of the guards, still carrying their huge guns.

"What will happen to them?" Alessandra asked.

"Only what they deserve." Martina smiled.

Watching her, Austin realized he knew her not at all. She had changed before his eyes, morphing from a woman to a predator. He didn't understand. Why was she being so cold and uncaring? He wondered if he was imagining the malice. He didn't think so. Every part of him rebelled at the idea, but he had the distinct impression those men wouldn't live to see the sunset.

***

Los Banos – The next day.

He had to get away from the house. Austin felt as if he were choking on a cloud of confusion. More and more he was realizing he didn't belong here. Something wasn't right. The urge to just leave – walk off was more than overwhelming. He thought about stealing the keys and just driving away. The only problem was – he didn't trust his driving yet. He hadn't been cleared to drive and his headaches were still achingly persistent. But just as soon as he was given a clean bill of health by his doctor, he was out of here. Engagements could be broken. He was grateful for Tomas and Martina for saving his life, and he would pay them back – but not with his future. That belonged to him.

Heading across the manicured lawn, he made his way to the barn. The smell and sounds of the horses seemed to be a comfort to his soul. As he entered the dim interior, he heard a man softly humming. Walking closer, he saw a vaquero, brushing down a white mare. He was crooning to it, gentling her when her every instinct seemed to tell her to dance away. "Easy girl. Easy."

Austin didn't want to startle the horse, so he hung back until the man finished and returned the animal to its stall. "Hello. That's one fine looking animal."

Looking over his shoulder, the vaquero smiled. "I heard you back there. Yes, Reina is beautiful. But she is selfish, she demands my attention every day." He filled her trough with oats and gave her fresh water. "How are you feeling, Mr. Wade?"

Austin felt at a disadvantage. It was obvious this man knew him, but he didn't have equal knowledge. "I'm much better." And that was true, he did feel much improved. Like the horse, he needed to run and expend energy. There was a coiled urgent impulse to act – to rectify. Only he didn't know which direction he should take – not yet.

"Good. I'm glad to see you on your feet." The big man smiled at him. "Alessandra told me of your troubles."

The way he said her name told Austin volumes. There was tenderness in his tone. Ah, now he knew who Martina's sister had been waiting on the other day. "You're American." He stated the obvious.

"So are you."

An odd knowing smile was on the other man's face. Austin got the feeling this stranger had the answers he needed. But he also knew he would have to approach him carefully. "I think you're right."

"My name is Brock Phillips."

They shook hands. "Austin Wade, so they say. You couldn't prove it by me."

"No memories returning, yet?" Brock seemed to be choosing his words carefully.

"Not any I can make sense of." They were dancing around something – Austin just wasn't sure what it was.

"Be careful." Philips stated flatly. "The Patrona is a difficult woman to love, I'm sure."

Austin laughed harshly. "You have to understand something about me and 'the Patrona'. He said the name with emphasis. "I don't remember anything. These people, all of them, are strangers. This place is not my home. Hell, I don't even know my own name. Are we friends?" Austin pointed in between the two of them.

The cowboy turned his back and began to put up the curry comb and a blanket on a shelf against the wall. "I'd like to be to be your friend."

At the other man's admission, it was as if a damn broke inside Austin. He had held it in so long, he needed to talk to someone. "This is like the twilight zone for me, Brock. I don't know which end is up. Martina says she is my fiance, but I feel more of a connection to Tomas than I do her."

Philips turned around, looked to the right and then to the left, as if he were making sure they were alone. "You and I need to have a long talk soon, somewhere off this ranch. There are eyes everywhere. But I want to protect Alessandra before this place goes up like a keg of dynamite."

Austin didn't understand. "Go up like a keg of dynamite? What do you mean?"

"No. We can't talk here, I said."

"All right, I hear you. How about we go out for a beer tonight? Surely there's a cantina nearby?"

Brock continued to talk low. "Can you leave the ranch?"

Narrowing his eyes, Austin looked at his new friend. "Can I leave the ranch? Why shouldn't I be able to leave? I'm not a prisoner."

A wry laugh from Philips made the hair stand up on the back of Austin's neck. "No, I suppose not. If you say so. Let's do it. Eight sound good?"

"Yes. I'll meet you down by the garage. We'll have to take your vehicle." Looking at his watch, Austin noted the date. "Thanksgiving isn't far away. Shoot, it will be another three weeks before I'm cleared to drive." The image of a pick-up came in his head. A Ford. He drove a dark blue Ford pick-up. Now, that was progress.

"Great. I look forward to it. What will you tell Senorita Martina about our meeting?"

"Why, I'll tell her the truth. What else?"

Austin returned to the house and went up to his room to take a shower. No one seemed to be about, thank God. Of course there were always the ever-present guards standing on the front porch, rifle in hand. At first, he'd tried to reason that out and the best he'd been able to come up with was where the ranch was located and the likelihood of people coming through on their way to the US border, like they had the other day. He knew violence was prevalent down here. Drugs were everywhere and the cartels were powerful. But still, all of the weapons being bandied about seemed to be over-kill in his mind.

Staring in the mirror, he noticed his hair was growing back over the bald spot where he'd had the operation. All in all, Austin was becoming more and more used to himself. At first, he'd looked at his own hands as if they belonged to a stranger. In many ways, he felt like an imposter. No matter how hard he tried, his past always eluded him.

Picking up his shaving kit, he stared at it, trying to remember buying something so ostentatious. It was covered in silver. None of his things felt familiar, yet he wasn't tempted to unpack the contents. He felt like a visitor. Opening it wide, he dug in the bag, and was surprised when his finger touched something cold and hard on the bottom. He pulled it out. It was a coin. A gold coin. Austin turned it over and over, looking at the image of a woman on the side, her delicate profile and long hair giving him an odd feeling of recognition.

Something seemed to come over him. He could see underwater, like he was swimming. And then he saw a cave and a glimmer on the floor. A flashback ripped through his mind, causing an abrupt shaft of pain to seize his temples. He remembered! He'd found this coin while diving. A feeling of excitement overcame him. But it wasn't just the event he remembered – it was the feeling – the significance.

Again, he stared at the coin. Something about the woman stamped into the side was familiar. He stared at it. Who are you? He ran his hand over the grooves – over the profile. "Speak to me, beautiful. Tell me your name." Pressing the coin to his lips, he wondered at its significance. Did it belong to her? Clasping it tightly in his palm, he squeezed it, then raised it to his lips and kissed it. "I want to remember. I want to come home." Carefully, he placed the coin on the vanity table, shed his clothes and climbed beneath the spray. Once there, he cleansed his body, letting his mind wander freely. How many women had he known? His whole life was like a faded canvas where a detailed scene had once been painted. But the sun had beat down on it and faded the colors to just a vague pale outline. The tapestry of his life had become unraveled and he didn't know how to reknit the strands.

Leaning against the cool tile, Austin let the warm water sluice over him. It wasn't something he understood, but his body longed for someone he couldn't place. If he closed his eyes, he could feel her touch. Letting his mind meld with his dreams, he could feel her – she was here. Standing right behind him. Her lips, just those sweet, plump lips, placed a kiss right in the center of his back. He groaned, his cock immediately responding. Softly, she began to touch him, running her hands over his shoulders and down his arms. Austin held his breath as she stepped closer. Now he could feel her stiff little nipples grazing the skin of his back. Little licks ran all over his shoulders, if he was really still, he could feel her teeth graze his skin. She wanted him. "Touch me, please," he begged.

A lilting laugh made his heart race. And when he felt her palms rub down his arms, and her breasts press flat against him, he pushed back, needing more contact. "You're ripped. I love to touch you. I hunger for you. I ache," she purred.

"Don't torture me," he growled.

He shuddered when her hands skated under his arms and came around to massage his pecs. She was driving him mad – rubbing his muscles, paying special attention to his nipples. Austin threw his head back, turning his face to find her lips. Their mouths crashed together and he got lost in her kiss. All the while, she petted him, molding his chest, pressing her luscious little body against his. "Please," he was asking for something – anything.

And then she gifted him, letting her hand glide low until she made contact with his burgeoning erection. He was stone hard, leaking and aching for her touch. No one else would do. "Do you want me to stroke you, Cowboy?"

"God, yes," he moaned. "I'll die if you don't. Ahhhh," he sighed as her little hand grasped him, her fingers not quite meeting around his girth. And when she started to pump him, he almost lost his mind. She worked his cock, her lips and tongue still tracing erotic patterns on his back. Austin couldn't keep his hips still. Helplessly his hips bucked forward, needing to pound into her soft, wet pussy more than he needed life. "God, baby, this feels so good."

"There is no one like you. No one." She whispered. "I've loved you for so long. I'll love you forever."

Her words made his blood boil, the heat and desire rose in his balls, making him stand on tiptoe. God, he needed to cum. It had been so long – not since…. Lord, he could remember how it felt to pound into her – how tight she was, how perfectly they fit together. "L…Love," he cried as she jerked him off, the white, hot jets of semen splashed against the wall. Austin grunted, his whole body convulsing with ecstasy. For long moments, he pulsed – his heart pounding – her hands slid from his body. Her touch evaporated in the steam. Austin let his cock go and collapsed against the wall – spent.

"I'll remember you," he promised. "I'll remember you, or die trying."

Getting out of the shower, he toweled off. God, it had felt good to masturbate. Most men would say he was crazy to forego the pleasures of fucking Martina, especially when she offered herself to him so blatantly. But something, or someone held him back. And it had to do with this coin… Austin picked it up and looked at it once more. All the while trying to force himself to remember more, but there seemed to be a dead-bolt on the gate to his memories.

Dressing in all black from denims, to a western jacket, hat and boots – he was ready to go. Before leaving the room, he put the coin in the front pocket of his pants. It seemed to comfort him, somehow. Heading down the stairs, he was surprised to see Martina coming through the door.

"Darling!" She ran to give him a kiss. He hated to be so indifferent, but Austin couldn't shake the sense of betrayal every time he even casually touched her. There was someone else, somewhere who loved him – whom he adored. He was sure of it. He could feel it.

"Martina." He allowed the kiss on his cheek and gave her a smile. "You're looking well."

She seemed to bask in his faint praise. "Thank you." She grabbed his hand. "Come with me to the kitchen. I have something I want to show you."

He followed her, not willing to dampen her good spirits. "I want to talk to you about a few things, also. If you have the time."

Martina looked at Aron McCoy. "You are one gorgeous man." She ran an appreciative hand over the sleeve of the jacket. Her secretary had done a good job picking out clothes. Leaning in, she stole a kiss before he could even react. Tonight would be hard; she had to break the news to Alessandra that a marriage to Joaquin Rios would be the best for all concerned.

He didn't respond, but he smiled, taking down a couple of coffee cups from the cabinet. "Coffee?"

"Yes, please." After Esteban had voiced his proposal, she had considered it. Conceivably, at some point in the future, the cartels could be united under her leadership. At the thought, she stood straighter. Now, all she had to do was bring Aron/Austin into the fold. Together they would be a formidable team. "I am so glad you're with me." She confessed, sending a little oracion to the skies – and yes, she did still pray. Justifying her actions might be difficult, but providing for and protecting her family shouldn't be a crime.

"I am very grateful that you have taken care of me." Austin was careful how he answered. He was grateful. If what she'd told him had all been true, Martina had saved his life. He could have drowned. Then he'd never find... never remember – the woman who haunted his dreams.

She was feeling generous. "What did you want to speak with me about?" Adding sugar to both of their cups, she urged him to sit at the table with her. All she could think about was how it could always be this way – her and Aron – planning and sharing. And making love. A blush rose in her cheeks. She was going to go to his bed tonight. This time, he would not turn her away. She was sure of it.

Austin took the coffee and considered how best to approach the topic. "I'm feeling better these days and I need to be more active. More useful. I want to work around the ranch. I want to help Tomas."

Martina smiled, nodding her head. "That will not be a problem. It will make Padre very happy. You can be his foreman." She knew Aron had an intuitive knowledge of ranch life. He had run Tebow with consummate skill and she had no doubt he would turn Los Banos into a true profit-making affair. Now, if she could just coax him into the cartel. "Anything else?"

Austin smiled. "Yes, I'm going out after dinner with Brock. We're going to get a beer. I wanted you to know. I've been missing hanging out with a guy." He offered by way of an explanation.

Almost – almost she demanded that he not go. It wasn't that she didn't trust Brock. She did. He was a good employee, her father's favorite. But the idea of Aron alone with a man who might suspect her story about Austin's identity - was almost unbearable. She had strove to quell any talk of Aron/Austin and why he was here, but stemming the flow of gossip at operations as big as Los Banos and El Duro was next to impossible. "All right." She covered her hand with his. "But don't be long. I have a special night planned for us." Briefly, she considered planting a bug on him, to monitor his conversations, but she rejected the idea. As deceptive as their relationship was at the moment, Martina longed to build a future with him based on mutual trust and love. Because – yes – she loved Aron McCoy.

A special night? Austin compressed his lips. Well, he'd cross that bridge when he came to it. "You wanted to show me something?" He thought it might be best if he changed the subject.

He was wrong.

Martina pulled out a brochure, gave a very distinct feminine wiggle and spread it out. "Help me pick out our wedding cake. I want a Christmas wedding."

Chapter Five

Tebow Ranch

"Libby! You've got a package," Nathan called. He walked into the living room. Cady and Avery had begun to decorate for the holidays. Tricia, Avery's partner at the florist shop, had brought in huge wreaths and fall flower arrangements. On the porch were bales of hay, pumpkins, even a scarecrow. And he knew right after Thanksgiving, they would start putting up Christmas decorations. A feeling of guilt made Nathan hang his head. He knew why they were doing it; they were trying to make him happy.

Didn't they understand?

Aron was gone. Being happy just felt wrong. How could they celebrate anything when Aron might be dead? Or what if was hurt somewhere or lost?

Nathan went to the refrigerator and looked in – staring. He didn't even know what he was looking for. It was hard to put his thoughts together. Awful ideas were going through his head. What if a shark ate his brother? What if he'd drowned and been swept out to sea? What if he'd been kidnapped by pirates? The worst part was – no one would talk to him about any of it. They were trying to protect him, but what they were doing was shutting him out. And it hurt.

"Need something?" Libby stood behind him. "Can I fix you something to eat?"

Nathan turned, closing the fridge. "No, I'm not hungry." Lately, he couldn't look Libby in the face. He didn't know if it was because he didn't want her to see how much he was hurting or if he couldn't stand to see the hopeless pain in her eyes. "I laid your package on the table."

"Nathan," she began, her voice was soft. "I've missed you." Libby knew she had shut everyone and everything out after the shock of Aron's disappearance. There was a time, not long ago, when she and Nathan could talk about anything. She made him brownies. She helped him with his homework. They talked about his brothers, his mother, Bess – even girls.

Nathan felt tears prickle at the back of his throat. "I've missed you, too."

She lifted her hand and touched his arm. They were the same height, but still – she was so important to him. He wanted to…. "Oh, Libby."

He walked into her arms and she held him tight. Laying his head on her shoulder, Nathan cried. "I miss him, so much."

"I miss him, too." She hugged him hard. His tears were splashing on her neck and hers were running down her face.

"I' m so afraid." He sobbed.

"Don't be afraid." She soothed him. "We won't let anything happen to you. You have all of us – Jacob, Joseph, Isaac and Noah – plus all the girls. We'd do anything for you."

"I'm not afraid for me," he whispered brokenly. "I'm afraid for Aron."

Silence. "Oh." Libby shook. Nathan's hold on her tightened. "I'm afraid for him, too. I lay awake some nights and just try to feel him. I try to connect with him, to know where he is and how he's feeling."

"Me, too," Nathan confessed. "I dreamed about him last night." She led him to sit down at the table.

"Tell me." She urged him. Pouring them both a glass of milk, she got the cookie jar. "Snickerdoodles. Cady made them."

"Thanks." He took a couple. "I saw him on a horse. He was riding in a desert looking place. It wasn't green there like it is here. And there was another man with him. And they rode up to this house which was made of pale orange stone. There were arches all across the front of the house. And everybody there spoke Spanish."

Libby didn't know what to think. "That was some dream. What else?"

"Not much," he admitted. "Only they didn't call him Aron. Everybody there called him Austin."

"Did he look happy?" That was a stupid question, she knew. But sometimes dreams meant things.

"Yea, I guess so." He smiled.

"Well, if you dream about him again. Will you let me know?"

"Yes." He bit a big bite of cookie and washed it down with milk. "You know what else?"

"What?" She munched on a cookie, too.

"I met a girl. Her name is Tina."

"Oh, really?" She reached out for another cookie. "What's she like?"

"She's pretty and smart. Reading is her favorite past time." He rolled his eyes.

"Hey, you're getting better all the time." His dyslexia was something they had worked together to beat.

"Yea, I know." He blushed. "We're gonna talk on the phone tonight."

"Oh, my goodness." Libby smiled, grabbing another cookie. "I'm glad.

Nathan laughed and pushed the whole platter toward her. "You're eating a cookie out of both hands."

Libby looked and sure enough, she was clutching one snickerdoodle in her left hand and one in her right. "I'm a two fisted cookie eater, because I'm pregnant with twins."

"Yea, likely story. Did you look at your package?"

"No." She picked it up. "But I'm going to now. And you," she wrapped both cookies up in a paper towel for later. "Invite that girl over her for supper. I want to meet her."

Libby glanced down at the return address on the box and nearly sat back down in the chair. Kerrville Photography Studio. It was her wedding pictures.

***

Los Banos

Well, butter my butt and call me a biscuit. A wedding? Oh, shit. "I thought girls needed, uh, years to plan."

"No. No." Martina laughed. "A Christmas wedding will be perfect for us." Perhaps a double wedding. She had returned Javiar's phone call and Joaquin wanted to meet Alessandra. Now all she had to do was break the news to the bride-to-be.

Speaking of.

"Hello, you two!" The younger Delgado sister came breezing in. A waft of sweet smelling perfume accompanied her.

"Join us." Austin pulled out a chair for Alessandra. He was glad for the company, maybe it would get his so-called fiancé's mind off of orange blossoms and honeymoons. Bam! Another feeling of deja-vu struck him as the word passed through his mind. He looked down at his hand, no mark of a wedding ring. Yet, he could almost see someone walking down the aisle toward him, his heart pounding as he waited to take her hand.

"What's going on?" Alessandra picked up the brochure, then widened her eyes. "Are you getting married?"

"No." "Yes." He and Martina answered simultaneously. Then, he added. "Not anytime soon."

"We're thinking of a holiday ceremony." Martina took her sister's hand. "I have good news for you, hermana menor."

"What?" Alessandra brightened. "Do you want me to be your maid of honor?"

"Why, yes." Martina smiled. "But this isn't about my wedding, it's about yours."

Alessandra froze. "You know about…" She coughed. "How did you find out?"

Her sister ignored what she was saying and just plunged ahead. "You have been chosen by one of Mexico's richest, most eligible bachelors."

Her smooth forehead wrinkled. Now, she was really confused. "Chosen for what?"

Austin was looking back and forth between them like he was watching a tennis match. He had no idea what was going on.

"Chosen to be his wife!" She spread her hands in a grand, dramatic gesture.

Austin had to hand it to Martina, she delivered devastating news like she was passing out a Publisher's Clearing House Winner notification.

But Alessandra's reaction shocked them both. He had never seen anyone collapse in on themselves before. The beautiful woman just crumpled and a fountain of tears started to flow. "No!" She screamed. "I will marry no one but Brock. I'm in love!"

There was one advantage of two women having an intense argument… any man in the room could sneak out undetected.

So, Austin made his escape.

He knew how Alessandra felt. He couldn't marry a woman he didn't love. Martina would just have to understand when he lost his memory that changed things for him – if she was telling the truth. He hated to be suspicious of someone who'd saved his life. But things just didn't feel right for him, plus there were these dreams he kept having. The woman on the coin seemed to call to him.

As he walked across the lawn, he thought of all the things which didn't make sense to him. One of them was the claim she made that he was from Wyoming. Austin would bet his life he was from Texas. The memories of another ranch, another family and another woman were beginning to become clearer and clearer. In fact, he didn't plan on being here very much longer at all. Certainly not long enough to get married at Christmas. By then, he'd be just a cloud of dust going down the road. But one thing bothered him. If this was true and he was wrong – then the blow to his head did more damage than he realized. But if he was right and Martina was lying – the question was – why? Could all of this just be wishful thinking? Or was he the pawn in some kind of crazy game?

Austin hadn't been waiting long before Brock came driving up. He'd figured the man was the one seeing Alessandra, but now he knew the situation was much more than casual. "Ready?" Brock rolled the window down.

"Yea," Austin went around and crawled in the cab of the truck. "Where are we going?"

"There's a bar about a half hour away, Rosa's." Without any more of an explanation, he pulled out and they were soon on their way.

Austin watched the surrounding country-side with interest. He hadn't been awake the last time he'd arrived. Tomas had told him he came by ambulance. It seemed there was a full medical facility on the ranch and another at Esteban's house in town. That confused Austin. Perhaps it was because they were so far out in the country and maybe Mexico didn't have the network of physicians and hospitals that America had. In fact, nothing was as he expected it to be. Not even the entrance to the ranch was normal. It looked more like the exterior of a prison, and if he wasn't mistaken, the fence was electrified and topped with barbed wire. "What the hell? What kind of place is this?"

Brock laughed. "You have no idea what kind of mess you're embroiled in do you?"

"Apparently not." He rolled the window down to get a little breeze in his face. "Care to enlighten me?"

Looking him in the eye, then back to the road, Brock looked dead serious "You really have no idea?"

"No."

"Well, let's wait till we're in the bar. You're going to need a drink before you hear what I have to say."

***

Tebow Ranch

Libby's hands shook as she carried the packet of photographs. Almost running, she headed up the stairs, going straight for her and Aron's room. Throwing open the door, she escaped inside, closing it and leaning against it – out of breath.

Running her hand over the slick cardboard, she had to decide if she was strong enough to do this. Would it be easier to stick them in a drawer and not look at all – or could she steel herself to gaze at his face? God, she couldn't not do it – this was Aron – on their wedding day.

"I love you so much." She whispered. Going to the bed where they'd slept, where they'd made love, she crawled up in the middle of it. Then she changed her mind and moved over on his side of the bed, scooting back up to lean on his pillow. Silly her, she hadn't changed his pillowcase from the last time he'd slept on it. When she'd come back from the Caymans, Libby had been grateful no one had changed the sheets. Oh, she'd washed them since then – switched them out, but not his pillow case. It still smelled like him, his own unique scent of soap, leather and the sweet scent of grass and hay. Burying her head in the soft cotton, she rubbed her cheek against it, pretending it was his shirt and he had his arms wrapped tightly around her body.

A deep, sharp pang of grief dug a gash in her heart. Where was he? The family hadn't quit looking, but she could tell their faith was starting to falter. How could it not? There had been no trace of him. Oh, plenty of leads, but none of them concrete. None of them had panned out.

A bolt of thunder outside made her jump. The sky had darkened, she could hear the wind blowing. Libby leaned over and turned on the bedside lamp. A storm was coming.

Taking a deep breath, she took the package in hand and began to open it. Tugging at the edges, she finally broke the seal. With trembling fingers, she slid the photographs out.

"Oh, my God," she whispered. There they were. Swirls of happiness collided with piercing thorns of regret. There were photos of their rehearsal dinner and the rehearsal itself. Everyone looked so happy. She touched Aron's face as he handed her the sculpture he'd made for her. She had given him pictures of their unborn babies. And here was one of them dancing. Libby swayed, remembering the sound of the music and how it had felt to be held close to him. He was so big and strong – she knew she was safe with Aron. When she'd been sick, it always seemed to her that if she could just hold on to him, nothing could ever hurt her again.

One by one, she picked up the portraits. They were so wonderful. The photographer had performed miracles with her. She was actually beautiful. But Aron... he looked so incredible. With one finger, she touched his face. They were standing in front of the preacher and he was looking at her with such love in his eyes. She could recall exactly how she felt as she gazed up at him. He had whispered – 'I love you, Libby-mine.' How lucky she was. And the kiss they shared on their wedding day, she almost swooned at the memory – he had literally picked her up. Her feet hadn't touched the ground. When Aron kissed her, he consumed her – he inhaled her. She always felt so cherished. There was no other man in the world like Aron McCoy. He was her hero. He was her protector. He was her life. "Aron, come home to me. Please." Clutching the pictures to her chest, she prayed. "I need him, God. We need him. Please give him back to me."

***

Los Banos Ranch

"You have gone too far, Martina." Tomas consoled one daughter while he confronted the other. "Your obsession with power and money has stolen your humanity."

Martina stood her ground. She was regal in her bearing, but not untouched by the tears of her sister. Yet, logic should prevail. "Not long ago you were concerned with all of the deaths and bloodshed, Padre. Now, I offer a solution and you reject it? Because of emotion? This has been the way of powerful families since time immemorial."

"If you want someone to marry Joaquin Rios, marry him yourself!" Alessandra yelled at her older sibling.

"I agree." Their father chimed in. Your involvement in this lifestyle makes me sick, but letting Alessandra marry into it, also – would kill me. It would be like throwing her into a pool filled with blood-thirsty piranha with a paper-cut on her finger. They would devour her!"

"But, I cannot love marry Rios, I am going to marry…" Martina stopped, her thoughts turning somersaults in her brain. "So, you love this vaquero?"

"I do, so much." Alessandra pleaded with her sister, standing before her with her hands outstretched. "Help me, Martina. Don't make me run away from you. I can't live without him."

Oh, she could rectify this situation. Brock could go missing with a snap of her fingers, but then her baby sister would hate her. God! She was going soft. The head of a drug cartel did not go soft and survive. Martina hung her head, wondering what to do.

***

Rosa's Cantina – near Los Banos Ranch – Sonora, Mexico

Austin was surprised by Rosa's. He had been expecting mariachi music and he got country western. In fact, the interior of the bar looked so familiar; he knew he'd frequented one similar to it somewhere else. "All right. Spill." He drained his first long-neck and motioned for another.

"Do you know who Martina Delgado is?"

"I don't know." Aron smirked. "Could she be the sister of the woman you're in love with?"

Brock didn't look that shocked. "You are one perceptive cowpoke."

"No, not really. I just heard Alessandra screaming her love for you at the top of her lungs back at the house."

"What? Why?" Brock looked concerned, upset and scared – for Alessandra he presumed.

"Her sister, my beloved," he said wryly, "just informed Alessandra that she has been chosen to marry the most eligible bachelor in Mexico, Joaquin Rios."

As Austin watched, Brock's face blanched white. "Over my dead body. Do you know who Rios is?"

"No. Hell, I don't know who I am, much less a Mexican lothario." He assumed it was not a mere rival for the senorita's affections.

Brock looked around the bar, carefully.

"Who are you searching for?"

"Snitches. They're everywhere."

Austin was feeling like he was playing a bit part in an old movie. "What are you talking about?"

Philips leaned over and whispered. "Rios is the son of the second most dangerous drug lord in Mexico."

"What?" To say Austin was shocked was putting it mildly. "Why would Martina even suggest such a thing? Why would she even consider marrying her innocent younger sister to a kingpin?"

Brock didn't answer straightaway. He just stared at Austin Wade. Then, he asked… "If Rios is second, do you know who is considered the most lethal drug lord in Mexico?"

"No, I can't say I do." Austin had no idea where the conversation was going.

Brock smirked. "Diosa de la Guerra, Queenpin of the El Duro Cartel." Austin felt sicker with every work Philips spoke. "Martina Delgado. Your fiancé."

***

Tebow Ranch

"Jacob!"

Jessie's voice yelling his name made Jacob levitate out of the bed. "What? What's wrong?" He hadn't been asleep too long, he didn't think. "Are you sick, Sweetheart?"

"No. We've gotta go."

"Go where?" He sat up in the bed.

"To the hospital. My water broke."

"Oh, Lordy." Jacob got up and grabbed his pants, heading for the door.

"How about me?" Jessie was trying to get out of the bed. Her stomach seemed to be in the way of everything.

"Oh, yea, I guess we need you." Jacob smiled sheepishly. "Not much use of me to go without you." He helped his wife up, kissing her face every few seconds. "Do you feel okay?"

"Yes, I'm not cramping. There's no labor pains to speak of…" Her voice sort of trailed off." She watched her husband throwing things out of the closet, over his shoulder, one thing after another. "What are you doing?"

"Hunting the suitcase, we packed a suitcase. Didn't we?"

"You already loaded it in the car. Remember?"

"Oh, yeah." He turned to her. "Are you ready to go?"

Jessie sighed. This did not bode well. "I need to get dressed. My gown is wet."

Jacob rubbed his face and took a deep breath. "You're the one having the baby and I'm falling apart."

"That's okay." Jessie kissed him. "I have it under control. Just help me to the bathroom."

In a few minutes, Jacob was carrying her downstairs. "Isaac! Noah! Joseph! Nathan!" He yelled at the top of his lungs. "The baby's coming!" People began pouring out of bedroom doors – shouts and whoops and laughter from the men and concern from the women. All were there but Noah. "Where's Noah." They were following him down the stairs. "Lord, look at that rain!"

"I don't know. I'll look for him. Maybe he had a date." Joseph offered.

"Let me get the car for you. Just stand here." Isaac took off. "I don't want Jessie getting wet."

Avery came up to them. "We're coming with you."

"Yes, we're all coming." Libby had joined them and Cady was hunting umbrellas.

"You don't have to, I'm sure this is going to take a while."

"Are you kidding, this is the first McCoy. We wouldn't miss this for anything." Nathan was grinning from ear to ear. "I'm going to be an uncle!"

***

Rosa's Cantina – near Los Banos, Sonora

"Martina Delgado is no damn fiancé of mine." Austin barked. All right the damn jig was up. "What the hell are we going to do?"

"Get ourselves killed if we're not careful." Brock drank a long swig of beer.

Austin held his head in his hands. "Let me get this straight. Martina runs a drug cartel?"

"Yep, a huge operation, she runs drugs from South America all over the United States – heroin, cocaine, marijuana, meth – hell, I've even heard she's selling women. That's why this shit doesn't really surprise me."

"Tell me the truth." Austin had to know. "Have you ever seen me before? Did I live with the Delgado's before my surgery? Were we really engaged?"

Brock waved his beer bottle in Austin's face and bent over to be sure he could be heard over the music. "I don't claim to know everything." He paused for emphasis. "But I've been at Los Banos for two years and I've never seen you before in my life."

"Son-of-a-bitch." Austin muttered. "So, who the hell am I?"

"That I don't know. Since you've been here, they've been close-lipped on everything. Martina has commandeered newspapers and magazines. She's even put the ranch on closed circuit television. We only see the programming she approves of. All I can tell you is this – if your name is Austin Wade – I'll eat Tomas's sombrero."

"We have to do something. I want out of here."

Brock studied the tabletop, like he was reading a manual. "You can't just walk off, you don't know what you're dealing with. Shit, she'll have you killed in a heartbeat if she thinks you're betraying her. That's one of the reasons that Alessandra and I haven't eloped. She hopes to negotiate some type of separation from her. My baby thinks her sister loves her enough to let her just walk off – with me – if she convince her how much we love each other and how much happier she'll be just living a normal life."

"You don't look convinced." Austin observed dryly.

"I don't trust her, but I love Ali to distraction. I'd die for her, man."

"So, you think Martina will just let you two walk away?"

Brock was silent for a moment. Then, he shook his head. "I don't think there's a chance in hell."

"Then, I think we ought to take down the whole damn operation."

"I'd think you would want to get out of here and go back to where you came from."

Austin slammed his beer bottle down. "I don't know who I am."

"I bet there's information at the house, somewhere. Or you could go to one of the newspapers in town. I bet they'd know."

"Do you think that would work?" Austin looked skeptical.

"I think you'd be dead in an hour."

"Hell – so do you have a plan."

"Well, maybe." Brock pulled his hat down over his eyes. "The thing is - I don't want Alessandra hurt. I love her. I fully intend to marry her if I get her out of this hornet's nest."

"Yea, I don't relish hurting Tomas, either. We need to think." Austin sighed. "First, I need to find out my name." He put a hand to his head. A headache the size of Bevo was tromping through his head. He groaned. "I graduated from the University of Texas." The memories were coming back. The headaches seemed to bring them.

"Well, don't let her know, for God's sake. Act dumb. You're more on the inside. Why don't you play along and start gathering evidence? Find out your name and get lists of suppliers, dealers, lieutenants – hell, get a hierarchy of the whole hell-hole."

"To give to whom?" Austin had no knowledge of the political workings of the Mexican government.

Brock smiled. "This I know. We'll give the information to Cisco Salazar. He's the newly elected Attorney General of Mexico and I think he's on the up and up. The war on drugs was his platform, we can gather documentation and help him build a case."

"This is war." Austin held out his hand.

"War." Brock agreed.

A sense of urgency and purpose filled Austin's heart. Everything within him wanted to get to the bottom of this fiasco and fast. He wanted to go home – wherever the hell that was.

***

On the way to the hospital – between Tebow and Austin

"Skye, huh?" Joseph grinned at his younger brother.

"Skye, yea. You gotta problem with that?" They had just made a run for the truck in the pouring rain. "God, this is some storm."

"Bad night for a baby to be born."

"Turn on your brights, Joseph. I can't see a damn thing." Noah was still buttoning up his shirt. Joseph had come banging on the door to the hunting cabin to inform him that Jessie was in labor. He had been visiting the beautiful Skye Blue, their foreman Lance's sister. "How did you find me?"

"Well," Joseph laughed as he flipped on the lights and illuminated the narrow country lane which connected the hunting cabin road to the main ranch highway. "It wasn't that hard. You were gone. Your truck was still at the house. Your horse was gone, so you couldn't have gone far. You're perpetually horny."

"Very funny." Noah grumbled. "Nothing happened."

"Only because I interrupted you," Joseph pushed his Stetson back on his head and grinned.

"No, I want to get to know her, take her on a date. Skye's a lady. I like her."

"Well, I do, too." Joseph affirmed. "We've all been hoping you'd start seeing Skye. We want you to be happy, Noah." He said that like he was worried Noah didn't believe him.

"Joseph. I need to tell you something."

"What?" He slowed down at the stop sign and turned left onto the main highway toward Kerrville. "Hold on, let me see where the rest of them are." Joseph called Cady and talked for a few seconds. "They're almost at the hospital."

"How's Jessie?"

"The contractions are pretty far apart. She's afraid this might be a false alarm."

"You think so?"

"Hell, I don't know. They said her water broke." Joseph shrugged his shoulders. "This is our first baby. We're all sorta new at this."

"I guess by the time your babies are born, this will be old hat."

"Yea, Aron's will be next." They grew quite. Joseph cleared his throat. "What did you want to tell to tell me?"

"I dreamed about him tonight." Noah confessed. "That's why I was with Skye."

"You did?" He slowed the truck down a bit, listening to his brother.

"I woke up in a cold sweat. The dream was his funeral. We were all standing around his casket. I watched them lower him into the ground."

"God."

"I couldn't stay in the house, so I took Shawnee and just rode. When I stopped, I was at the cabin and Skye was running out toward me. Lightning was striking all around us."

"It was just a dream, Noah. That doesn't mean it will come true."

"No, I know that."

Both sat silent. "This is crazy." Joseph sighed. "We have such a wonderful family. Jacob's baby is being born. We're all finding love. And Aron has to go and get himself damned lost!"

"What do you think happened to him?" Noah asked quietly, as if it were wrong to even say the words out loud.

Joseph hesitated before he answered. "Cady says he's coming home. Harley says he's coming home. I believe in magic, brother. So my money's on Aron McCoy being home for Christmas. What do you say?"

"I say, I hope you're right."

Chapter Six

Los Banos Ranch

On the way from Rosa's, the two men firmed up their plans, agreeing on the next time they'd talk. They decided to meet at the ranch dump site, not too many people were eager to go there. It was where all manner of garbage was hauled, including the dead bodies of livestock. "How about in a week, high noon?"

"Agreed." Austin felt like his head was about to split in two.

After they'd parked, Brock asked him to keep an eye on Alessandra. "If things go to hell, get word to me and I'll take Ali out of here."

"You got it." Austin nodded. "To tell you the truth, I've got to come up with a plan, I don't have a clue how to start this."

"I'm just glad we've decided to do something." Brock drove off, leaving him standing in front of the ranch house. He stared at it for a moment, sensing another time when he'd looked at this same vista. The home was typical Spanish stucco, with fountains in the circle drive and beautiful arches all across the wide front. He'd come to buy cattle, which made sense. Tomas had known him. Hell, it was all slowly coming back.

Two sentinels stood on the front, their guns undoubtedly close at hand. Knowing him, they nodded respectfully. Making his way into the house, he noticed all was dark. He didn't linger, even though he stomach was growling. His head ached like a son-of-a-bitch, all he wanted to eat was painkillers. As he walked up the stairs toward his suite, he wondered if she kept files in her room. He'd check and if she didn't, he'd just have to pay attention to her, shadow her – she would think he was being romantically attentive, which was the farthest thing from his mind.

When he came to his room, Austin didn't even turn on the lights. He fumbled his way to the bathroom and did his business, finding something in the medicine cabinet he hoped was close to acetaminophen. Foregoing another shower, he turned off the bathroom light and moved to the bed, throwing back the cover and crawling in.

Only to find it was already occupied.

Goddamit! "Martina!" After what he'd learned tonight, he felt like he'd just found a fuckin' viper between his sheets. This woman was the head of a high-powered drug operation. She was responsible for countless deaths and she'd kill him and anyone he cared about at the drop of a hat – of that he had no doubt. "I can't deal with you tonight. My head is splitting. I feel as bad now as I did before the surgery. I'm having nightmares, seeing visions - people and places that I have no idea who they are or where they're coming from." If Austin had been thinking clearly, he wouldn't have said so much, because the Diosa honed in on the fact his memory might be returning like a blue tick hound on a fox's scent.

"I'm so happy!" She laid her upper body on top of his, cradling his face and pressing kisses on his chest. "You are finding yourself, Austin. What have you remembered? Tell me, so I can celebrate with you." At her words, Austin realized his mistake. Her words were warm, but there was an icy layer beneath them. The lie dripped from her tongue like acid. She was crafty; he had to hand it to her.

"Oh, nothing specific, really. I'm getting impressions of a ranch and college." Surely that was generic enough not to set her off. Nausea made his stomach roll.

Interesting. Okay, he was here in her arms – and she intended him to stay there. Snuggling up to him, Martina decided it was time to put the second part of her plan in action. "I'll make you feel better." She soothed her hand over his chest, tangling her fingers in his chest hair. "Tomorrow, I'll make you a doctor's appointment. We need to see how you're progressing. Maybe there's a shot or a pill they can give you for the pain."

Austin didn't doubt that he needed to see the doctor. Brain surgery was nothing to mess around with. But could he trust her? Not as far as he could throw her – that was for sure. "I don't know, Martina."

"All I want is for you to be all right." Truer words had never been spoken. "Hopefully there is a drug the doctor can give you to ease your pain." It was time to call Emily Gadwah. If anyone had an answer for her, it would be Emily.

"This has been hard for me." Austin confessed.

"I know." She leaned up and pressed a kiss to his forehead. He was sweating. "I want to take away all of your troubles." If only she could, she'd replace all of his forgotten memories with new ones full of love and happiness – with her. Another thing she needed to do was make peace with her sister and get Esteban off her back. After seeing Alessandra fall apart at the suggestion she marry Joaquin, Martina could not force her. She had two soft spots in her heart – one was her sister and the other was Aron. Now, being in his arms was sheer heaven.

Austin took it as long as he could. His head hurt – true. But sleeping by this lying Jezebel was making his skin crawl. "I can't lay here. The pain is making me sick to my stomach." Pulling his arm out from under her, he left the bed, walking to the window. "You just rest, darling." The word stuck in his throat like a cockle burr. "I'll rejoin you as soon as I feel better. I'm going to take a walk." Grabbing his pants and a robe, he stopped by the bed." In for a penny, in for a pound. He pressed a kiss to her forehead and felt the bile rise from his gut.

"All right." Martina purred. "I'll be waiting. Don't be long."

If she only knew, Austin wiped his mouth on his sleeve. "Sweet dreams." Bitch.

***

Hospital – Austin Texas

"The baby's not coming tonight." Jacob let out a long breath. "Jessie's not in labor. They've induced and induced and little B. T. McCoy is refusing to budge. I guess he's gonna be stubborn like his uncles." He looked at his brothers.

"Is there anything we can do?" Isaac asked. He'd just flown in from Mexico. He and Roscoe had gone down to check out a lead on Aron. It was another dead-end. This time the family was relieved, remains had been found, but they proved to belong to a much older man.

"No, you might as well all go on back to Tebow. I'll call you when something happens." He walked the whole family down to the lobby before returning to Jessie. Walking into the birthing room, he smiled at his lovely wife, who was at the moment trying to push herself up in bed. "What do you think you're doing?"

"I want to get up and walk around."

"Hold on, hold on." He got to her and put his hand around her middle.

"I'm so fat." She sighed. "The doctor says I may have developed gestational diabetes and that's one of the reasons he was inducing, even though he says the baby might not be ready to come."

"You aren't fat." He hugged her. "You are perfect – pregnant and pleasantly plump." He smiled. He'd heard what she said and it worried him. If she had gestational diabetes, why were they just mentioning it now? "Don't you worry; everything is going to be fine." She might be walking, but he had her covered. The slightest stumble and he'd have her up in his arms before another heartbeat sounded. "He wants you to take a little breather and then he's going to put you on another drip and see if we can get this little rascal to budge."

"I know." Jessie laid her head on his shoulder. "Bowie is going to be fine. Speaking of, did you call him?"

Jacob knew she meant Bowie Travis Malone, his friend and the man their baby would be named after. "Yes, he's on his way."

"What's wrong?" She could tell by the sound of his voice. Her rock, Jacob, had been under so much pressure lately, they all had. Aron's disappearance had hit them all hard – Libby, the most of course. But Jacob had stepped into his shoes, and they were a mighty big pair to fill, especially when having to deal with a pregnant, cranky wife.

He led her to the end of the hall. They looked out at the skyline of Austin. "Are you okay? Need to sit down?" She sighed no, and leaned into his arms. He rubbed her tummy. When he realized she was waiting on him to talk about Bowie, he relented. It wasn't a secret. Bowie would tell her himself. "He's met somebody."

"Really?" Boy, that perked her up. Jacob chuckled. Nothing like a little talk of romance to put a woman in a good mood. "Who?"

"I don't know her name, but Bowie is smitten." He turned her and they started back towards the room. "I've never seen him like this. He's even thinking about renovating his house, I'm not sure what's going on."

"Things are that far along?"

"No, I don't think so." To tell the truth, he wasn't sure. Bowie had sounded strange about the whole thing, sorta mysterious. "She's been injured, somehow." He wasn't sure about the details.

"What happened?" Jessie had that motherly tone down pat. She was going to be hell on wheels if anything ever threatened her baby.

"I don't know." Jacob shook his head. "It wasn't recent. Maybe he'll talk to us about it when he comes to see his namesake."

By the time they'd reached her room, the nurse was waiting to put her back on the drip. Jacob helped her into the bed and he stepped out to get a cup of coffee. What would the family think if they knew what he'd done?

Pouring a Styrofoam mug full of thick coffee, he wondered if he'd done the right thing. They'd tried everything else and he would never forgive himself if they didn't do all they could. So, he'd offered a reward. If the family didn't want to pay it, he had no problem doing it himself.

Five Million Dollars for information on the whereabouts of Aron McCoy.

***

Los Banos Ranch

Austin hadn't returned to his bed. If Martina moved into his room, he'd never sleep again. Last night he'd just walked around outside. He'd sat outside on the patio, in the chill and stared at the moon. The face of a woman kept dancing in and out of his mind. She was so beautiful, with a voice as warm as a soft summer breeze. Her name still eluded him, but he could remember her kiss. He was seeing images of her writhing beneath him as he made love to her. Sweet gentle mornings after, holding her close in their bed, her cuddled against his side. An image of her in a wedding gown, walking down the aisle to him, kept repeating in his head over and over. He could feel the longing, the way he cherished her, she was his world. "I want you. I need to be with you."

A tortured whisper left his lips as he held his aching head. "Who am I?" Lifting his eyes, he tried to fight back the loneliness and confusion seeking to overwhelm him. Austin felt lost.

In the hours before dawn, while the whole ranch seemed to sleep, he took a chance. A risk. Martina slept in his room, so he went to hers. Even though she'd invited him, he'd never been in there before, and when he entered, he was surprised. What he'd been expecting, he didn't know – but it was a feminine room, done in soft blues and white. The bed was a queen size and a portrait of her and Alessandra as children hung over the bed. An uneasy thought came to him, what if it was bugged or what if there was a camera. But he realized she would have never allowed that – this was her private place. Walking around, he made note of her furnishings, her closet – an entertainment system. And a desk.

Holding his breath, he sat down and began opening drawers. Nothing, it was relatively disappointing. And then he saw a laptop on the credenza. Opening the lid, he turned it on. Dang, he realized he wasn't as comfortable on the computer as... damn, there was a person in his life who was a computer whiz. Who was it? Shit.

He pressed enter and looked at the icons. Going into Word, he started looking at documents. A creaking noise out in the hallway made him freeze. What if she came back? The jig would be up. But – nothing. Scanning down through the files, he saw some clearly labeled – Suppliers, Transport, Employees, Financial Records, and Emily Gadwah. He started to open a file, but another noise in the hallway let him know people were stirring. Crap he had to hurry.

Opening the drawers one by one, finally, he was rewarded. A thumb drive. With a few clicks, he saved the files. Closing the lid, he rose. Now, if he could only get out of here without getting caught.

Pulling open the door, he looked right and left. The coast was clear – well, at least he had the information; he would put it in the shaving kit with the gold coin, his two most prize possessions.

***

Hospital – Austin, Texas

"Jacob!" Jessie screamed as the doctor gave her the news. Something was wrong with their baby.

"I'm sorry, Mrs. McCoy, but you're going to have to calm down. I need to get this IV in your arm; you have to have a C-section now. The baby is in distress."

Jacob tried to get to her, but the nurses kept pushing him back. "Jessie, I'm here." He wanted to yell. Why was this happening? "What's wrong with him?" He asked anybody who would listen.

"It's his heart."

His heart. Jacob reeled as if he'd been slapped. They began to wheel Jessie out of the birthing room and toward the operating room. "Will she be all right?"

"We're going to do everything we can." The doctor informed him solemnly.

He stood back against the door as they went back, pushing the gurney down the hall. He took out his cell phone to call his family, needing them. Joseph answered.

"Am I an uncle?"

"Something's wrong, Joseph. The baby's having trouble. They're on the way to give Jessie a C-section. Come down, please."

"We'll be right there."

He paced. He cursed. But more than anything, Jacob missed Aron. He needed his big brother, the one who'd always stood by him in times of crisis. It wasn't long before they began pouring in – Isaac and Avery, Joseph and Cady, Libby, and Nathan. Noah and Skye came last. They had been to the Cattle Baron's Ball. He felt like he was drowning. They comforted him all they could, but nothing was sufficient until the doctor came out to give him the news. "Your wife is resting, but the baby has complications."

The whole room tensed, Jacob most of all. "What kind of complications?"

"Your son has a heart valve abnormality." Everything seemed to fade. Jacob was listening, but terror seemed to be sapping his very breath. He could feel the touch of his family as several stepped up to place a hand on him in sympathy.

"What are you going to do about it?"

"Surgery, when he's stronger." The doctor went on to explain that the baby was too small and too weak to undergo such a dangerous procedure at the moment. He would be placed in NICU until he was stronger and better able to withstand a serious operation to replace one of the valves in his heart.

"When can I see my wife?"

"Give us a few minute, someone is closing the incision." When he'd left, Jason had hung his head, but the rest of the McCoys had stepped up, assuring him he wasn't alone. They promised to stand by him, stay with him – Noah even offered to give blood, but in Noah's typical way he put his foot in his mouth.

"I know he's not a McCoy, but if you need blood..."

Jacob had reeled on him, blasting his brother with both barrels. "You don't have to be blood related to be family, Noah! Someday, you'll understand that."

Noah had pulled back, Skye taking him by the arm. "It's okay. He misunderstood."

They'd stayed a few more minutes, but Noah was the first to leave. Jacob hadn't seen him go. Joseph had talked him down and he knew he had messed up. "Tell him I'm sorry. I'm just torn up." Jacob said.

"It's okay. We've all had a hard time." Isaac spoke up. "But we're McCoy's, we'll pull through."

Jacob had faith. He knew scripture said we'd never be asked to handle more than we could bear – but he was reaching his limit and there were still battles to be fought.

*　*　*

Emily Gadwah's lab – Hermosillo, Sonora, Mexico

"I'm loyal to a fault, Martina. My memory is a long one. I haven't forgotten what your family has done for me." Emily Gadwah sat at her desk, arranging and rearranging the stacks of papers in neat, perfectly aligned piles. She fingered the staples, letting the sharp edges of the ends almost prick her fingers. She needed to stay alert. The woman in her office was a friend – but a very dangerous one.

"We take care of our own, Emily."

Which was true. To an extent.

As long as an employee or a friend was loyal, Marinta was loyal. But if they slipped, the consequences were dire. She stared at the woman across the desk. Her pink hair was startling. If she walked out from behind the desk, Martina knew her sandals wouldn't match and she would be wearing no socks of any kind. But she was brilliant, and she could be trusted – and that was all that mattered.

Emily swallowed hard. "Would you like some coffee or a coke?" How she'd gotten mixed up with a drug cartel was one of those mysteries of life for Emily. Her work was her world – other than her son, and sometimes trade-offs had to be made. Cartel money bought the best lab equipment. It funded research when government grants dried up. All she had to do was test their coke, perfect their meth recipes, keep their reputations intact as to the grades of heroin offered, and the rest of the time she could dabble in whatever her heart desired.

And her heart desired recognition.

If she was correct, her work would ensure her a place in history. All she had to do was keep her nose clean, stay alive and continue getting enough money to fund her testing. What she'd found was a drug which would almost halt the progression of certain forms of cancer – namely leukemia. Ibrutinib effectively stopped tumor cell multiplication in its tracks.

"What can I do for you, Senorita?" Staying alive had to be her first priority and keeping this woman happy went a long way in ensuring she would be around to see another day. Other unsavory types came knocking on her door. Without the protection she received from Ms. Delgado, it would be like a mouse living in a glass cage full of anacondas.

"Let me tell you a story." Martina knew she was risking everything, but if Emily knew exactly what was happening, she would the best course for her to take. "Several years ago, I fell in love." She hated to show her vulnerability, but that might be exactly what would convince this brilliant chemist to give her what she needed – if it even existed. "The man, a Texas rancher, did not return my affections. At the time, he did not realize who I was – the granddaughter of a drug lord. I had not picked up the reins of power." She twirled her engagement ring on her finger. The ring was real, but the love it represented was false. "So, he didn't reject me because of my association with El Duro, he just wasn't interested. At the time, I don't think he was in love, but I was lacking somehow."

Emily felt sorry for this woman, she couldn't help it. Anyone could see there was a longing in her for tenderness, to lay down the guns she carried and just be a sensual human being. "What happened?"

"I have thought about it a lot. If he'd shown me any encouragement, I would have done anything he wanted. I'd never have become the Diosa. I would have been happy becoming his wife."

"It didn't work out?"

Martina laughed. "He didn't look at me twice. His ranch purchased cattle from us. More than once. After that, I never heard from him again. I became embroiled in the 'family business'."

"Okay, so what happened, then?" Lord, Emily thought, this was like pulling teeth.

"A few weeks ago, while sailing off the coast of the Cayman Islands, we pulled a man out of the water. Saved him. He'd almost drowned. A diving accident, we think." She blew out a long breath. "It was the man I love. And he was hurt, badly. His memory was gone. And I made a decision to bring him with me, to get the help he needed and to sail away from whoever was searching for him."

Emily tensed up. Damn. She didn't let on, she thought it wise not to – but Emily Guadet knew exactly who she was talking about. The American – Aron McCoy. "Were you able to help him?"

"Yes," Martina nodded. "He's had surgery and recovered. But his memory was still missing when he awoke." She smiled, slightly. "Well, he's remembering now." She stood up and walked across the room and then back. "I've lied to him. I told him he'd sold his ranch and lived with me. I told him he was my fiance. I gave him a new name, a new identity – everything."

"His memory is returning?" At Martina's nod, she continued. "And what do you want me to do?"

"I want to know if there's a way you can stop him from remembering, but I don't want him hurt. I don't want him impaired." She thought of the strong virile man he was. "I want him to be who he is, but just not remember his family... or his wife."

Emily pondered the question, staring at the Diosa. She could tell how important this was to her. A twinge of guilt and fear hit Emily. This was huge. Aron McCoy was as important and powerful in his own right as the queenpin was. "Give me a day or two and let me see what I can do." She wasn't certain, but maybe there was a way she could appease Martina and protect Mr. McCoy at the same time. Maybe.

***

Tebow Ranch – the day after the Cattle Barron's Ball

"You need to take it easy, Libby." Joseph led her back to the room. "Those babies of yours need you to be strong."

"I know, I didn't mean to get upset. It wasn't Noah's fault." She pulled herself together. Libby didn't want to be a burden to her family. "It was just a shock. For the Cattle Baron's Association to honor Aron as if he were dead..." her voice trailed off.

"They meant well."

God, she had to be strong. Aron wouldn't want her falling apart every few minutes like this. She brushed the tears off her face. "I know it. I'm sure it was as big a shock to Noah as it was to me."

"Well, Noah, you know, he's a little anal." Joseph laughed. "Everything has to make sense, it all has to add up. He doesn't like surprises or uncertainties." He touched Libby's shoulder. "That's why he keeps questioning everything about Aron. You've got to understand, Noah would give his right arm to bring your husband home. So, he keeps grasping at straws about where he might be or what he's doing – that's Noah's way of working it all out in his head. He wants Aron to be alive, no matter what."

Libby knew what he was talking about. One of the private eyes had told Noah it was possible Aron had just walked out of the surf and left. That he didn't want to come home. That it was intentional. "I don't believe it, but I understand their thinking." She had been through enough in her life to know tough things happened. Pain and grief made some people do strange things. "But, he was happy. If he could, Aron would come to me."

If he could come home, Aron would. There. She had said it. It had been over a month, Thanksgiving would soon be here. Then

Christmas would come. If Aron could come home, he would. And if he didn't, neither her life nor the lives of his family would ever be the same again.

**

Emily Gadwah's Lab – Hermosillo, Sonora, Mexico

When Martina left, Emily began doing some research. A colleague of hers was working on a compound which was being designed to make subjects forget traumatic experiences, or at least that was the legal, public reason. It was being labeled the innocuous name of Zip. Such a drug was what the Diosa was hoping for. But Emily didn't want to tamper with an innocent life, any more than had already been done. In addition, the tests on Zip weren't conclusive. Most of the results chronicled had been on lab rats. Only a few human subjects had been tested. But as far as was known at this point, the effects of the peptide were thought to be a complete erasure of whatever memory the patient was recollecting at the time the drug was administered. In the trials, the people were asked to discuss their trauma and while they were speaking, the dose was administered.

She had no wish to permanently harm Mr. McCoy, so what she needed was something she could give Ms. Delgado which would pacify her by doing what she wanted, but only on a temporary basis. But to do that, she needed to know more about Zip. It was time to make a phone call and see if she could make a trade, Royce had been hounding her about the cancer cure. As much as she hated to share credit, she would do it to save a good man's life. Dialing the phone, she put her plan into motion. "Royce, this is Emily…"

**

Tebow Ranch

He couldn't handle it. He just couldn't handle it. Here he was running out of the house again, facing a storm far more devastating than the first one which had driven him from his home. The other time it had been a dream, a nightmare of Aron's funeral. This time it was a reality. What Noah had found changed everything. He wasn't who he thought he was. His whole life had been a lie. The woman who'd held him when he was sick, who had taught him how to walk, the woman he had called 'mama' hadn't given birth to him. He didn't know who the hell he was!

Climbing in his truck, he started the engine, gunning it as he spun out of the driveway. Would this ever feel like home again? Blindly he drove on instinct, following the same path he'd traveled the other night. To Skye. He needed her. Right now, he couldn't face his brothers. "Hell!" He laughed sharply. Were they even his brothers? Did they know? Was that why he couldn't do anything right in their eyes?

He glanced in the rear-view mirror. Taking a hand, he ran his fingers through his unruly long mane so unlike Jacob and Joseph's and the rest. All of his life he had wondered why he looked different. Neither of his parents was blond. He remembered Sue - he couldn't use the word 'mother' right now – telling him he was special. That she'd asked for a boy with sun-kissed hair. "Why?" He choked out the word.

What he'd found in Sue McCoy's diary had knocked the very foundation out from under his feet. What was he going to do? Whirling into the driveway at the hunting cabin, he saw Lance and Skye standing by her truck. His foreman lifted a hand in greeting, then walked away toward his own vehicle. Skye, his beautiful Princess, stood watching for him – waiting. She was about to leave on a trip to 'find herself' and he was going to ask to go with her. For he'd surely lost himself more than any man ever could. Maybe together, they could make sense of it all. Maybe together they could find something to hold on to, even if it was just one another.

***

La Dura Headquarters – Cananea, Sonora, Mexico

On the way home, Martina went to the hacienda to check on the operations. A shipment of cash was coming in today. People would be amazed if they knew how much money she had control over. During the last month, she'd taken in a hundred and ninety-two million dollars or six million four hundred thousand dollars a day. Actually, they didn't count their money, they weighed it. Twenty pounds of hundred dollar bills was a million dollars. There were business expenses of course, primarily the bribing of Mexico's law enforcement officers and a few random assassinations here and there.

Today, she drove the Bently. Aron hadn't seen the luxury car, she'd tried to introduce him to their lifestyle slowly. He'd seen the yacht, or part of it, but he'd been too out of it to appreciate the one-hundred-twenty foot, ninety million dollar Nauta. Her father, Tomas, refused to upgrade Los Banos with drug money. The ranch was a shack compared to the hacienda in town. Esteban lived in style. There were gold faucets in the restrooms, marble floors in the garage, a multilevel swimming pool, a full size discothèque and even a private zoo for his enjoyment. One day, she and Aron would live in the same luxury. Martina was making sure she put back money for their future. Perhaps she wouldn't always be in the business. Lately, she had considered giving it up, maybe to have a family. So, she was putting money in U. S. banks, Swiss banks, even Canadian banks.

Martina had also purchased legitimate businesses – apartment complexes which covered entire hillsides, diamond mines, shopping malls, even two professional soccer teams. She had as many legitimate employees as she had drug runners. So, keeping herself and her trusted associates organized was imperative. But this part of her job was enjoyable, she had a good head for business. The only distasteful thing she had to do was inform Esteban that Joaquin Rios would not be acquiring one of the Delgado sisters as a bride.

"Buen dia, Senorita," one of her people greeted her. She struggled for a name, but couldn't think of it, so she just smiled. Taking a few minutes, she visited her accountants and the dock where the crates of money were unloaded. Bales of cash came in to the hacienda by eighteen wheeler trucks, most bore legitimate U. S. company labels. Corrupt custom agents on the border waved the trucks through without inspection. The money would be packed in crates with padlocks on them. For a few minutes, she stood and watched a few of the boxes be opened – seeing that much money in one place still gave her a little thrill. Now the cash would be laundered back through the legitimate businesses and make its way back into banks in Texas and Arizona. If she had her way, they would soon cut a step out. Martina's thinking was that the drug money was made in the U. S., it might as well stay there, so she was fostering relationships with several men and businesses to handle a substantial amount of her money on the north side of the border. Ah – it was a game, but an exciting game.

"Martina, do you want to go with me to the church?" Esteban's request sounded strange, but she knew what he was referring to.

"Today's the day?" No, she didn't want to go to church.

"Yes, I'm expected." Once a month, he would go hold court in church and hundreds of peasants and dirt farmers would come from miles around to ask favors, to get disputes settled, to ask for loans for businesses or grants for education. Martina knew Esteban got off on this whole medieval, lord of the land, kick.

"No, I need to get back to Los Banos. I wanted to check the deliveries and to give you an answer on Rios's proposal." She put her hand on her hip and looked at her uncle. She was about two inches taller than he, about five in her heels and she enjoyed looking down on him. "You can tell him the answer is no, the Delgado women will marry for love."

Esteban sneered. "If you think you are headed for a happy-ever-after with Aron McCoy, you are mistaken. A price was put on his head, I understand."

"What?" She was shocked. "What do you mean? No, one will harm him – I will see to it."

Her uncle laughed. "Not that kind of price. His brother is offering five million dollars for information on him. For that price, someone will tear up your playhouse, nina."

Anger made her face flush pink. If there wasn't one thing to worry about, there was another. His returning memories seemed like the biggest hurdle. She'd been so hopeful that she could somehow stem Aron's recollections of the McCoys and his wife, whatever else he remembered would just be part of the tapestry of his life – something she could live with. Replacing the memories of his past with new events centering around herself and Los Banos was the goal. Despite her manipulation, Martina only wanted to be good to him, to give him his every heart's desire, as long as that didn't include reuniting with Libby Fontaine or Tebow Ranch. Yes, she knew about his wife. Martina had watched the news. She knew they were searching for him, she had read the articles and seen the reports. Thankfully, the news coverage had died down. The possibility Aron would stumble on a report about his disappearance was getting less and less likely. Soon, it would have dropped off the radar completely. But, if they were now offering a reward – a substantial reward? Joder!

He walked off with a smug smile on his face. Martina stared after her uncle, if her eyes could have shot lasers, he'd be dead. The buzzing of her cell phone broke her antagonistic glaring. It was Emily. "Hablar!"

Back over in her lab, Emily jumped at the harsh greeting. "Diosa? I have good news."

She heard the drug lord sigh, "Bueno."

"I have an idea, I think I can help you. There is a new drug called zip." She had worked out a deal with her friend, they would trade their projects and share credit on both. That is, if Emily lived through this dangerous deception. Her plan was to prepare a low-dose form of Zip which would disrupt specific memories for several months, but not permanently, like a full dose would. Now, all of this was highly speculative and she was risking her life and Mr. McCoy's well-being, but if she didn't do this, the Diosa might find someone else who would and the outcome for all concerned might be worse. Especially for her, and Emily wasn't ready to fail. What she had found out from Royce was that the Zip peptide was a PKMzeta inhibitor and chemically blocked specific, identified long-term memories, but not personality or learned behavior. In other words, with her Zip-mini, she could help Aron recall memories, then chemically put them on a shelf in his brain, where hopefully they would reemerge at a later time. Or at least that was what she was hoping.

In layman's terms, Emily explained to Martina the effects of full-strength Zip and that she, Emily, should be the one to treat him. "Now, it will be up to you to convince him I'm a physician, I do have a doctorate, so Dr. Gadwah is not a lie."

"I can do that." Martina sounded gleeful.

"I can't guarantee this will solve all your problems, but it's the best I have." Telling a drug lord that all you can offer is your best was dangerous, but she had no other way to put it.

Martina twirled in a triumphant little dance, all smile. She trusted the eccentric chemist. "All right. You get me the peptide and I'll make it worth your while."

Emily could live with that, she just hoped Aron McCoy didn't suffer from the results of her manipulation.

Chapter Seven

Los Banos Ranch – Two Days Later

Tomas and Austin rode side by side. "The basic source of our water are the thirty-five natural springs scattered throughout the ranch. In addition, there are four medium deep wells run by wind and solar power. There are also five large water ponds or tanks which store run-off water from the rain."

"Solar power. Good. That's smart. Do you have it hooked up for irrigation and to control the gates between the grazing pastures?" This seemed to be a topic he knew.

"No, this is relatively new technology for us."

Austin got excited. "I may have some ideas on how to implement some changes, if you don't mind."

Tomas looked pleased. "If you are to be my foreman, my son-in-law, I welcome your input."

Austin had nothing to say to that – foreman was one thing, son-in-law was another. What he planned on doing was fitting in until he could figure a way out. Part of him wanted to just walk off, put as much distance between him and this web of deceit as he could. But that wouldn't be smart, he needed to gather evidence on the cartel while he worked to find his real identity.

They rode over a creek and down a small canyon to a herd of Corriente grazing on buffalo grass. "There's an American coming in today to look at Rey Moteada." He pointed at a dappled bull that had stopped to watch the men on horseback. "I want you to be there. I'm having him brought to the front viewing corral as soon as we return."

"No problem." Austin agreed, but he wasn't really into the conversation. He'd just had another memory, a woman rising from the waters of a stock tank, holding her arms out to welcome him to her embrace. God, she was beautiful.

"Austin…" Tomas started to speak, but then he stopped, seeming to weigh his words. "You are a good man. My daughter is lucky to have you. I want you to be happy."

A wave of regret assailed Austin. Why couldn't things be either black or white? He didn't know what to do with all of these shades of grey. "Thank you, Tomas. I want to be happy, too. I want my memories back." Tomas didn't comment, he only sighed.

When they returned to the ranch house, Brock was waiting for them, a strange look on his face. "Three bodies were just discovered hanging from the gate up on the main road. They were decapitated."

Tomas cursed and Austin felt a chill run down his back. The reality of what he was embroiled in was becoming more and more evident.

"Were they removed? Given a proper burial?" The elder Hispanic gentleman wiped his brow. "Why can't I live a normal life?" He shook his head.

"Your daughter took care of it." Brock answered as he put fencing supplies in the back of his truck. "Tomas, Sir, I need to talk to you."

Austin felt this was the time to leave. He didn't know what Brock was about to say to Tomas – if it was about Alessandra or the dead bodies, but either way, he had an agenda of his own. In a couple of days he'd speak to Brock at their designated meeting place. If he was going to take over as foreman, even for a little while, he needed to get the whole picture. Martina's father had given him a key to the office in the barn and he intended to dive right in and get an idea of the operation. He knew he had to maintain the illusion, to fit into this life for now. His survival depended on his ability to blend in and not give away his true goal. Even the most clever prey knew the value of playing dumb.

To acquaint himself with their system, he glanced through the files. Everything looked to be in order. Opening the top drawer, he saw the normal things – pens, staples, paperclips and a couple of thumb drives. Remembering Martina's laptop and the information he'd seen, he slipped one of the small devices into his pocket for later. Then he went to work. As he sat there, immersed in the ledgers and receipts, he familiarized himself with the sales numbers, the feed bills and the listings of buyers for cattle and semen straws. As he looked over the records for the last few years a name jumped out at him. Aron McCoy of Tebow Ranch. It was like a bolt from the blue – his hand shook. Why was this so familiar? Did he know this McCoy?

"Austin." He jumped at the voice at the door. It was Brock. "Tomas said the American buyer is here. He'd like for you to come meet him."

He rose from the desk and followed his friend. "Our meeting still on for tomorrow?"

"Yea, I have news for you." Brock whispered.

They found Tomas and a big dark-haired cowboy standing next to a corral. They were checking out the bull from earlier. "Ah, there you are Austin." They both turned to greet him.

"Austin Wade, this is Jaxson McCoy from the Highlands Ranch in Texas. Jaxson, this is my foreman." McCoy. There was that name again. Was this just a coincidence? Austin held his breath, staring at the face in front of him. There was a vague resemblance to the image he looked at in the mirror every morning, but not enough to get excited about. He carefully studied the eyes of the other man, but if McCoy recognized him, he couldn't tell. Maybe he'd get a chance to ask him.

The three men discussed price, bloodline, transportation – Jaxson wanted to arrange for delivery of the bull to his central Texas ranch. As they talked, flashes of familiarity about towns – hell, even zip codes came to mind. Austin, Wimberly, San Antonio, Houston, Kerrville, Fredricksburg. There was no doubt, he lived in Texas on a ranch and he had a family – and dammit, he had a wife! The certainty of his memory almost bowled Austin over. He felt excited, dizzy, anxious to learn more.

"Jaxson, come into the office and we'll fill out the paperwork." He motioned toward the door, rehearsing in his mind what he'd say to the stranger.

"Oh, there you are!" Martina and Alessandra came walking up. Before he could react, Martina kissed him and he saw a confused look pass over the Texan's face. "We've been looking for you, sweetheart." She rubbed a smudge of lipstick off his cheek. Brock embraced Alessandra which would give anyone the impression they were one big happy family. "Dr. Carlos is here to see you. Can I steal him, Padre?"

"Of course, I'll be glad for Austin to see the physician. Brock and I can finish up with…" he paused as if thinking twice about what he was about to say, "our guest."

"Can't this wait?" Austin asked Martina. This was critical – he had to talk to McCoy!

"No, he has another appointment to get to." She wanted this over and done with. "I'm sorry, but this can't wait. Your health is more important."

Austin clenched his fists, frustrated, wondering if his one chance to find out his true identity was slipping through his fingers.

"Nice to meet you," Jaxson McCoy held out his hand. "Maybe we'll run into each other again one day." The man lifted one eyebrow and Austin almost said something right then and there.

But Martina's "Darling," in that insistent tone she had, reminded him he couldn't risk the life of this guy. He wasn't dealing with ordinary people here, he was immersed in a situation so volatile – his whole world could blow up at any moment and the fall-out could be permanent. And deadly.

Back at the ranch, he sat in a chair in one of the downstairs rooms surrounded by the doctor's equipment. "So tell me how you're feeling?"

"Is all of this necessary?" He pointed to the heart monitor, an x-ray machine, and other equipment filling the room.

"Yes, it is." His answer was short. "Now, tell me, are you still having headaches?"

"Monster ones."

"Pressure changes in the skull can trigger pain." The physician explained as he put cathodes on Austin's skin. "The brain is covered by layers of membrane which contain fluid to cushion the brain. During surgery, this system is disrupted and the pressure can drop in the skull which causes debilitating headaches. Also, the trauma of surgery itself can cause swelling in the brain. We need to see which possibility is causing your problems. Have you been nauseated?"

"Yes," Austin answered truthfully.

"Pressure changes can also contribute to nausea. We'll check this out. There are any number of medications we can give you."

Martina had come in with them, but the doctor had asked her to leave. Austin was relieved. "Thanks, doc. I've had a lot of aches and pains in my life, but you can ignore it if it's your foot or hand. But when it's your head – that's where you live. You know?"

"I understand." He led him to the portable x-ray machine. "So, you are remembering things?"

Austin hesitated, he'd said more than he should. "A few."

"Well, let's take a look at that brain of yours." After a few minutes, he had some shots. The doctor looked at everything carefully. "Yes, there is swelling, too much." He pointed to two areas on the x-ray. "Here and here. But this is not unheard of for someone who has suffered as you have." Laying them down, he leaned back in his chair. "Tell me about your memories. Sometimes it helps to talk about them."

Austin balked. Was this a trick? A fishing expedition? Probably. He wasn't stupid, he'd be vague. "Well, I'm picturing people in my head. No one in particular." He thought of the young woman in the wedding gown. A feeling of elation nearly took his breath away. She was his wife. The name Liberty Belle kept coming to him, but that didn't sound like a girl's name. "Both men and women." He could see other men who looked similar to him, but one was blond. One was young. Were these his family? "And a place. A ranch. Could be anywhere." Tebow. Yea, the more he said it or thought it – the more familiar it sounded.

"Is that all?" Martina's personal physician knew the chemist, Emily Gadwah, was set to erase these memories. Frankly, he didn't know how much time the Diosa had before her captive lover would remember everything. Something told Juan Carlos that this man might not be as easy to control as Martina had figured. "Today, I'm just going to give you a shot for the nausea. Tomorrow, I'm sending you to a specialist. From the look of these x-rays, you still have swelling on the brain and we need to give you something to counter that."

"I never have liked shots." But he could tolerate them a lot better than Nathan could. He used to scream blood murder every time they took him to the doctor. "Damn!" It was all coming back like a tidal wave. Jacob. Joseph. Isaac. Noah. Nathan. Tebow. And, God – his darling Libby. He groaned at the picture he had of her in his head. A storm of love almost overpowered him. He was Aron

McCoy. "Raw honey," he groaned, remembering that T-shirt she had on the first time he laid eyes on her. And the stock tank, he remembered it clearly now, watching her touch herself and call his name. All the times they'd made love – the picnics, holding her close as they danced. Kissing her on the back of the neck as she stood over the stove, cupping her breasts as he pressed into her perfect bottom. He remembered the sharing – the laughter. God, she was pregnant. With twins! His babies. And then it hit him, the cancer. Fear barreled through his body. He jumped up from the chair.

"What's wrong? This should make you feel better soon."

Aron pulled the wires from his body. "I need a drink."

"Let's get the shot first."

Aron forced himself to remain still while Juan Carlos gave him an injection. "You need to relax. Tomorrow the specialist will help you, Mr. Wade."

"Don't call me that." He growled, walking out of the room. Martina was waiting for him in the hall. He remembered her now, too. The trips he'd made down here to buy cattle and the spectacle she'd made of herself to get his attention.

"How are you, darling?"

"Never better," he spat. "Give me your keys." He held out his hand.

"No, you're not cleared to drive yet. Tomorrow, after you see the specialist..."

"I'm not seeing a damn specialist. Give me the keys." At her look of concern, he played her, smiling softly. She wasn't the only one who could act. "Look, darling." He touched her cheek. "I'm not leaving the ranch, I just need to drive and clear my head." The times she'd tried to make love to him turned his stomach. Once you've known heaven in the right woman's arms, nothing less would do.

The look in his eyes caused her to obey. "Alright." She went to the counter and gave him a set of keys. "To the Land Rover."

"Fine, I'll be back. Don't wait up." With that, she watched him walk out.

As soon as he was out the door, she ran back to Juan Carlos. "What happened?"

He shook his head. "I can't be sure, but I'd say his memories are coming back quickly. He's overwhelmed with it all." He touched her arm, braving the familiarity. "You'd better be careful. I'm not sure what he'll do if he realizes the game you've played."

"It's not a game for me, Senor." She smiled sadly. "I've played God and now I have to deal with the devil." What she had to do next, filled her with regret. But it was the only way. She picked up her cell phone and placed a call. "He's in the Land Rover. Follow him, discreetly. When he stops, take him. Use the tranquilizer. I don't want him to wake up until I have him at the lab tomorrow."

After she'd finished, she closed the phone. There was no going back now. Either she would be successful or she'd lose the only man she had ever loved. Permanently.

***

"I remember." He whispered. "I'm Aron McCoy." The first time behind the wheel and he was shaking with fury and fear. What the hell was he going to do? Libby must be worried sick. They had been married on the sixteenth of October, leaving soon after for a honeymoon in the Caymans. God, he remembered – he remembered it all. The love. The hope. The plans for the future. How he'd made love to her. How they'd played and the fateful day he'd went into the water with her, never to return. How she must be suffering. "God darlin', I'm so sorry." He didn't even have a cell phone, or he would call her. Would she want to hear his voice? A horrid thought struck him. Did she think he was dead? "Fuck!" His whole family thought he was dead, they had to.

Turning down one of the dirt lanes, he careened into a ditch, just righting the vehicle before it flipped. The thought of being gone from home this long, Libby missing him – crying for him. God, he wanted to scream! "All right, McCoy. Get it together." He admonished himself. Plans began to race through his head. He'd go back to the house and copy those files on that drive he'd confiscated earlier. Then he was getting the hell out of Dodge, or Mexico, or wherever the hell he was. As soon as he could find a phone, he'd call Libby and his brothers. The enormity of what Martina had done to him began to dawn to Aron and he clenched his fists at the absolute audacity of the bitch. Oh, he remembered her and Tomas, now. Back then, he'd had no idea they were involved in the drug trade or he'd never done business with them. Shit – what had he got himself into?

Slowly, he came to a stop. His head was literally killing him. Brain damn surgery. What a hell of a mess. He shut off the engine and just rested his face in his hands. He couldn't help it, he laughed. He was gonna be a daddy! "Oh, Libby-mine, I miss you so. I remember you. I remember you."

One second he was reminiscing and the next the door of the Rover was jerked open. He turned to look up and there was a pinch on the back of his neck. Aron struck out, landing a good blow to the man's face – he recognized him as one of Martina's bodyguards. But things went from clear to blurry. He'd been drugged. He blinked, trying to look at his assailant, but everything was swimming in front of his face. "Libby…"

$$***$$

Tebow Ranch

"How was your trip?" Nathan ran out to meet Noah, closely followed by his black Lab. "Was that Zane?"

Noah hugged his younger brother. There were still plenty of unanswered questions, but since spending time with Skye, he had some answers about himself. One of them was the fact he could face his uncertain parentage and still rest in the assurance that the McCoy's were his family. Him learning of his adoption, or whatever the truth would reveal, wouldn't change the fact he loved his brothers and they loved him. "Yea, he came to pick up something I found that I thought might help your cousin Philip win his court case." They hadn't told Nathan all the details, but he knew enough to understand what Noah was saying.

Apparently his answer was enough to pacify Nathan, because he went on to another topic. "Were you with Skye?"

Noah smiled. "Yes, nosy, I was." He ruffled Nathan's hair.

"Good. I like her. She's nice. Are you going to marry her?"

Laughing, Noah, answered. "Not today. Give me time, but I am in love with her."

Going to the back seat, Nathan pulled out some of Noah's luggage. "Will you take me to Galveston to see Tina?"

"How is she?" Before he had left Tebow, word had come that Nathan's friend had been in a car accident.

"She's improving, but I'd love to see her."

"We'll go. I promise. Where is everybody?"

"Jacob's still at the hospital, they're supposed to hear from the doctor today. Isaac's at the bar, I guess. But, Joseph's inside." They walked to the porch. "You go on in, I promised Lady a walk."

He made his way in the house. Before he could get more than a few feet past the door, Avery waylaid him to help her with a problem she was having on her computer. Just the general chaos of family coming and going was a comfort. As soon as possible, he wanted to talk to the family about the diary, but Isaac came barreling in with a frown on his face. "I need to see everyone in the den."

Jacob called to give them an update on the baby, who'd been approved for surgery. They asked him to come home, if at all possible. As soon as he arrived, Isaac dropped a bomb. "They've pulled something from the water." He showed them the photos, one of them was a part of a wet suit which had been partially shredded by fish and the other was a snorkeling mask with a sliver of bone stuck in the purge valve.

"What does this mean?" Joseph asked.

"It means..." Noah started.

"We don't know what it means, but we've got to find out." He called Vance and ordered the tests which would tell them if the blood and bone belonged to Aron.

All of them stood around, numb. Soon they might have irrefutable proof that Aron had been killed. A huge weight seemed to press them into the ground and Noah was about to add to it. "I found out I'm not a McCoy."

"What the hell?" Joseph asked.

As Noah scanned the faces of his brothers, it was Jacob's solemn face which caused his heart to sink. He knew something, but his words were confusing. "You are a McCoy. You are our brother."

"What made you say that?" Isaac demanded.

"Because what I found in Sue's diary." Noah called the woman who'd raised him Sue, because he needed to know the truth.

"Sue? Why did you call Mom, Sue?" Joseph looked as upset as Noah.

"You've got to understand, Noah. This never mattered. They never let it matter. Not where you were concerned."

"What are you saying, just spit it out." Noah needed to know.

"You're Daddy's son. By another woman."

"Holy shit." Isaac breathed.

Noah talked to his brothers for another hour, Jacob telling them about Sebastian bringing Noah home and how his mother had reacted. It was a shock to Joseph and Isaac that their dad had ran around on their mother. As Jacob was leaving, Isaac ran out to him. "Who was Noah's mother?"

Jacob stopped in his tracks. "I don't know her name, but I do know one thing." He stopped and looked down.

"What?" Isaac prompted, clearly upset.

"I shouldn't tell you this before I tell him, but I think he's had enough thrown at him lately." Jacob headed to his truck. "The week before our parents died, she came to see them asking about Noah."

"Did you see her?" Isaac stood at the door to the pickup, holding it open in case Jacob would leave without answering.

"No, but I know where she lives."

***

Emily Gadwah's Lab

A knock on the door alerted Emily that the Diosa and her entourage had arrived. She had worked tirelessly to come up with a formula which would fool her into believing Aron McCoy's memories had been permanently erased. The bad part was, Emily wasn't a hundred percent certain herself what this concoction would do to McCoy. She had analyzed Zip and cut it down to the smallest dose she thought would work, combining some of its characteristics with that of propofol and scolpamine. Hopefully this would dull the memories of his wife and family enough that it would satisfy Martina Delgado and not do him permanent damage. "Hell, if I can pull this off I'll deserve an Oscar."

Martina, her two bodyguards, Juan Carlos and a handcuffed and gagged Aron McCoy stood on the other side of the door. "Come in." She stepped back, noticing the trouble the two men were having controlling their prisoner. He struggled against his captors, only the gun to his neck kept him from attempting to break free. Looking into his eyes, she could see a mixture of anger and fear. If Emily could have reassured him, she would have, but that would have done neither of them any good. "Put him on the table. I affixed some straps, he'll have to be kept still for this procedure."

Fuck. What was happening to him? Were they going to kill him? Fury made Aron stiff. How in the hell was he supposed to endure this? Libby! His heart cried out for her. Just as soon as his memory returned, these idiots were about to do something to him. He stared at the unusual woman with the pink hair and the mismatched sandals. She looked too kind to be dangerous, unlike the velociraptor who held him prisoner.

Martina held her breath. This was not going as expected. She could see the hate in his eyes. "I'd like to speak to you, privately please." Walking toward an adjacent door, she expected the chemist to follow.

Emily held up one finger. "Just put him in the chair next to the steel table," she instructed the muscle. Dreading the conversation, she followed Ms. Delgado out the door.

"All right. Tell me what you're going to do to him and what I can expect."

If Emily wasn't mistaken, there was actual concern in Martina's voice. She cared for Aron, but she didn't have the capacity or the luxury for a 'normal' relationship. Almost – she felt sorry for her - almost, until she thought about the countless folks who died from drug overdoses, those killed by people under the influence and the many, many casualties of the cartel drug wars – both innocent and guilty. No, she didn't feel sorry for the near billionaires who played with people's lives like one played Battleship.

"I will be giving him a shot which should eradicate long term memories." She sought her words carefully. "The chemical is called ZIP and it's a PKM enzyme blocker." Keeping the conversation technical would hopefully confuse her enough she wouldn't question too much. "When we finish, he won't recall his past." Or at least that was the goal. An exterior of calm was what she was projecting, on the inside Emily was trembling like a leaf. If she fucked this up, she might find herself stuffed in an oil drum and dropped into the Sea of Cortez.

"Will the effects be immediate?" Tenseness was leeching off of the woman in sheets.

"Yes, I think so," Emily pulled a piece of paper out of her wallet. "But I have to tell you that this procedure is the very earliest testing phase."

"Will the results be permanent?"

Now, this part was sticky. Guess she'd see how good a liar she could be. "ZIP should permanently erase memories if they are recalled during the administration of the drug. But, I make no guarantees." Simply put, she was covering her ass.

"I don't understand."

"Simple. I have to make him talk about the things he wants to forget."

"But, you make no guarantees?"

"The drug is too new, to be able to say that for certain would take years of testing, but this is your best bet." She was spouting shit, but she had to give herself an out.

"I don't like this…"

Gulping, she took her life into her own hands. "I have nothing else to offer you."

A scuffle inside the room and a cry halted their conversation. "Diosa!"

They opened the door to find that Aron had broken loose from the guards and was fighting them both. He was still groggy from the drugs, but had managed to knock one down while the other one had pulled a gun and had the barrel pointed right at the Texans' heart. "Aron, stop!"

Aron wheeled on Martina. "Why are you doing this to me?"

"Sit him back down," she instructed, coolly, watching the two slightly smaller men wrestle the big cowboy down.

The whole thing made Emily uncomfortable. To see a man subjected to the will of another was demoralizing. "Let's get this over with."

"Get what over with? Are you going to kill me, you liar?" He stared at Martina. "You know exactly who I am, don't you?"

Emily was shocked to see Martina Delgado shake.

"No one will harm you, Aron McCoy." The queenpin spoke a bit haughtily. Clearly she did not appreciate being dressed down.

"You can understand if I don't believe you? What did you do, kidnap me, drug me?" Aron was yelling. The guns of the body guards were still trained on him.

Emily was afraid Martina would give the order to shoot. She did not want to see Mr. McCoy die today. "I will give you something, you'll feel better, I promise."

He didn't respond to her, instead he glared at the woman who he considered to be his greatest enemy. "You won't get away with this. My brothers will find you."

All of this was getting to Martina, because she sneered at Aron. "They haven't found you, yet. And you've been missing for over a month. Perhaps you are dead to them."

"I'd rather be dead than have anything to do with you." Aron spat out the words. He'd pulled so hard at the ropes binding his wrist that blood was running down his fingers.

"Are you in pain?" Emily asked, touching his shoulder.

"What does it matter?" He didn't take his eyes off Martina. "There's no telling what she's done to me already."

"I think it would be better if you left us." Emily told Martina, giving her a meaningful look. "He has to be calm for this pain medication to be effective." When no one moved, she tried again. "You can guard both exits, there is no other way out of the lab."

"All right." Martina motioned for the guards to go before her.

Emily stood up, following them to the door, then she turned to see the big man hunched in the chair, his head bowed. She debated on how to play this. There was no doubt she had to give him the drugs, her life depended on it. But she could be merciful. She decided to play both ends against the middle. Having her cake and eating it too was something she had always wanted to do. Lord, she could have looked at this man forever, he was truly a handsome specimen. But it wasn't because of his looks she wanted to help him – oh, that might have played a small role – she liked to think it didn't. No dog deserved to be treated this way. "I'm going to give you something to take those headaches away." That much was true. One of the injections would be a dose of steroids laced with mannitol to reduce the swelling in his brain. But the other would be the cocktail to harness his memories. – for a season at least.

Aron followed her movements. "Help me get out of here."

She grimaced at him and got close enough he could hear her whisper. "You know as well as I do what those people are capable of – our only hope is to cooperate, or at least pretend to."

She could tell Aron was considering her words. "Why am I having so much pain, is it normal?"

She considered her answer. Piling one more lie on her list of sins wasn't her first choice, but she could give him information, even though she wasn't a medical doctor. "It is not uncommon and your stress levels have aggravated the situation."

"I have never experienced pain like this, at time it's debilitating." Aron's voice changed, almost confiding. "If you could help me, I'd welcome it."

She took his reasonable tone as permission, picking up a syringe she approached him. Lying it down on the table next to him, she reached out to touch him – drew back – it seemed so personal. When he didn't jerk away, she rolled up his sleeve high enough for her to be able to give him a shot.

"Just a pinch." Something she'd heard the pediatrician say to Hadley numerous times. Her son was alive and for that miracle, she owed the Diosa. And now she was betraying her. Actually there were no right answers in this conundrum. With care, she let the drug feed into the strong muscle of his arm. He did not react.

Now, for step two. "You have remembered your past." She did not ask a question, she stated a fact.

"Yes."

In order for the Zip elixir to work, she needed for him to speak of what had come into his mind. "You are Aron McCoy of Texas?" She tried to modulate her voice to an easy conversational tone. Not waiting for an answer, she asked another question. "Where in Texas did you live?"

Aron looked over her head as if he were looking at something a great distance away. "Tebow Ranch is a beautiful place on the Guadalupe River near Kerrville, deep in the heart of Texas."

"I've been to San Antonio," she smiled. "The River Walk is a very fascinating place." Discarding the used syringe, she stood to retrieve the other one. "Do you miss your family?" She was attempting to word her questions to sound as little like an inquisition as possible.

"I miss my family. I ache for my wife." He smiled. "She is the sweetest, most loving woman in the world."

"What's her name?" Emily retrieved the syringe filled with Zip and the other elements.

"Libby, her name is Libby."

She took his arm.

"What are you doing?" He stiffened and drew back.

Emily lowered her voice. "This will save your life and mine."

"I don't believe you!" He stage whispered and Emily heard movement in the hall.

"Shush!" she mouthed harshly as she pressed the needle into his flesh. "I have risked my life to preserve your past. This is not permanent. This drug will wear off. Your memory will return." He tried to pull away, but the ropes that bound him to the chair held steadfast.

"No! No!" He screamed. His shouts brought the others back into the room, but the injection was complete. "You are all insane!" Aron screamed. "I want to go home! I want Libby!"

"Ms. Gadwah, what is amiss?" Martina rushed to their side.

Emily held her breath. If Aron gave her away, she'd be dead before nightfall. "He resisted, Diosa."

"Did you tell him what you were doing?" She was aghast.

"I had to make him talk or the drug wouldn't work on the memories you wanted eliminated."

"Bitches." Aron barked, but his words weren't as loud or as clear as they had been. "You've drugged me," he shook his head.

"Yes," Emily admitted. "There is a relaxant included, it will make the transition easier for you." Forgetting would be as hard as remembering for Aron McCoy.

"No," he groaned. "I will not forget." With every bit of strength and determination he had, Aron desperately tried to hold on to his thoughts. "Libby, my love," he mourned, whispering her name like a prayer. "I won't forget. I won't forget. I will remember you." The drug began to take hold. Valiantly he fought to keep his eyes open, to keep his mind clear – but a haze began to form, a cloud rose in his mind. It was as if a curtain was falling behind his eyes. "Oh, Libby. I love you, Libby."

His eyelids drooped and blackness engulfed him.

Emily watched as he tossed and turned, mumbling and thrashing. Guilt tore at her conscience. This drug was not fully tested; all of the ramifications as yet were unknown. Soon, he quieted. Settled down. But he still groaned; a sound full of sorrow and loss. "Libby." Was the last word he said...

Dreams turned into a nightmare. It was as if everything he held dear was being ripped from his grasp. Visions which had been clear were receding – going farther and farther from his reaching hand. "Aron, please." The plea of a dear voice seemed to echo through eternity.

"I'll remember you. I'll remember you. I promise." He stared at her until she faded from sight – and when she did, he was left with nothing.

Blankness. Hopelessness. An empty, dark despair.

Chapter Eight

Hardbodies Bar – Kerrville, TX

Isaac put the pedal to the metal. He raced into the wind like there was no tomorrow. Sometimes there was just nothing else to do but ride his Harley as hard and fast as he could. The roar of the engine was almost loud enough to drown out the horrible thoughts racing through his head. When he'd been notified that a bloody, shredded portion of Aron's wet suit had been found with a piece of bone lodged in the face mask – he had wanted to break something. Was this it? He'd kept his cool and asked how long it would be before DNA tests would either confirm or deny that the remains were Aron. The lab was putting a rush on the work, but the waiting would be almost unbearable.

Putting on his brakes, he slid into the parking lot of Hardbodies. He needed Avery, nothing else would do. Between the DNA tests and finding out Noah wasn't his full brother, he'd had as much as he could handle. A trip to his dungeon and a chance to lose himself in her sweet submission was all that was going to keep him sane. His church girl was meeting him here, he'd called her.

Cause when his good girl was bad, there was nothing any better in the whole damn world.

"Hey, Badass, Sir." Her sweet voice ran over his senses like sugar cane syrup. Just the thought of loving on Avery gave him a hard-on the size of a Louisville slugger.

Lord, she had dressed up for him. All black, a halter dress, cut short with heels that made her legs look a mile long. "Inside, now." He growled at her. They went in the back to his private domain and when the light hit her body, he saw she had dusted herself with that vanilla flavored body glitter which drove him mad. She would shimmer for him – his favorite place to lick the powder off her body was those succulent, bouncy tits. God Almighty!

He started shedding clothes. Avery went ahead of him and he followed – tossing his leather jacket, vest, leather pants – motorcycle boots. The clink of chains sounded loudly as they hit the floor. She knew right where she was going, she had been there before. In fact, she loved it – he could tell. And Isaac hadn't touched another woman since the day Avery had waltzed into this bar and informed him she had decided the bad-boy of Kerr County was the right man for the preacher's daughter.

And when he flipped on the light and started walking down the stairs, the sight below him caused his heart to stop. She was on her knees in front of him, head bowed, her legs spread with her hands behind her back. "Sweet Jesus." Would he ever tire of looking at her? Touching her? Loving her? Not in this lifetime.

"Stand up." She did.

"Strip." She reached down to the hem of her dress and slipped it over her head – and there she stood – lush, curvy, hourglass perfect and all his. "Beautiful." Her nipples were already tightly puckered, so hard and distended he couldn't help but reach out and rub them. A whimper of gratitude whispered from her lips. His Avery loved to have her tits touched and sucked. He could make her cum just from playing with her breasts – and he did it, often. Some night, they'd sit and watch television on the couch, or it would start out that way. But he would put his head in her lap after a bit, undo her shirt and while she tried to watch one of those lifetime movies, he would mold and shape and fondle and suck those gorgeous mounds until she was moaning. Oh, she never left him out – her hand would stray down to his cock and she would massage him through his pants until they couldn't stand it another moment and he would tear off her clothes and bury his dick deep into her pussy, trying to slake the lust that rose between them several times a day. She was his woman – his submissive, soon to be his wife, and he would die for her – in a heartbeat, no questions asked.

Her body was perfection, from that wealth of dark hair which spiraled in big bouncy curls to her tiny waist, to generous hips, the face of Aphrodite, and the prettiest, pink pussy in the world. "Command me, Master."

A rumble of approval rose from his chest and he stepped up to her – close – so he could feel her bottom pressing against him from breast to thigh. "Not tonight." He needed her too much. With one powerful movement, he put his arm beneath her knees, swept her up and walked over to the king size bed. Laying her down, he gave her one more directive. "Watch me, eyes on me."

Like she could look anywhere else. He didn't have a clue how much she loved him. Oh – yea – he felt loved, but he didn't know she worshiped him, adored him, would give herself over to any manner of punishment to save him one moment of heartache. This thing with Aron was killing him and she felt so helpless, so desperate to ease his pain. So, whatever he asked – he got. Avery would turn the world upside down for him if she could. "Yes, sir." She answered, mesmerized, watching him shed the last of his clothing – a pair of briefs which had been straining to bare threads trying to contain his cock. He was beautiful. His chest was twice as wide as hers and covered in slabs of muscles which she could have spent hours tracing and licking. But what lay between his legs was magnificent – long and thick, jutting upward toward his middle with a heavy sac hanging down that she loved to tongue.

To her absolute delight, he stood in front of her and touched himself, weighing his sac, then fisting over his length, pumping once or twice. A sigh of pure longing floated from her lips, making his eyes darken with desire. She wanted to touch him, but that wasn't to be – not yet. "Hands over your head, Sable." He called her by her penname and she smiled. The fact she wrote erotic romance turned her man on. He knew he had no reason to be jealous. Isaac McCoy was her inspiration. Every book she'd ever written cast him in a starring role. He came down on top of her, covering her, his body touching her all the way up and down – the sensation made Avery feel faint. She craved to be taken by him anyway he cared, but old-fashioned missionary where he pressed her down into the mattress, let her bare his weight as he powered between her thighs was her absolute favorite. She would do anything for him – and she did – but when he wanted to reward her for good behavior, this is how he took her – hard, deep and all night long.

Covering her mouth with his, they kissed. Mild term. Isaac consumed her, he licked her lips, sucked on the bottom one – teased the seam with his tongue then thrust inside, lapping and caressing the inside of her mouth like it was made of pure candy. "I know what you want," he smiled a devil-may-care grin, making her quiver. Sitting up over her, straddling her hips, he took her breasts in both of his palms and set out to drive her nuts. Rubbing them with a circular motion, he massaged the nipples – fondling, kneading, lifting, shaping – he had her moaning, lifting her hips, making the sexiest little kitten whimpers he had ever heard. "Are you wet?"

"What do you think?" She said before she thought, then she tried to look repentant, but she giggled and he growled. Sometimes her sub slipped and she let her bad-girl out.

At his raised eyebrow, she lowered her eyes and answered. "Creamy wet."

"Damn," he bent over and began sucking at her tits – voracious pulls, mouth wide, chewing on the flesh, tugging at the nipples – first one breast and then the other until she was sobbing his name.

"Open your legs." He rolled to one side, so he could still suckle from her tits while he slid a hand between her legs and began to massage her vulva – cover the whole thing which his hand, the heel pressing against her clit and two fingers fucking in and out of her pussy. Avery lifted her hips, moaning and begging, needing him more than she needed air.

"You are so beautiful," he praised her. "I can't wait. I've needed you so much, today." Coming over her, he spread her legs wider, just gazing at his prize. She was breathing hard, her breasts heaving, quivering, jiggling a little bit in her excitement. Her pussy was swollen, and a deeper shade of pink, showing him how aroused she was, how much she wanted him. "Every time is like the first time," he groaned out the words as he took his cock in hand and slid the head up and down her slit, coating the tip in her juices. She let out a soft sigh as he bumped her clit with the blunt end of his dick. "Feel good?"

"Makes me hungry," she purred, bucking her hips up in invitation.

He chuckled. "Well, let me see what I can do." Guiding himself to her little hole, he pushed in – slowly.

Avery exhaled – never, never in her born days would she take this feeling for granted. He slid in to her, the pressure was exquisite as he filled her up, stretching her sheath to accommodate his extra-large cock. She never broke eye contact with him, her Isaac was worth looking at – a warrior, a cowboy, a badass biker with long, dark hair – midnight blue eyes, the face of a fallen angel. "Heaven," was all she could say.

As always, she took her cues from him. He was the master. He was in control. When his eyes became hooded, and his lips pulled back from his teeth in a grimace of passion, she squeezed down on his cock, causing him to groan, his whole body jolting in reaction. Bringing him pleasure was what it all about for her. Oh, he rocked her world – daily, but the greatest gift he gave her was making her know she was wanted, craved. Avery wouldn't trade that feeling for all the tea in China.

Sinking in till he bottomed out, Isaac stretched out over her, needing to feel her body next to his. She spread her legs even wider, like wings, inviting him to plunder the very depths of her. He hummed when her walls tightened down on him, clasping his cock in a silken vise. In and out, he fucked her, his hips pistoning in, impaling her over and over again.

He went on like that for what seemed like hours, their passion mounting and mounting – Avery held on, digging her nails into his shoulder, loving her until she was mindless and begging for release. Isaac could hold her just on the edge for eternity, for he had trained her well – she wouldn't come until he gave her permission. It was if she was wired to his specifications, responding only to his commands. "Please, please – more, don't stop," she chanted. All she could comprehend was the pull and surge of his body into hers. "God, you're good, baby. So big."

In response to her mewls, he thrust harder. She was completely overtaken by him, her body and soul no longer belonging to anyone but him. Their joining was an ecstasy she would die for, being taken by Isaac was her purpose, the reason she'd been created. For him. "I love you, Isaac McCoy." At her offering of devotion, he paused – kissing her hard, swirling his tongue in her mouth.

"I love you, Avery Sinclair." Then he went wild, lowering himself more firmly onto her. His hips slammed into her repeatedly, shaking the entire bed, banging the headboard against the wall in one of the most erotic symphonies in the world. Beat after beat – the noise of their lovemaking overwhelmed her. She felt her orgasm rise, crashing through her like a storm. Her cries and the fluttering of her pussy seemed to rev his engine as he plunged into her faster and faster. Rising up, he looked down to where they were joined – desperate growls of lust tearing from his throat, "love this, me in you, mine, mine." Taking one of her knees in each of his hands, he pushed them toward her head – splaying her open and tilting her hips so he could jackhammer down into her. "Hold on. I have to do this, I can't help it."

Avery grasped the sheets in her hands. He didn't have to apologize – this was her favorite part. Watching Isaac lose himself in her was indescribable. Holding himself up on his arms, he drove into her, thundering – stroke after stroke – hard, pulsing, grinding down on her until she was screaming his name. "Isaac! Yes! God, yes!" As she came, so did he – his big body quaked, shuddering, as he pumped her full of his white-hot essence.

Their movements slowed, but he stayed inside of her, enjoying the aftershocks, the pulses. Making love to Avery healed him. He needed this to remind him never to take one moment of their life together for granted, no one was promised tomorrow. Love was meant to be celebrated – today.

***

Los Banos Ranch

When he awoke, Austin was exhausted. It seemed as if he'd run a marathon – and lost. Rubbing his face, he tried to remember what the hell had happened. Oh, yeah. He had met with the doctor about his headaches. A dull thud still resounded in his skull, but the sharp pains were gone. Well, he had work to do. If he was going to be foreman of this outfit, he had to get busy.

While he'd been asleep, he'd dreamed. But he had no memories of what those dreams had been. He only recalled a sad fear and an aching longing for home. Why were memories so elusive and the nightmare so clear? Hell, he needed to get his act together. His past continued to elude him. Hell, what if there were things about Austin Wade he didn't want to know? The not knowing was killing him.

For the next couple of days, Austin worked tirelessly fixing fence, ordering grain, and herding cattle. He even verified the delivery of a bull to a buyer in central Texas. To keep up with the ranch business, Tomas presented him with his own laptop. He really liked the old man. As for his relationship with the woman who claimed to be his fiancé, he was endeavoring to give her the benefit of the doubt. She seemed to be trying also. Nothing would do Martina, but they make plans to go into town so he could meet her uncle, Esteban, and have dinner. He'd asked why Esteban never visited the ranch, but he got no answer. Maybe he would learn more if he just cooperated and listened.

Everything felt strange. He felt disconnected. And it wasn't just his memory loss. He was having odd incidents of déjà vu, like he was repeating the same things over and over again. Even Brock acted weird, he'd come up to him and whispered that Austin had missed their meeting and asked if there was something wrong. Austin had said no, he didn't think so. Then Brock had whispered something which kept repeating itself in his head, over and over again. He'd looked at Austin, grabbed his arm and said, "What happened to you? Did they drug you or pay you off?"

The look in the man's eyes spooked him. "What do you mean?"

"We were supposed to work together to get out of this mess. Don't you remember?"

"No." Austin didn't know what to say. "What do you mean?"

"Fuck!" Brock threw his hat on the ground. "Forget I said anything, I don't even know if I can trust you anymore." He walked off.

Austin stood there – confused. Shit. He didn't know what to do. He didn't know what to believe.

Thanksgiving came and went. He was surprised they celebrated it, actually. But they had turkey, dressing, pumpkin pie and all the trimmings. Austin had a sneaky suspicion they did it all for him. He appreciated it. One thing struck him that day, though. When they were having their meal, there was a bronze statue sitting on the dessert table. He was drawn to it. It was a rendering of a cowboy roping a stampeding bull. There was no way he could not touch it – it drew his hand. The metal was cool, but so familiar. Looking down at the plate on the base, he saw the artist was Aron McCoy. Nice piece, but he'd never heard of the artist.

***

Hill Country of Texas

Noah held Skye as tight as he could. "There's nothing I wouldn't do to keep you safe." She laid her head on his shoulder and he hugged her up.

"Can you believe all of this?" Over the past couple of weeks, she and Noah had become so close. He loved her. There wasn't a doubt in her mind. "What will happen to Langley?"

"He tried to kill you. I want him prosecuted to the full extent of the law." As he remembered the hit and run, the tampering of her truck, the way he'd burned down the hunting cabin and held her at gun point - as far as Noah was concerned, they could throw the idiot in a cell and throw away the key.

"But he's sick." Despite all the horrors Skye had known- the prejudice, the rape, imprisonment for self-defense, she still hated to be the instrument of pain for anyone else.

"Yes, he's dying and he wanted to take you with him." Noah kissed her full on the lips. "I can't feel any sympathy for him. He threated the person I love most in the world."

Skye stood up and climbed into his lap. "You have accepted me unconditionally. I never expected someone like you."

He picked up her hand and gazed at the ring he'd put on her finger. "Loving you is the easiest thing I've ever done. You've colored my world with joy."

They teased one another, playing and loving, celebrating the fact they'd found one another and battled their demons together. A good night's sleep, shower sex, planning and dreaming for the future can go a long way toward healing battered hearts.

The DNA tests had come back negative, proving without a doubt that the blood and remains on the dive suit were not Aron, so there was still a glimmer of hope he would be found. Noah had no idea what their next step should be, but at least they weren't planning a funeral. He knew he would still wake up thinking about his past and who his mother could be, but having Skye in his arms made it all bearable. Someday soon, he'd start asking questions about his mother, but not right now.

So the day after Thanksgiving, they woke ready to conquer their world together. "You do realize I don't have any clothes to wear."

Noah laughed. "Naked looks good on you. Who needs clothes?" When she'd playfully pooched out her lips, he pulled her to him, chuckling. "I'll have a good time outfitting you like the Princess you are." He looked forward to making her happy.

"I don't need much..." she'd started to argue with him, but as he picked up his phone, he saw there had been a call from Jaxson McCoy. The message was simple.

CALL ME. IT'S IMPORTANT. ARON.

Noah grabbed his phone and dialed. Jaxson answered. In a few minutes, Jaxson told Noah something which almost caused him to drop the phone. He said he'd seen a man who was the spitting image of Aron. "I was in Sonora, Mexico visiting a ranch called Los Banos. He's calling himself Austin Wade."

Noah's heart had started pounding. "Skye, we're going to Mexico. Jaxson thinks he saw Aron."

She squealed, jumped into his arms and kissed him hard. He was shaking. "See, prayers are answered, Noah." He decided not to tell his family anything, Noah didn't want to get their hopes up until he knew something for sure, especially Libby. So they left a note and slipped off, knowing the rest of the McCoys and their women would assume they just needed some time together.

In the car, Skye put a loving hand on his thigh and squeezed. "Smile, be happy. As long as Aron is alive, anything else can be worked out."

"I know." Noah agreed. He was so excited; he had to calm himself in order to think clearly. "Let's see. We need to get you some clothes, first. I thought we might go to the airport boutique, but we have to go right by the mall. Let's stop there, and while you're shopping, I'll call Roscoe and tell him what's going on."

"Good idea." Skye was still trying to get used to her new role as Noah's fiance. The ring on her finger was a visible proof it was all real, but the huge turn had life had taken for the better was still hard to comprehend.

"I love you, Princess."

His out-of-the-blue declaration made her heart leap. "I love you, too, Noah. More than the rest of the world put together." She leaned over and kissed him tenderly on his cheek. Skye's heart was so full of happiness, she could hardly be still. If the vehicle had a convertible top, she just might lift off and float away.

"I can promise you, when all of this is over, we'll start building a life together." He looked at her as he parked in front of a name-brand women's clothing store. Getting out and opening her door, he escorted her inside. "I'll be right out front. Buy anything your heart desires" He handed her his credit card. She gave him a skeptical look. "I mean it, you'd better buy so much we have to have help carrying the bags to the truck."

"You're so sweet." She hugged him. "I'll get all I need."

"You better." Noah kissed her on the end of the nose. Stepping out towards the entrance, he dialed the PI, who picked up after two rings. "Roscoe."

"Did you have a good holiday?"

"I did, Noah. What's up?"

"Jaxson says he saw Aron at a ranch down in Mexico. I'm on my way to the airport. I want to see for myself before I tell Jacob or the rest. But I wanted to tell you where I was going."

"Hold on. Where are you?"

"I'm in Austin. The ranch is Los Banos in Sonora, Mexico."

"Let me do a little research before you just take off. I'm in San Antonio, I can be with you in a little over an hour. Don't hop a plane yet. Meet me at Mandola's in the Triangle on Guadalupe."

Noah hated to delay, but he thought perhaps Roscoe was right. He hoped an hour was enough time for Skye. Waiting on a woman to shop was new for him, but she shocked him by finishing in less than a half hour. "Three bags... not enough." He fussed good-humoredly.

"Later, I'll make you sorry you offered." She handed the card back to him.

"You keep it." He hugged her up. "I talked to Roscoe and he wants to check out Los Banos and see what we're dealing with. We're meeting him at a restaurant up by the University of Texas."

"It's probably best we know what we're getting into." She stood by while he opened the door and put her packages in, then shut it. When he was seated, she reached over and played with a strand of his hair. "Where were we going to fly to, what city?"

122

Noah had to admit he hadn't thought this through. "When we get to the restaurant, we'll get a drink and do some research."

The Italian restaurant was comfortable and the waiter highly recommended the pizza. "I'm starving," Skye studied the menu. "Oh look, everything is in half portions."

"Great," grumbled Noah. "I'll have to have four half portions." They ordered their food, plus some for Roscoe, and a pitcher of tea. By the time their pizza had arrived, so had the P.I.

"Are you sure Jaxson said Los Banos?" Roscoe asked the question before he even sat down.

"Yea, that was it. If I'm not mistaken, the name sounds familiar." Noah berated himself. "I should have checked the records at home before I left, but I'm almost certain we've done business with them before, several years ago. I think Aron went down there a couple of times."

"It's possible. Tomas Delgado runs a clean operation, unlike how his daughter runs her business."

"What do you mean?" Skye asked, her fork paused in mid-air.

Roscoe looked between the two of them, pushing his Stetson back on his head. "Let me explain. Delgado raises cattle, but he married into the Rodrigo family, who run an entirely different kind of business."

"Like what?" Noah had no idea what he was getting at. He had stopped eating, realizing he was about to learn something he wasn't going to like.

"Martina Delgado, daughter of Tomas, runs the El Duro drug cartel."

"Drug runners?" Skye was aghast.

"Drug lord," Noah corrected her. "Why would Aron be mixed up with people like that?" All he could think was that his brother had known these people before. What did this mean?

"First, we don't know for sure it's Aron." Roscoe reasoned. "And second, if it is, we can't assume what his situation is there. But what we do know is that you'll have to be careful, you can't just waltz in there and ask to see him."

Noah thought. "You're right. We need a plan. These people could be dangerous."

"Dangerous?" Roscoe laughed harshly. "Try deadly. If it is Aron, and they know his true identity, the name McCoy would be like waving a red flag in front of a bull."

The waitress brought them their check. Noah took it. "There's no way Aron is working with them willingly." He dry scrubbed his face. "Do you think he's undercover?" The idea that Aron was a spy of some kind almost caused him to laugh. "He isn't known for his subtlety."

"I agree with you, but we still need to have a plan."

"But I want to go now," Noah protested. "What if he's there now, but if I wait too long, he disappears?" He wasn't pretending to make sense, the idea that he could see his brother again soon was incredible.

"I agree we can't waste time, but you need help."

"Who?" Skye asked, knowing they needed to keep this from Libby until the information was more concrete.

"You tell me," he looked at them both. "We need a real rancher who can contact them to get us an appointment to see Tomas."

"Our cousins won't do." Noah admitted. "Unless one of us uses a false name."

"Too risky," Roscoe countered. "You have to know these people are sharp. They are technologically savvy. In seconds of them meeting you, they'll run your image through a computer and know your real name and your dog's name."

"Unless you have a fake identity."

"True, but we don't have time to manufacture that, not if you're in a hurry to verify he lives." Roscoe told the waitress to bring them coffee. "So, think. Who can you ask? More importantly, who can you trust?"

Noah racked his brain.

"And it can't be someone who is readily associated with your family."

Noah huffed. "Well, it's going to be hard to find someone we can trust and them not be associated with the family." Skye rubbed the top of his hand, giving him support. "Micah Wolfe." He said at last.

Roscoe paused, thinking. It was his business to know the family's business, history and associates. He took his ipad and checked some notes. "Good choice. He's been out of the country for several years. Former SEAL. Has valuable connections. Plus, he's Aron's friend." He looked up. "Call him. See if he's willing, and if he is, ask him to meet us at the airport."

***

Los Banos Ranch

"What did she do to Austin?" Brock asked Alessandra. Her head lay on his shoulder as they nestled down into the hay.

She faced him, feeling more at home with him than she ever had with her family. "I don't know the details, but I am sure she did something to ensure he didn't recover his memory."

"Drugs?"

Alessandra laughed. "Well, that is what we do."

"Not 'we', mi amor, you are an innocent." Brock caressed her face.

"Not completely innocent," she sighed. "You can't live as close to this as I have and not be tainted by it to a certain extent."

"Can you tell me what's going on?" He asked, carefully. "I just want to protect you."

"I could," she spoke slowly. "And I hesitate, not because I don't trust you, but because I do not want to endanger you."

"I want to be where you are. If you are in danger, where else would I be?"

She smiled wanly. "Austin Wade is a man named Aron McCoy. Martina fell for him a few years ago when he came to the ranch. He wasn't interested, but she never forgot him." He was listening to her intently, so she continued. "I'm sure you saw the news or read the papers. On his honeymoon, he disappeared while snorkeling off the coast of the Caymans. Thousands turned out to search for him, but they didn't find him because Martina picked him up from the water and brought him on the yacht. He was severely injured and had no memory of who he was or what happened. We took him to Mexico City where he had surgery, and then we brought him here. But his memories began to return and my sister took him to someone who could ensure those memories were lost and would not surface again."

"Jesus!" Brock knew it was something like that, but to hear it stated so baldly made him realize how cold-blooded Martina actually was. He had to be careful. It didn't matter if Alessandra loved him or not, her older sister would kill him in a heartbeat. "What can we do?"

Alessandra buried her head in his chest. "I don't know. But the deception won't last much longer. Aron's brother has offered five million dollars for information on him."

"Five million is a lot of money."

"Yes, and even though she's tried to hide his identity from people in the organization, there are many that know. She controls by fear, but there will be someone who is brave enough to take the risk. It's only a matter of time."

Brock agreed, because he planned to make the phone call himself.

Chapter Nine

Austin, TX

"Of course, I'll help you." Micah answered after Noah had explained to him what was going on. "I think we ought to be prepared for anything."

"I agree, what do you have in mind?" Noah listened.

"We need to be armed and since we can't take weapons on a commercial flight, I think we ought to go by private plane."

"We don't have a plane, and I'm drawing a blank on who to ask. If we have to charter, it's going to take a while. We'll also have to be honest about what they're getting into."

"True, but I have a suggestion. Let's ask Kyle Chancellor, he has a plane, plus he was on the SEAL team with me. He knows Aron and would want to help. Besides, the guy will come in handy if we get in a gunfight too."

"Gunfight – shit." Noah was realizing this wasn't going to be a piece of cake. All he'd envisioned was flying down, tapping him on the shoulder and bringing him home. "But as far as your suggestion goes, hell yes. If Kyle Chancellor will fly us down there, that would be great. I didn't know he was back in the states." He had played for the Longhorns along with Micah and Aron. Heir to Chancellor Industries, he'd won the Heisman trophy his senior year at UT. "How soon can you ask Kyle?"

"Actually, he's sitting across the couch from me and is on his cell having his plane fueled up. Hold on." Micah was speaking to Kyle, then he was back. "He said for you to meet us at the Austin Executive Airport off of I35. We'll bring the guns."

Noah pocketed his phone, turning to Skye. "I don't know if you should be going, Princess. This could be dangerous."

"Oh, no." Skye shook her head. "Where you go, I go."

Roscoe didn't say anything, he didn't want to get in between a McCoy and a female.

Noah ended up losing that argument. He paid their tab and they drove out to the airport. When they arrived, Micah was waiting for them at the gate to direct them to the right hangar. Once they boarded, Noah realized Kyle wasn't flying the plane himself. He had brought another member of the team along to pilot, Tyson Pate.

Once they were in the air, Roscoe got their attention. "We're flying into Hermosillo. Vance will have a car waiting on us and he's found a house in a town closer to the ranch, a village called Cananea. He'll have a sweep done before we get there. We just can't be too careful."

Skye's eyes got big at the 'sweep' notion. She knew they didn't mean with a broom.

Roscoe looked at Noah. "Once we land, let's get some food and place the phone call to see when Tomas Delgado will see you."

Micah and Kyle had several questions for both Noah and Roscoe. They knew the same details of Aron's disappearance as told by the news media, but there was some information the family had managed to keep under wraps – some leads, the wedding ring and the dive suit. None of those things were ever made public.

"Noah, I have some news for you."

Roscoe had his attention, immediately. "What news?" After so much had happened, he didn't think anything would surprise him.

"Your brother, Jacob, has offered a reward for anyone who has any information on Aron's whereabouts."

"Really? I had no idea." He wondered if the rest of the family knew. Not that Jacob needed to ask their permission, he had his own money. But, like Noah, the rest of the brothers would want to be involved too. "He doesn't know about Jaxson phoning me."

"I'm sure your cousin didn't call for that reason." Skye injected.

Noah nodded his head. "No, Jaxson didn't know about any reward money and wouldn't take it if he did." Considering that new bit of information, his eyes met Roscoe's. "You'll get the chance to review any claims before he pays off, of course. I'd hate for him to have to pay for information we already possess."

"True," Roscoe got up to get himself a bottle of water. "We'll just have to play that part by ear."

Micah had been quite for a while, with a guarded look on his face, like he was analyzing the situation and seeing a problem. "On the way to the airport, I called Saxon, our team's computer expert. If there's anything to be found on these people on the net, he'll find it. He's going to be checking things out and told me he would call tonight. But what he did say was this, Martina Delgado is deadly. She works with her uncle Esteban Rodrigo and together they run a conglomerate which pulls in about 2.3 Billion dollars a year. Esteban is the brains behind the outfit to some degree, but Martina is the clear-cut leader. She's the one the people develop a loyalty far. She is the deal-maker and when someone displeases her or betrays her, she has no compunction about ending their life. At least five hundred deaths have been attributed to her, a few by her own hand." All eyes were on him as he spoke. "Saxon also said, to the best of his knowledge, the cartel operates out of an estate just outside of the town of Cananea."

"How do these cartels keep such a stronghold on the country?" Skye asked. She'd heard a lot of talk during the time she'd spent in Eddie Warrior. The violence was spilling over into the United States, especially in the border towns of Texas.

Kyle Chancellor spoke up. "I can answer that," he offered. "The cartels are essentially organized crime, they are Mexico's mafia. They offer an illegal substance to those who can pay for it. Unfortunately most of their customers live in the U.S. and Canada. So, they are the supply, but we are the demand. It's crazy. And in order for them to be successful, they have to be protected to a degree. So, they bribe the police, the government – even the military."

"Is there no one who is fighting to stop them?" Chills of apprehension covered Noah's skin. To think his brother might be exposed to this amount of danger made his belly ache.

Kyle shook his head, sadly. "A few have stepped up, but they usually don't live very long. Although at the moment, Mexico has a new Chief District Attorney, Cisco Salazar who is determined to make an impact and bring some of the cartels down. He is calling for help. One of the things he's asking for is a list of the suppliers and snitches. They can't do a lot about the users from this end, but if they could eliminate the source that would mortally wound the beast."

Skye listened at them talk. She was glad they weren't alone. Micah and Kyle seemed knowledgeable.

Roscoe and his partner, Vance, had been traveling extensively through Mexico following leads about Aron, but none had been up in the state of Sonora. It sat just below Arizona and they'd been concentrating their efforts on the territories which bordered the Caribbean and the Gulf of Mexico. She was so worried for Noah, not so much about the danger they faced, but for what he might discover. He'd spoken to her about his fears and his doubts. Was Aron dead? Had he stayed away from home on purpose? She knew he idolized his older brother and what Skye knew of him only reinforced the opinion everyone else had – if there was any way in the world it was possible, Aron McCoy would come home. She held his hand, listening and looking around the Lear jet. She'd never been in one before and its sleek elegant interior was entrancing.

When they began their descent, she watched out the window, seeing quite a bit of desert, barren land. But the city of Hermosillo was quite large, seeming to her to be about the size of Austin, or a bit smaller. She liked that – she wanted them to be able to blend in rather than sticking out like a sore thumb. After they'd exited the plane, the promised car, a dark SUV awaited them. Roscoe called Vance and got the directions to Cananea and the house which had been reserved for them. He'd said it was in one of the better neighborhoods. Skye didn't know what to expect, but when they pulled up to a white stucco home, what she would classify as a ranch house, but with arched window and a circular drive – she was impressed. The interior was quite barren, just the required furniture, but it was spacious. The kitchen was fully equipped and all the bathrooms had linens. It wasn't 5 star, by any means – not that she'd stayed very many fancy places, but this wasn't really a vacation. This was a rescue mission.

After putting their things away, they met in the living room to discuss their plan of action. Big cloth couches covered in dark red material flanked a white brick fireplace. There was a fully stocked wet bar, but no one helped themselves, they all wanted to be sharp and alert. Much to Skye's surprise, they checked and cleaned their weapons, even arming Noah. The guns of choice were a Glock 40 caliber and Colt 45's. He wasn't unfamiliar with guns, and neither was she, but she wasn't about to volunteer that information – not unless she had to.

"All right, let's go into town and get some food. While we're there, we'll keep our ear to the ground. After dinner, Micah will call Tomas Delgado and see about arranging a visit."

Loading up in the SUV, they drove into the main part of town looking for a promising place to eat.

***

El Duro Cartel Headquarters – Cantanea, Sonora, Mexico

"It's good to meet you, Mr. Wade," Esteban Rodrigo greeted Aron. Martina held her breath, anxious to see both of their reactions. Since returning from Emily Gadwah's, Aron had been almost docile. She smiled to herself. The pink haired chemist would have to be rewarded accordingly. It was early, but for all extents and purposes, her injection of the Zip peptide seemed to have worked. Aron/Austin hadn't mentioned his wife or family anymore. Nor did he seem dissatisfied. Today on the drive over, he had laughed and joked with her about eating hot foods. Now that wasn't to say he'd made love to her yet, he hadn't, although it certainly wasn't for lack of trying on her part. There still seemed to be something holding him back. Nausea and sickness had been a factor at first, but surely that reason was mute now that he was feeling better.

Sometimes she felt as if it were her, her lack of sexual appeal. Men rarely came on to her. This bothered her until Alessandra had explained that most men were afraid of her. She was the Diosa, the Queenpin of the Duro Cartel. She held the power of life and death in her hand. That idea made her laugh. Until Aron, she hadn't really cared whether men were drawn to her or not. When she felt the need for sex, there were two or three of her lieutenants who would perform upon demand. They pleased her, but she felt nothing for them – not like she did for Aron.

"Mr. Rodrigo, it's a pleasure." Austin shook the other man's hand. "Martina has told me so much about you."

"Oh, really?" Esteban looked mildly shocked.

Martina smiled. What Aron said wasn't necessarily true, but it was about to be. Now that the procedure had been completed, she felt like it was time to introduce him to the family business. "I hope to share everything with Austin, soon." She rubbed a bit of imaginary lint off the sleeve of his black shirt. "Nothing would please me more than for him to work alongside me one day very soon."

"I see." Esteban said dryly. "Do you think this is wise?" He directed his question to Martina.

"Of course," she gestured broadly. "Once we are married, he will share in all aspects of my life."

Austin wanted to protest. He knew they were engaged, but his memory hadn't returned yet and the feelings newlyweds were supposed to have for their spouses was missing. The night before, he'd tried to talk to her about it, but it was like trying to have an argument with a stump, she was less than cooperative.

Her uncle didn't comment about the marriage. Instead he gestured them toward the garage. "Well, let's celebrate. We never had an engagement party for you. Why don't we begin by having a nice dinner at my favorite seafood restaurant? Champagne is in order."

Martina almost balked. "Is it wise?" Going out in public was always a risk for them.

"It will be safe, I promise." Esteban looked confident. "I have a plan."

***

Maricos Fresco Seafood Restaurant – Cananea, Sonora, Mexico

"This looks good." Kyle Chancellor stared at the menu. "I think I'll have the lobster."

"That's what I'm thinking," Micah studied the selections.

Skye and Noah held hands under the table. He casually rubbed his thumb on the back of her hand. "The grouper looks good to me. How about you, baby?"

"I think I want a salad." She answered.

"A salad?" He looked at her with a frown. "You'd better eat more than that."

A waitress came and they placed their order, Skye added a bowl of soup to her salad which appeased Noah somewhat. After she was gone, Micah leaned toward Noah. "Let's talk about what I'm going to say to Tomas. He had bulls for sale, right?"

Noah took a drink of beer. "Yes, but they also sell straws of semen and young heifers for breeding stock. But the easiest to discuss would be the semen, and that way if we got so far as to actually having to make a purchase, it would be easier to deal with."

They were deep in discussion when Skye punched Noah so hard in the ribs, he hollered. "What?"

"Look, on my God, look!" she whispered, then when they started to follow her instructions, she said. "Don't turn around, for god's sake, don't turn around."

Of course, they all turned around and Noah almost fell out of his chair. His brother, Aron McCoy came walking through the door – in the flesh. His breathing became labored, his heart was pounding ninety to nothing and every muscle in his body was clenched. It took sheer determination to remain in his chair. Every instinct Noah possessed demanded he get up and go to his brother, throw his arms around Aron's neck and hug him. He was alive! "Easy, Noah, easy," Roscoe muttered. "Let's be steady and see what happens."

The tension at the table was palpable. Everyone held their breath. Aron wasn't alone. He was accompanied by a beautiful young woman. Skye was shocked at her grace and elegant way of dressing. "Look at her," she marveled. Compared to this woman, Skye was plain stuff.

He also led in a gentleman who looked to be about fifty with longer hair, wearing a light grey suit. Four men walked beside them and Skye was shocked to see they carried guns – big guns.

Austin had seen the guns. He'd asked if they were necessary and was told they were. He didn't really understand what was going on. Things were always dangerous in this part of the world, so he didn't belabor the point.

Noah watched Aron's every move and once, when his brother had glanced toward Noah, he had held his gaze. They had looked into one another's eyes for a couple of minutes and there was absolutely no recognition. At all. "He doesn't know me," Noah marveled. "He looked right through me." He started to get up, but Tyson and Skye both pulled him back down.

Roscoe spoke. "Realize who he's with. You can't just go over there. In fact, quit staring, we don't want to show our hand."

"Look at all of the muscle with them." Micah observed. "That man isn't Tomas, I take it."

"No," Roscoe answered. "He's an older man. I think this is the uncle."

"Look, at that," Kyle observed. "What the heck is going on?" Two of the armed men went to the front and back door, effectively closing it. The others milled through the crowd, checking every table.

Noah grabbed Skye's hand. "What the hell is going on?"

"You have to be calm," Roscoe warned. They watched as the armed guards covered the room, obviously taking control.

"No one will enter or leave." They announced. The owners of the restaurant looked nervous, until the man in the grey suit rose and began to speak.

"Please, please, everyone remain calm. We wish to cause no one any distress. Everyone continue with your meal. I am Esteban Rodrigo and today your meal is on me. No one will be allowed to come and go while my family and I have our food, but when we are finished and depart, all of you will be free to go with no one paying for anything. So, please, order what you'd like, and champagne for everyone!"

"Oh, my God!" Skye muttered. "Can you believe this?"

"I'm confused." Noah muttered, almost feeling sick to his stomach. To sit this close to his brother and have to pretend he didn't know him was torture.

At the other table, Austin Wade was putting two and two together. His fiancé and her family were more than just rich people. Commandeering the restaurant was something a celebrity like Elvis Presley would do. But they weren't movie stars. Something was niggling in his brain, information, things he felt like he should know, but couldn't put his finger on.

"This is new," Martina murmured, glancing around at the shocked patrons who stared at them openly. Of course, men with AK-47's always commanded attention.

"Mind telling me what's going on?" Austin asked casually.

"Lunch, Rodrigo style," she smiled coolly.

When asked what he'd like to eat, Austin chose shrimp even though he had very little appetite. He might not be the smartest cowboy at the rodeo, but he wasn't dumb either. Things were beginning to stink to high heaven. Austin wondered what in hell he had gotten himself into.

Micah and Kyle looked at one another, then at Roscoe and Noah. "Can't deny they have a pair of balls." Kyle said.

"Even the woman," Noah grimaced, watching her rub Aron's arm. Fury for Libby just washed all over him. "He doesn't know who he is or he's the best actor I've ever seen." There was little doubt in his mind.

"What are we going to do?" Skye felt so sorry for Noah. She could see the pressure he was under.

"Look, he's getting up." Micah whispered as they watched Aron make his way to the restroom. One of the guards took note of him, and trailed him slowly.

"I'm going." Noah threw down his napkin.

Roscoe put a hand on his arm. "Hold on a second, don't draw attention to yourself."

He waited a few more seconds, then he rose and walked across the crowded restaurant. With a casual nod, he passed the sentinel, anxious to see Aron up close and personal.

Austin stood at the urinal, taking care of business. He heard the door open and close. Looking into the mirror he saw a young man with longish blond hair enter. He was dressed in requisite cowboy gear; jeans, hat and boots. Austin didn't speak, but he did raise his head in a nonchalant greeting.

Noah's hands shook as he unzipped his pants. He observed his brother closely in the mirror, noting that he had lost weight. What to say. Noah struggled with the possibilities. But before he could open his mouth, Aron zipped up and went to wash his hands. Closely following suit, he just jumped in. "Aron."

Austin stopped and turned. "What did you say?"

"Problema, Senor Wade?"

"No, no problem." He looked at the young man one more time, then patted the big guard on the shoulder. "I appreciate your concern, but I think I can handle my bathroom trips alone." With that, he left.

The bodyguard gave Noah a calculated glance, then left. If the situation hadn't been so serious, Noah would have laughed. At least he knew Aron's sense of humor hadn't changed. After he'd returned to the dining room, he watched Aron reseat himself, never once looking around.

"What happened?" Skye was anxious

"Not much, I called him by name and he asked me what I said, but there was no emotion in his question. We didn't get a chance to say more, that armed gorilla interrupted us."

"Well, what's the verdict?" Micah spoke, then stuffed a piece of roll in his mouth. "There's no use making that cattle viewing appointment. We don't need to verify Aron's identity. That's definitely him."

"Hell, I don't know what to do." Noah sighed. He was torn and disappointed. "We have to get him back, one way or the other. But, there's one thing for certain, however we handle it." They all looked at him. "We're gonna need bigger guns."

***

Los Banos Ranch

God, he had indigestion. Aron dug in the medicine cabinet for some antacids. He took two and chewed them up. He didn't know if it was the seafood making him feel like shit or the unanswered questions. What he'd seen tonight wasn't normal. People, no matter how influential, didn't close down restaurants and hold the customers hostage. Something crazy was going on. He had struggled with the possibilities, and nothing he could come up with was good. Yet, he had no proof.

The meal with Esteban wasn't the only thing bothering him. He felt like he was missing something. Like you'd feel if you left the coffee pot on and your subconscious kept trying to jog your mind until you thought of it.

At least he had some time to himself. Martina had dropped him off and said she had business to attend to. He had no idea when she'd be back. Tomas had gone to bed early and Alessandra's whereabouts was none of his business. Deciding he needed to shave and shower before he relaxed, he grabbed his shaving kit. When he'd taken out his things, he saw the gold coin. "Damn, I'd forgotten about this." He rubbed it between his fingers, gazing at the woman on the face. A sentimental feeling passed over him. This must have meant something to him in the past. Smiling sadly, he wished he could remember. Dropping it, he noticed something else, a thumb drive. What was this? He tried to remember what it was for. A sense of excitement coursed through him. Hell, he'd just find out.

Going to the desk, he turned on the laptop and slipped the thumb drive in the slot. A few clicks later he had his answer. Shit! As he studied the damning details, he remembered downloading it from her computer. Martina was a drug lord, head of a dangerous drug cartel! How had he repressed that memory? Austin rubbed his eyes. Was he going crazy?

Considering his position and what he now knew, his skin crawled. He felt dirty. Here he was, sitting in the home of a mass murderer, supposedly engaged to be married to her. Well, to hell with that! Searching through her supplies he found another small flash drive and downloaded the information, copying it onto the other drive – just in case. "Gotcha!"

Standing up, he gathered a few things and threw them in a small duffle, making sure not to leave the coin behind. He wasn't staying in this house one moment longer than necessary. Putting the thumb drive back in his pocket, he considered his options. He needed to tell somebody, but who? Hell, he didn't know where to go or who he could trust. What he needed to do was get back to the states and there was no time like the present.

Without looking back, he left the suite he'd been given. Heading downstairs, he laid his bag by the back door and jogged to the bunkhouse, hoping to see Brock without drawing a great deal of attention. Luckily, he was standing outside, drinking a beer. "Hey."

"Mr. Wade." Brock looked at him suspiciously. "What can I do for you?"

"Look, I don't remember much. I know enough to realize everything is fucked up and I'm getting out of here. I hope my instincts are right and that we're on the same side, if not I'm signing my death warrant."

"What are you talking about?"

Aron handed the flash drive to Brock. "I don't have time to go into detail, but I do know my name isn't Austin Wade. And I know who Martina is. This is enough to take her down, if we can get it into the right hands."

Brock took it. "Look, I think we need to…"

They heard the whir of helicopter blades. "I gotta get out of here."

"But...."

"There's no time. I'm leaving this place while I can. If I can get in touch with you, I will."

Aron hurried back to the house and went around back to get his bag. Damn, he wasn't thinking clearly – he needed keys! There was no way he could walk out of here, it was miles to the nearest town. Easing back into the kitchen, he made for the cabinet where the car keys were housed. Flipping through the assortment, he took the fob for the Land Rover. Good, as soon as he had them in hand, he felt better. Now, to get out of here and leave the ranch. He had very little cash, but that wasn't going to stop him. He'd get back to America if he had to walk across the border like the illegals.

"Austin? Where are you going?" The shock in her voice vibrated through the room.

He stopped. She was home. Turning around, he let his eyes rake over her. She was really a beautiful woman, but knowing what he knew, she was loathsome in his sight. They stood in the foyer and he couldn't deny he was leaving, he had a bag in his hand. Her mouth tightened and those dark eyes flashed with anger.

"Answer me!" She spoke with authority. "Where are you going at this hour?"

Austin sneered at her. "I'm going to Texas." She looked alarmed, but he didn't care. "Tonight's little outing got me to thinking. I guess I've been blind. It took me this long to put two and two together." He walked up to her, pointing a finger in her face, grinding the words out between his teeth. "You're a crook, and that's putting it mildly. You sell drugs and exploit people. Hell, you probably even have blood on your hands. And I am not your fiancé. I don't understand why you ever assumed I would fall for this farce!"

He was angry. But by the time he finished speaking, it was obvious she was angry too.

"You know nothing." Her voice was like ice.

"I know I'm going to take you down." He promised her. "The world needs to be rid of trash like you."

She was shaking, she was so angry. "I am not trash!"

"Why do you do it?" he asked. "You have plenty. I don't understand."

Martina narrowed her eyes and stared holes through him. "I do it because I am good at it. I do it because I can!"

"But, you're beautiful, Martina. Any man would lay the world at your feet if you gave him the opportunity."

This seemed to jar her out of her raging stupor. Visibly she softened and walked toward him. "I want you to lay the world at my feet. You."

"Not going to happen. I would say I'm sorry," Austin started to step around her, "but I'm not."

"Oh, Aron," she put her hand out to stop him as she pressed a button on her phone. "I too am sorry, but there's no way I can let you leave."

He was already so angry, he almost missed what she called him. "Aron?" The name reverberated through his soul. Before he could challenge her or ask more questions, the doors were flung open.

"Take him. Take him to the hacienda and put him in one of the rooms we reserve for our 'unwilling' guests. Restrain him, he's strong." She said with regret. Aron swung around, throwing a punch, but he was slammed upside the head with the butt of the gun.

***

Tebow Ranch

Libby debated with herself. Was she just being foolish? Maybe she was, but she couldn't even consider letting December 25th go by without her buying Aron McCoy a Christmas present. She was still holding out for a miracle, even though the likelihood of one happening seemed to grow slimmer by the day. But if miracles were easy to come by, they wouldn't be miracles, would they?

She had thought long and hard about what to get him. What did you buy a man who seemed to have everything he wanted? If she could have bought him a ticket home, that would have been what she would do – but that was foolish. A tie was out of the question. She had given him copies of her ultrasound for their wedding present. A beautiful photo of their unborn twins.

It was Noah who had given her the idea of a scrap book or a photo album. He was gone now, off on a trip with Skye or she would have consulted him. The family had suffered so much – little B. T. being born with a heart valve abnormality, Skye almost being killed – and Aron. God, her losing Aron was the most horrible of all. But on top of all this, Noah had discovered that Sue McCoy wasn't his mother. The information had floored her. Noah was as much a McCoy as Jacob or Aron. They were all family – period. She had tried to show him how she felt, how much she cared and maybe she'd succeeded. No one knew better than Libby that she'd been hard to be with – she was hurt, heartbroken and scared to death. Her moodiness didn't excuse her behavior, and Noah had borne the brunt when she lashed out – more than once.

The day he had discovered Sue's diary, he had left open a box of papers and photos. Libby had found them when she was straightening up. Among the pictures had been portraits of Sebastian and Sue, even ones of their parents. There were also many candid shots of the boys as they were growing up. So, she had taken them all and had copies made, just in case the other boys would want some, and lovingly fashioned Aron a legacy book. He could go from front to the back and see their family throughout the years. At the end she'd put photographs of them, their wedding, even the baby's ultrasound pictures.

The only problem was, she hadn't been able to wrap it. She looked at the images over and over again, especially the ones of him – on the football field, riding bulls on the rodeo circuit, with his art – riding his horse at Tebow. But most of all, she stared at the ones where he was looking at her with that special look on his face, the look of love.

Libby clasped the album to her heart and cried. If she never saw that look again, she didn't know if she could go on. "Aron, I love you. Please come home."

***

Somewhere over Mexico

The Learjet was winging its way home. The return trip, unlike the first one, was made with the assurance that Aron McCoy was alive and well.

At least for now.

He was in danger. There was no question of that. Aron was living a life as dangerous as walking through a minefield. And he needed to come home. That was the next step.

"Okay," Noah spoke out loud. "What's the plan?" All of them had been pretty quiet. Everyone was lost in their own thoughts. Well, it was time for them to be aired.

Roscoe took the lead. He had been making notes and looking at something on his Ipad. "First, I'd like to hear what you think, if you don't mind?" He directed the question at Noah.

Noah wasn't dense, he knew exactly what Roscoe was after. "Well, I don't believe he's went to the dark side, if that's what you mean. The thought of Aron McCoy willingly throwing his hat into a ring full of drug lords and drug cartels was ludicrous."

"I agree." Kyle chimed in. "I know Aron. He's as straight as an arrow. There's no way he's doing anything illegal, not if he's in his right mind."

Micah picked up on that 'if'. "Do you think he's been brainwashed?"

"Brainwashed?" The thought made Noah uncomfortable. He was on edge. It's a wonder Skye's hand had any feeling in it at all, he was hanging on to it for dear life, it seemed. "Do you mean hypnotized?"

"No," Kyle said. "But look what we're dealing with here? Drug-runners, drug manufacturers. People with no scruples and unlimited resources. There has to be some reason this is happening."

"I see what you're saying," Roscoe lifted the blind on his window so he could look out at the clouds. "He didn't recognize you, Noah. There's no way he could have ignored you, not reacted to you in some way, especially when he was with you, alone, in the restroom. Our Aron would have hugged you, whispered his plan in your ear and let you know how glad he was to see you."

"So, where does that leave us?" Micah crossed one booted foot over his jean clad knee. "How do we proceed?"

"There's no way we're leaving him down there, that's for sure." Noah was adamant. "I want to go home, tell my brothers what's going on and come up with a plan." He looked at all of them. "I'm going to need your help."

"So, we're going on the premise that he's being held against his will? Doesn't know who he is? What?" Kyle asked. "I just want to make sure we're on the same page."

Skye couldn't keep quiet to save her life. "Aron loves Libby. He's about to be a father. He would want to come home if he could remember."

Noah kissed her. "Damn straight." He looked at everyone else. "After seeing him, I tend to believe my brother has lost his memory – I don't know how, or why, but Aron has lost us and we need to help him. We need to bring him home."

"I can't see any way this is going to be easy." Roscoe admitted.

"He's in enemy hands." Kyle shook his head, leaning back in the seat. "My team," he pointed at his friend, "Micah, Jet, Saxon, Tyson and Destry – we have flown onto foreign soil and extracted people right out from under the enemy's nose. And we have an advantage here, we know where Aron is, we don't have to search for him. Count my people in."

"That's right," Micah nodded his head. "This will require some strategy. We've got to find out everything we can. There's no telling how many guns we'll have to go up against."

"You're making this sound like war." Noah wasn't arguing, he wanted Aron back.

"I'm afraid it will be war." Roscoe picked up the phone to place a call to Vance. "Let's start assembling our forces. We're going to have to put together an army."

***

El Duro Headquarters – Cananea, Sonora, Mexico

"I don't want to do this," she pleaded with him. "Give me a little hope."

"Tell me who I am." He demanded. "Aron, my name's Aron. What's my last name?"

She shook her head.

"You know what you need to do." Esteban stood by, still as a statue. "Nothing has ever given you a pause, before. This man is more deadly to us than any enemy we've ever had. Kill him."

Martina didn't say anything. Aron lashed out at them both. "You fuckin' cowards. You make a fortune on the backs of other people. You deal in death. Killing me won't save you from what's coming. I have a family." He didn't remember them, but the assurance of their existence was branded into his soul.

"Yes, you do." Martina spat at him, his words seeming to infuriate her. "And you have a pretty little wife who cries for you. She thinks you're dead. And she's pregnant!"

"Bitch!" He yelled.

Martina turned to stone. Her eyes froze to ice. "Guard!" She looked at Aron. "If you know what's good for you. You will cooperate. You will forget your little family and pledge your allegiance to me." She stepped closer to him. "The only way you and your precious little wife will survive this is if you kneel and give me your fealty. If not…" She spat on the ground. "I will make you pay. I know where she lives. My reach is long and my strike is deadly."

With almost superhuman strength, Aron lunged at her, but his bonds held him tight. "I'll kill you, Martina. I swear by all that's holy, if you threaten my family, I'll kill you and not have a moment's remorse." He trembled. Aron couldn't say their names, he couldn't even picture her face. But he knew he loved her more than life itself. His mind might not remember, but his heart would never forget.

"Whip him." She walked out and didn't look back.

Chapter Ten

Tebow Ranch

"Where have you been?" Isaac asked when Noah and Skye walked to the door.

Noah smiled. "I need to talk to you. Where is everybody?"

"The girls are all down at the hospital with Jessie. Little B. T.'s surgery has been scheduled. The doctor has given a green light, he says the baby is much improved. They're celebrating."

"That's wonderful," Skye accepted Isaac's hug. "I can't wait to see him."

"We tried to reach you, but your cell didn't have service."

"Yea, we were in a pretty desolate area there for a while." There had been no cell phone service at points on the drive between Cananea and Hermosillo. "I didn't get any messages. But that's great about Little Bowie. I'll go see him as soon as we deal with this."

"Deal with what?"

Noah was still grinning.

"Tell me, dammit!" Isaac wanted to hit his little brother. "What, did you two get married? Did you elope? Have you been to Vegas?"

"No!" Skye laughed.

"No, it's..."

"Better?" Isaac was teasing Skye. "What could be better?"

"Not better." Noah was about to bust. "Different. Call Jacob and Joseph. We need to talk before the ladies get back." He turned to kiss Skye. "Honey, I want you to take all your pretty clothes up to my room and warm the bed for me." He whispered in her ear. "Can you keep this from the girls until we figure out how and when to tell Libby?"

She winked at Isaac, stood on her tiptoes and hugged Noah tight. "I'd do anything for you, you know that. No questions asked."

"Damn, brother." Isaac laughed as Skye left the room. "You're a lucky man."

"Don't I know it."

"Now, what's going on?" He refused to get his hopes up, he'd been disappointed too many times.

"Call Jacob and Joseph, I only want to tell this once."

"How about Nathan?" Joseph asked, as he and Jacob walked up behind them. "We were down by the corral when you drove in."

"Nathan will find out eventually, but let's discuss it first."

"Alright." Jacob sauntered over to the desk and sat on the edge, crossing his arms. "What's going on and where have you been?"

Noah decided to start slow. "I hear you offered five million dollars for information on Aron."

Isaac and Joseph looked as surprised as Noah had felt when he heard.

"When did you do this?"

"I'm glad, but why didn't you tell us?"

They both spoke up.

Jacob didn't look disturbed. "I had been thinking about it and decided it couldn't hurt."

"Don't blame you a bit." Noah admitted. Then, he smiled. "I got a phone call about Aron from Jaxson."

They all three straightened. "Jaxson, our cousin?"

"Yes," Noah put his hands on his hips. "He called on Friday." Two days had passed.

"Quit stalling." Isaac fussed. "You're killing us."

Noah nodded, he understood. "He'd been down to Sonora Mexico at the Los Banos Ranch. He said he saw Aron there."

"Goddamn," Joseph breathed. "Let's go."

Isaac and Jacob stared at Noah who looked like he was about to explode with excitement. They both began to smile, hope finally settling into their minds.

"I've already been." Noah confessed. As all three of the others started talking at one time, he spoke over them. "He's alive, but he needs our help."

Silence.

Joseph started pacing. "He's alive? How does he look? What's wrong?"

Noah sat down on the couch, facing his brothers. "He looks the same, maybe thinner. And I don't know what's going on. He's

146

living with a Hispanic family and as far as I can tell, he doesn't remember who he is."

"Did you talk to him?" Isaac was confused. "Did you bring him home?" He started to walk to the door. "Aron?"

"Hush," Noah admonished him. "No, he's not here and yes, I talked to him briefly." He began to explain what had happened. "Skye and I took off the moment I got the call." He looked at Jacob. "They notified me because I'd been up there a while back with information that might help Philip. Remember the drive I found in the cave?" They said they remembered. "I didn't say anything to you, and I asked them not to, because I was afraid of what I'd find when I went down there."

"What do you mean?" Isaac looked worried.

Noah looked down. "Well, despite what I told you, I still had this dread that maybe Aron had wanted to start over. I even wondered if it was because of me."

"Shit, he'd never leave Libby, even if he did want to toss you off a cliff." Joseph drawled.

Noah smiled, knowing his brother was kidding. "I know, I've been as torn up about all of this as you have. I guess it affects all of us differently."

"Go on." Jacob wanted to hear it all.

"When we left, I was heading for the airport, but I called Roscoe and he made me wait while he checked everything out. And it's a good thing he did. Because he unearthed some information that just blew me away."

"What would that be?" Joseph was getting antsy. He wanted to do something – right then.

"I can't explain it, but Aron is with the drug lord of the El Duro Drug Cartel."

"What the fuck?" Isaac snarled. "I thought you said he was at a ranch."

"I did, but the ranch is owned by Tomas Delgado, the father of Martina Rodrigo Delgado."

"Martina?" Jacob looked as if a light had come on in his head. "Dammit, I know who she is. She had a huge crush on Aron. I flew down to Los Banos with him once to look at some cattle." His brow was furrowed with worry. "What has Martina and her father got to do with the drug cartel?"

Noah snorted. "Martina is the most powerful drug lord in all of Mexico. She's ruthless and somehow – she and her family have Aron."

"I don't understand." Isaac looked ready to explode. "A drug lord? How in the hell did that happen?"

Noah held up his hands. "Roscoe wouldn't let me go down there alone. My first inclination was to go to the ranch on the excuse that I wanted to check out Tomas's bulls, but he told me the name McCoy would sound a huge alarm for them."

"Yea, it would." Jacob agreed. "There's no way they don't know who Aron is. She used to all but throw herself at him, the girl was in love."

"Then that's what this is about." Joseph whistled.

Noah continued. "I called Micah Wolfe to go with me, just in case I needed him to call the ranch. And Kyle Chancellor flew us down in his plane. Roscoe and Vance took care of all the arrangements, but before we could go to the ranch, we – uh- ran into Aron and Martina and her uncle at a restaurant."

All three of them were hanging on Noah's every word.

"We were sitting there when the three of them came in with four armed guards." Noah ran a hand through his long hair. "By armed, I mean, automatic weapons. AK47's. Serious shit. We were shocked. I kept looking at Aron and he saw us, but there was no reaction."

"You don't think he was just covering up? Could it be working with the FBI or something?" Joseph was grasping at straws.

Noah shrugged his shoulders and chuckled, wryly. "FBI? I don't think so or the DEA either. At one point, he got up to go to the bathroom and I followed him. I said his name. I said 'Aron'."

"What did he do?" Isaac asked.

"He asked me what I said, but then one of the big armed goons came in and wanted to know if 'Mr. Wade' was having problems."

"Mr. Wade?" Jacob repeated the name.

"Yea, Austin Wade, Jaxson had told me that, too."

"Well, enough of this – when are we going after him?" Joseph wasn't taking 'no' for an answer.

Jacob held up his hand. "Hold on." He had a phone call. "McCoy." He listened for a few seconds, then his eyebrows rose.

"You have information on Aron?" They all tensed. "Okay, Mr. Brock Phillips, I'm listening."

***

Pop! Pop! The lash came down hard on Aron's back – over and over again. He winced, closing his eyes, but he never cried out. Martina stood behind him, watching the rivulets of blood run down his wide back. He was tied with his arms up and stretched out, almost as if he were being crucified.

"Stop it!" She finally cried out. "Enough!" She motioned to the man wielding the whip. "Leave us." The man went.

She walked up to Aron and touched his shoulder. He was wet with sweat. He flinched. "Don't touch me."

"I can help you. I can stop this." Her whisper sounded desperate. "All you have to do is promise me, help me convince Esteban you won't betray us."

Aron laughed. "You're going down, Martina. If I don't do it, somebody else will."

Her stomach muscles were clenching and unclenching. Exacting revenge, carrying out death sentences was her specialty, but this was the man she loved. Every molecule in her body was rebelling against the idea of eliminating him. The tables had turned. Esteban was rallying support among their troops for her to dispose of Aron McCoy, saying he threatened their very existence. And he did. She knew this. Normally, she had complete control, but Aron made her weak. She was losing the battle. "I can't stand this." Her hand hovered over the raw stripes crisscrossing his skin.

"Then let me go," he taunted her. "You are the Diosa. Show me how powerful you are. Turn me loose. Do something right for a change. Let me go home."

"Your home is with me." She insisted with an uncharacteristic whine to her voice.

Aron pulled on the rings in the ceiling which held the chains imprisoning him. He wanted to bellow with rage. "Tell me about her, Martina. Tell me about my wife." She wouldn't do it, he had no illusions. But he wanted to torment her like she was torturing him.

He watched as her face transformed, changing from attractive to a sneering mask. "Your wife's a fat slut. She didn't wait on you. Her babies aren't even yours."

Aron laughed. "I don't believe you. My wife is beautiful and faithful. She loves me. She waits for me." He had no doubt of this. The wife he was holding onto in his dreams was an angel. "Tell me, Martina, how did you pull this off exactly?"

She didn't answer; instead she turned to look out the small barred window.

"What kind of a woman has to kidnap a man?" He watched her shoulders square and her back stiffen.

"Do you want to die?" She lunged at him. "Don't you realize it is only I standing in between you and the executioner's sword?"

Aron weighed his words, aching to go home. But the truth was the truth. "If my choice is to stay with you or die..." He paused. "I choose the sword."

***

Jacob listened carefully to what he was being told. His brothers stood silently by, their bodies tense with anticipation. "Of course. I appreciate anything you can do. Yes, we'll do whatever it takes." He cut his eyes toward Joseph. "If what you're saying is true, the money is yours."

Isaac and Noah looked at one another, wondering what the rest of the day would bring.

"We'll take any help you can give us." Jacob stopped to write down a number. "If we can pull this off, we'll offer you whatever protection we can." In a few moments he hung up. The other three brothers stood, waiting. "Well, Noah, you were right."

"How so?"

"Brock Philips works at Los Banos. He's in love with the youngest Delgado girl and wants to take her out of danger, away from the life she's living. At some point, he and Aron teamed up to work together."

"Start at the beginning," Joseph urged. "I don't understand. How did Aron get to Los Banos? Did he say?"

"We might as well sit down," he pointed to the couch. "Who wants a drink?" They all decided they could use one. "While he poured them each a shot of brandy, he talked. "Apparently, Aron was injured while he and Libby were snorkeling. Martina was on her yacht off the shore near Seven Mile Beach and found him in the water, badly injured. They took him on board."

"Damn," Isaac muttered. "So, all the time we were looking for him, she had him."

"Exactly," Jacob sighed. "While he was knocked unconscious, she elected to sail off with him instead of contacting the authorities on the island. Undoubtedly, she knew what had happened. She just chose to ignore his rights. Brock said that Alessandra, the sister, was on the yacht with them and when he told them he didn't know who he was or what had happened to him, the queenpin just decided to manufacture him a life different than what he had."

"You said he was hurt?" Noah was concerned.

Jacob let out a harsh breath. "Aron was seriously hurt. He had brain surgery in Mexico City, and he's had a lot of trouble since with swelling and headaches."

"Is he okay?" Joseph stood up. He seemed on the verge of flying off the handle or running out the door. He couldn't be still.

"That's debatable." Jacob sat on the desk. "Martina convinced Aron his name was Austin Wade and that they were engaged to be married."

"Son of a bitch!" Isaac cursed. "What about Libby?"

Noah and Jacob both held up their hands. "Hush, Isaac!" Jacob frowned at his brother. "Libby is not to know a word of this. Brock says Aron never showed one speck of interest in the Delgado woman. He says our brother began to remember. At one point he and Philips had a plan to gather information and take down the cartel. He says Aron was planning on coming home."

"What happened?" Joseph's face was full of worry.

"Aron got the information, enough to bring her down if we can get it in the right hands. He gave it to Brock."

"Why did he do that?" Snap! Isaac broke a pencil in half he'd been holding.

"According to Philips, when Aron started remembering, that bitch did something to him. Alessandra says they took him to a chemist and gave him some kind of a shot and when he came back, he'd forgotten everything about us and Libby that he'd gained back."

"Shit," Noah hung his head down and held it with his hand, his forearms resting on his knees. "Will he ever get his memory back?"

"I don't know." Jacob was solemn. "We'll have to try and find out what they've done to him. But it gets worse…"

"Worse, how the fuck could it be worse?" Joseph was yelling now.

"As far as he could tell, Aron had figured out who Martina was and he'd decided to leave. He gave Brock a copy of the files on a flash drive, enough for the authorities to arrest her. Aron was leaving when she came home. They had an argument, a confrontation. Aron showed his cards and now he's gone from being a fiancé, to being a prisoner."

"We've got to rescue him." Isaac was adamant.

"I agree." Jacob's mouth was set in a determined line. "Brock doesn't think we have much time."

***

Los Banos Ranch

She's my sister, Brock." Alessandra spoke quietly, head bowed. "How can I betray her?"

This was hard. He knew she was torn. "What do you want, baby?" He pushed a strand of silky hair behind her ear. "What kind of life do you and your father have? Is this what you want?"

A tear rolled down her face. "I love her."

"I know you do."

"But, I love you." She looked up at him with limpid brown eyes. "And I want a future and a family. I want babies." Her voice hiccupped with a sob. "And I don't want them to grow up in El Duro." She threw herself in his arms. "I'll help you. What do you need?"

Rubbing her back, he let his mind race. "Blueprints of the hacienda."

Alessandra stiffened. "How do I find that?"

"I don't know." He murmured. "I'm a damn ranch hand. But we need a body count, how many mercenaries are on the grounds at any particular time."

"What else?" She wasn't offering any answers, but she was listening.

"We need to know where Aron is, what room, and his condition."

"I'll have to go over there, I can do that." Chewing on her bottom lip, she was too pretty for Brock to resist, he stole a kiss.

"That's my girl."

"But, the blue prints are out of my league." She looked up at him. "We'll have to get help."

"Who can we trust?" She'd lost him.

"Papa, we can trust Papa."

***

Galveston, TX

The sound of crashing waves comforted Harper Summers. They were always on time. The tide rolled out, then rolled back in with precision. She craved predictability. More than anything, Harper hungered for structure in her life. She needed boundaries. In the past year, it seemed her life was careening out of control. Nightmares of Noah and Ajax were all mixed up with her insecurities and fears. God, how she wished she were normal. No one understood her, at least no one she loved. Her parents had rejected her. Noah had rejected her. And there were others who only wanted to use her or hurt her.

She sat on the wood plank floor, in the corner of the deck. Her knees were raised and she hugged her legs as close to her chest as possible. Harper tried to make herself small. Sometimes she just wanted to disappear.

Her days were half-way normal. She got up, went to work, then returned. If it weren't for Natalie, she wouldn't have made it. This beach house belonged to her. And the job she had at Joe's Crab Shack kept her sane. Harper didn't ask for much out of life. She didn't seek out a club anymore, it was just too dangerous. Even though she couldn't function sexually, in the vanilla world, she'd vowed never again to seek out a Dom. Men and pleasure. Love and sex. Romance and Marriage. None of those things were for her. Harper had resigned herself to just existing. What she was and what she needed was considered a perversion and she was weary of being condemned for what she was. She didn't know how to be anything else and she was tired of trying.

What she needed was a hero. A man who would walk into her life and accept her for what she was. Give her what she needed. Protect her, love her, cherish her for what she was. But a man like that didn't exist. Not for her. Once... once she'd known a man capable of that kind of unconditional devotion, but she'd pushed him away. And a girl like her – she wasn't worth a second chance.

As the sound of the sea roared all around her, the wind steadily blowing, the seagulls crying, Harper began to weep. If she could just turn back the clock. Just be different. Dare she say his name? Closing her eyes, she let her mind wander to the bayous of Terre Bonne Parish, to the dark still waters, to the Spanish moss dripping from the trees. If she were really still, she could conjure up his voice.

"Harper, what are you doing out in this cold, Baby?" Strong arms wrapped around her, picking her up and carrying her inside. God Almighty, she had lost her mind. Her imagination was going crazy. "Let's get you warm. Do you have any idea how long I've been looking for you?"

This was real. She had been so deep in her sorrow, for a few moments she thought her dreams were overtaking her. But he was here. She ran her hands down his arms. He was solid. Looking up into his dear face, she couldn't believe her eyes. "Revel?" Her voice broke on the word. "What are you doing here?"

"What do you think?" He smiled at her tenderly. "I've come to take you home."

***

On the highway between Bandera and Austin

Cassie." Bowie said the name and smiled. "Sweet Cassie." He hadn't kissed her, but it was just a matter of time. When he'd shown up at her house a couple of days ago, she had been shocked. Bowie hadn't understood why. Didn't she know how precious she was?

The look on her face had told him all he needed to know. She was as lonely as he was. And she needed him. There was work to be done around her place. A woman like her didn't need to be alone. No, woman did. It just worried him sick thinking about her being all by herself in that house, miles from town. Oh, it wasn't just because she was in a wheelchair, although that did make her particularly vulnerable.

He could still hear her voice when she'd opened the door and found him standing on her porch. "Bowie, what are you doing here?"

"I hoped you might welcome some company." He'd waited for her to invite him in. For a minute or two he had doubted she would. "Could we have something to drink and just talk?" Maybe he should have called to ask her out on a date instead of just barging in unannounced. But Bowie knew, deep down, she wouldn't have agreed to see him. She would have come up with some excuse. He smiled, remembering. Bowie felt as if he were harder to turn down in person. After all, he was cute.

"Please, come in." She'd said. They had hit it off, even more so than they had at the Silver Dollar. Oh, she was shy. Every time she looked into his eyes, she blushed. Bowie's heart pounded just thinking about her. Her skin was so soft. The few times he'd been able to touch her hand, he had trembled with the privilege.

Once they'd started talking, it seemed they couldn't stop. Bowie was amazed at what they had in common – outlooks, beliefs, hopes, dreams. She shared his views on the environment and immigration – on the rights of animals and the protection of children and the elderly. Politics and religion. There was no topic they veered away from, and even though they had some lively discussions, it was clear they could become fast friends.

But he wanted more. He wanted to make her life easy. Her little house was good, but nothing was the right height for her. Bowie had watched her cope, seen her strain to reach something. She was making do, when she should have been taken care of. Her world needed to accommodate her, she shouldn't have to merely make-do. He found himself wanting to create a world for her where she would be safe, happy and at ease.

Everything about her enchanted him. Her lips were mesmerizing. Driving down the road to Austin, here he was day-dreaming about how soft and sweet her kiss would be.

There was only one problem. At the end of the evening, when he'd asked if he could see her again, she had said 'yes'. But there was a condition.

She just wanted to be 'friends'.

The thought had hit Bowie Travis in the gut. Oh yes, he could be her friend. He needed to be her friend. But he also wanted to be her lover. His body was fully engaged and onboard with the idea. As they'd sat and talked, he'd memorized her smile, the way her eyes lit up, the dimple in her cheek. He'd also seen the way her nipples hardened when she'd become excited. And he had excited her, he could tell. Several times, he had touched her – casually, or looked into her eyes, or winked at her. And he watched the blush rise on her chest, till it swept up her cheeks. And he could see her breasts swell, they wanted to be touched as much as he needed to get his hands on her.

So, when she'd turned those big eyes up to him and told him she couldn't date him, he was confused – so he'd pressed. Maybe he shouldn't have. God, he'd never meant to make her cry, but this was important. He covered his mouth, worrying the scruff on his jaw he could never seem to keep trimmed down. What she'd said to him would haunt him all of his days. He'd pushed. Why? Why don't you want to have dinner with me? We get along. We enjoy one another's company.

"Bowie, please," she'd implored him.

"I don't understand."

"I'm broken." She'd finally said, hanging her head. "I can be a good friend, but that's all I'm good for. Can't you see?" As he watched, she'd spread her little hands, showing herself to him as if he'd somehow missed the fact she was in that damn chair. In her mind, she was less. Stunned, he'd gone to his knees at her feet – making his case.

"I don't believe that. Please, let me show you."

God, his heart had ached when he'd seen fear in her eyes. Oh, she wasn't afraid of him. She was afraid of how he made her feel – he'd bet his life on it. "I can't. I've tried."

What had she meant?

And then it hit him – she meant sex. Cassie was afraid she couldn't be what he needed in a woman.

Well, to hell with that.

It became his mission in life to prove her wrong.

The wheels of his truck ate up the miles. Jacob had called him and the baby was scheduled to have surgery. And he was going to be right there to support him. All of the McCoys were his friends, but Jacob and this baby were family.

Now, he'd found someone else he wanted to welcome into his world. Cassie. And he would. He wanted her too much. There wasn't any room for failure.

As the scenery passed by, Bowie saw it – but he didn't. His mind was racing with the possibilities. Could she have an orgasm? Surely she could have sex? His heart pounded with questions. One thing for sure, he wasn't about to let this go. He'd ask, subtle questions. He'd woo her. She might thing they were friends, but he intended to court his friend, seduce her and make her fall in love with him. Bowie intended to do his homework. He'd learn everything he could about her condition and then he'd set about proving to her that she was not broken. She was a woman. His woman.

***

Breckenridge Hospital – Austin, TX

"Help me pray, help me pray." Jessie buried her face in her husband's chest. He was solid. He was her rock.

"I've put in my petition, Jess. The Lord isn't going to let me down." Jacob's faith was riding high. His son would be okay. Just hours ago, he had stood at the bassinet and let BT wrap his baby hand around his forefinger. He'd smiled at the little boy's strong grip. The operation was going to be tedious, but their doctor was a good one and the family had rallied again. The waiting room was full of McCoy's. His head was spinning, there was so much going on. The news they'd received that Aron was alive, and in need of their help, galvanized the brothers into action. True, they'd had to stop to be here together for Little Bowie, but as soon as he pulled through with flying colors, they'd take care of business for Aron.

Jessie nestled into his arms. She was still a little weak. "You wanna sit down? I could hold you." She nodded her head and he picked her up, heading to a corner of the waiting room. Cady and Joseph scooted down one so Jacob would have plenty of room. He had never been so grateful for his armful. After finding out about Aron and thinking how lost Libby had been, Jacob had vowed to count his blessings every day. He squeezed her tighter. Her soft breasts nestled into his chest. Lord in heaven, he couldn't wait to get his family home. He needed Jessie, in every way.

"How are plans for the wedding?" He tried to get his mind settled. Waiting was agony.

Joseph gave him a knowing look. "Everything is set. Tricia and Avery have everything handled. It's going to be amazing!" He winked at Avery and then smiled at Jacob. Joseph wasn't known for his subtlety. Since they'd been thinking about the rescue operation, everything they talked about had to be veiled.

"I've tried to keep it small," Cady confessed. "But the guest list keeps growing. We've invited the cousins, my family, and Joseph and Harley." A smug smile came on her face. "Why, you never know." Her voice took on a mysterious quality. "There may even be a surprise guest or two."

Hmmmm, Jacob thought. Cady and that sixth sense of hers! He didn't know for certain, and he wasn't about to ask – but he wouldn't put it past this woman figuring the whole thing out. Honestly, he didn't know how long they could hide big news like this from any of the women. He'd thought about just telling Libby, but he was so afraid something would go wrong, and the time frame would surely frustrate her – it was frustrating them. Because it wasn't something they could rush into, they had to be ready and getting ready took time.

"How's Tina, Nathan?" Noah asked.

Nathan was sitting between Isaac and Avery, he'd been working at trying to convince the Badass to teach him to ride a motorcycle. So far, he hadn't had any luck. "She's getting out of rehab in a week or ten days. I'm hoping she's home by Christmas." There was a secret he was going to have to tell his family sometimes. But it wasn't going to be easy. If Aron was here, he wouldn't be so nervous. But he wasn't. "Do you think she could visit soon?"

"Of course." Libby spoke up. She was sitting on the other side of Avery. "We'd love to have her, Nathan. You know that." She had leaned up to look at Aron's youngest brother when one of the babies gave a well-placed kick on her bladder. Libby jumped.

"What happened?" Avery laughed, putting a hand on her shoulder.

"One of these rowdy McCoy's letting me know he's awake." She rubbed her tummy, which was getting quite round. Seeing an opportunity, she took it. "Avery, I want to ask you something."

"Of course," Avery turned in her chair. "Anything. Do you need something?"

"No, no," Libby shook her head. "I just wanted to talk to you about your writing."

Avery's smirked. "Sable Hunter? Oh, that girl is trouble!"

"I want to write something." Libby confessed, lowly.

"Great!" Avery grinned. "I'll help you. I have connections. You write it and I'll get it published, we'll do some promoting, I'll help you choose a cover. What's the title?"

"Wait," Libby grabbed her arm. "I don't want to sell the book, I want to write about Aron and me and our love story. I want to preserve the memories."

"You're not giving up are you?" Avery was shocked.

"No, no." Libby shook her head. "I'm not, I never will. But I have to hold on to something, and maybe this will help me."

"Sure, I understand." Avery held her hand. "What do you want to know?"

"Well, just how to go about it. I don't know where to start."

Just looking at Libby's face made Avery's heart ache. "Well, if I was going to do it, Sable style. I'd start by writing about Aron and who he is, his family, show some of his personality. And then I'd do the same for you. I'd tell about how you met and relate every memory I could. Make it real with dialogue and put into words all the love and tenderness you've felt for each other. Write your love story. And when you come to the end – don't let it end – put a big TO BE CONTINUED on it."

Libby chocked back a small sob. "Okay. I'll try. I have to do something. I have all of this love in me for him, and it's got to go somewhere."

Avery put her arm around Libby. "It will be beautiful. Aron is going to enjoy reading every word."

"I hope so."

"Jacob." A voice at the door got their attention. Jacob carefully put Jessie down and jumped up. "Malone, I'm so glad you're here." He hugged his friend.

"Where else would I be?" Bowie Travis greeted Jessie with a kiss and spoke to the rest of the family. "What's the word?"

"We're waiting on the doctor to come out and tell us something." Jessie said, tremulously. "He's so little, Bowie. It just breaks my heart."

Cady came over to where Jessie was standing by Bowie and Jacob, putting an arm around her. "Come sit by me. There's something I want to tell you." Jessie followed Joseph's fiancé over to the other side of the waiting room. They sat down.

"What is it?" She studied Cady's face, carefully. "Do you know something?" Everyone knew Cady was psychic. She came from a family of unusual powers. Lately thought, her powers had seemed to be stifled by her pregnancy.

"No, not in the normal way." She grinned – normal for her wasn't normal for everyone else. "But I had a dream."

"A prophetical dream?" Jessie was listening intently.

Cady smiled. "Well, I don't know for sure, I guess we'll see. But I have been known to have dreams which did come true." She looked at Joseph McCoy. He was proof of that. "Last night, I saw a vision of Christmas Day."

Jessie's breath hitched in her throat. "Tell me."

"We were all there. Joseph and I were married. You were holding little Bowie and he was dressed in a light blue outfit which looked like a small snowsuit and you had wrapped him in a white blanket with blue snowball tassels."

"Wow," Jessie's eyes filled with tears. "I bought that outfit for him yesterday. No one has seen it but me."

"There, you have it." Cady smiled confidently. "So, now you know. Bowie is going to be just fine."

"What else did you dream?" She wanted more.

"Well," Cady leaned over and whispered to her, conspiratorially. "Aron was there."

Jessie let out a little squeal. "Are you going to tell Libby?"

"I don't know." Cady shook her head, about to say more. But a voice from the hall drew their attention. It was Kane and Zane with their families. Jessie excused herself to go greet them.

"What were you telling Jessie?" Joseph settled down beside his angel.

"I was comforting her." She laid her head on his shoulder.

"As only you can." He kissed the top of her head.

Chapter Eleven

Breckenridge Hospital – Austin TX

"Mr. McCoy."

The doctor's voice caused everyone in the waiting room to go quiet. Zane placed his hand on Jacob's shoulder. "It's good news, Jacob. Look at that smile."

He stepped toward the doctor, taking Jessie by the hand. "How is he?"

"He's going to be just fine." Everyone let out a collective sigh of relief. "The operation was successful. I replaced the valve and it will grow with your son. A procedure to expand it when need be won't be as invasive as what he's endured today."

"When can I see him?" Jessie was tingling with nerves. "I need to make sure he's okay."

The doctor patted her arm. "He's being taken to recovery. Give us a few minutes to get him settled."

"What's next, Doc?" Jacob wanted the full picture.

"We'll keep him in NICU for twenty-four hours and if all is well, we'll move you all to a private room. Babies are resilient. If he progresses as well as I think he will, you can take him home before Christmas."

"Praise be." Jessie threw her arms around Jacob and everyone hugged everyone else. Libby and Skye took Jessie to the restroom to repair her makeup while Avery and Cady escorted Nathan out for a celebratory ice cream cone. Jacob, even though he was ecstatic about his son, pulled Bowie and the Saucier brothers to one side. "Don't leave for a bit, I couldn't think straight until I knew my baby was going to be all right. But I have something to tell you and I need your help."

"You've got it, you know that. What's up?" Kane took his hat off and held it in his hand. The Sheriff of Kerr County was never off-duty, it seemed, but friends and family came first.

"We've found Aron."

"What? He's here?" Zane almost shouted and Jacob shushed him up. "The girls don't know yet. We've got to get a plan together before we let them know what's going on."

"This sounds ominous. What's going on?" Bowie could read Jacob last a book. "Is he in danger?"

"Yes. He's being held by a Mexican drug cartel."

"What do they want? Money? Is that what happened? Was he kidnapped and held for ransom?" Kane had slipped into official mode.

"Let's move." Jacob motioned for his brothers to follow them outside. "Hold on." He saw Jessie and went and told her they were going to grab a cup of coffee and he'd return before it was time to check on the baby. "Ring me if they call us before I finish, and I'll run right back."

"Okay," she smiled at him. He could see the relief on her face. They'd been through so much – her surrogacy, a crazy man who'd tried to kill her – they deserved some happiness.

Turning, he saw his brothers and their friends waiting on him by the exit. "Let's go to that coffee shop across the street. I need to sit down." Jacob was amazed at the events of the last twenty-four hours. Now if this thing with Aron would end as happily as BT's surgery, they would have much to be thankful for.

As soon as they entered the small shop, Isaac led them to a table and ordered a round of coffee. Kane spoke first. "Answer my question. Was all of this about money? Is that what happened to him?"

"Not hardly," Noah sighed. "Something much more dangerous, Aron was kidnapped for love."

"Seriously?" Zane couldn't help but laugh a bit. "Leave it to Aron."

Jacob motioned for Noah to explain. He told their friends the whole story, then finished by looking at them one by one – right in the eye. "We're going after him. Are you with us?"

"Hell, yeah." Kane didn't even blink an eye. "Remember the Alamo."

Joseph snorted. "Roscoe is waiting for our call. We've got to have a planning session."

"Brock is supposed to gather as much intel as he can and give us a ring sometimes tonight. But he thinks we could be up against a hundred men, maybe more if they have any inkling they're being threatened." Jacob checked his phone to make sure he hadn't missed any message.

"This is a big deal. Those people don't mess around. We're going to have to have every man we can get."

"I agree." Noah said. "You should have seen these apes. Mercernaries. AK47's. We'll be going up against an armed battalion."

"Have you called your cousins?" Bowie asked. "They'll help."

"Not yet," Jacob stated. "I had to get through today before I could concentrate. But I plan to. Harley and Beau will come and they're going to be a major asset."

"Sure will," Joseph agreed. "Beau can get us any weapon we need and Harley can blow shit up if we need her to."

"I thought she defused bombs for a living," Zane laughed.

"I figure if she can take them apart, she'll know how to make one." Joseph was as serious as a heart attack.

"You're right." Kane agreed. "I have a couple of contacts down on the border. I'll give them a call and see what they know."

"Good." Jacob was relieved. "We've done some wild things in our time, but declaring war on a drug cartel has got to take the cake."

"Kyle Chancellor is bringing his Equalizer's, they're a former SEAL team. He can fly us in and out, plus they'll be invaluable in the execution of our plan."

"You know who else would be good?" All eyes turned to Isaac. "Patrick O'Rourke and his buddies. Do you remember? We met them at Beau and Harley's wedding."

"How many is that?" Joseph paused to count.

"Twenty-four."

"Sounds about right," Isaac drawled. "A hundred of them, twenty-four of us, we'd never want to be accused of not fighting fair."

***

Graywolf Ranch – near Johnson City, TX

Jacob made calls. Roscoe made calls. They gathered information from Kane on El Duro's habits and Brock furnished them blue prints courtesy of old man Delgado himself. Noah was relieved to hear Tomas and Alessandra had decided to go to Europe for a week or two. It would get them out of danger. Kyle Chancellor brought all of the Equalizers to Hardbodies to introduce them and Isaac and Jet hit it off instantly. Jet was just another Badass. It amazed everyone to find out he held an MMA title and spent his spare time hunting treasure in the Caribbean. All of the Equalizers had specialties: Jet was a bomb expert and was recruited to help Harley, Micah was former intelligence, Saxon was their computer genius, and Tyson was a helicopter pilot and Destry was a sniper. It turned out Tyson had known Patrick O'Rourke in Afghanistan. Destry, a former clerk for the Supreme Court held the longest sniper kill at 3079 yards, or one and three-quarter miles, with a .50 cal. Barrett M82.

Patrick O'Rourke and his team were on standby. Noah was surprised to find out that Revel Lee Jones, the man who'd come to see him about Harper was Revel's best friend and team member. He also was bringing Jayco Johnson and Philip Hawke. Jacob was acting as top gun, but he was relying heavily on Kyle and Beau to coordinate everything.

As much as they wanted to just fly down and carry out the rescue mission, all of them realized they needed to train, plan and re-plan. So as not to alarm the women, they made Micah's ranch out of Johnson City their headquarters. Beau flew in targets, weaponry, flash grenades, everything they would need to conduct an all-out assault against an armed fortress.

The McCoy cousins joined forces with them, and they decided to split into three teams. Kyle had studied the blueprints and recommended to Jacob that they attack on two fronts. "If we storm the front gate and take out as many as we can, Harley can blow the side wall as a distraction, then I can get Tyson to come in by helicopter and get a team as close to the house as possible. They can enter, occupy the house and rescue Aron."

"Can we do this?" Jacob asked as he looked at the charts Kyle had drawn. "It's going to take at least two weeks to get ready."

"Do we have a choice?" Kyle fired back. "We can't go down unprepared."

"No, we don't have a choice. Bringing Aron home is nonnegotiable."

***

Galveston, TX

Harley's heart was breaking. This was so hard. Sometimes you had to put the welfare of another person ahead of your own. "I'm sorry, Revel. I can't go back to Louisiana. That part of my life is over." This wasn't the first time he'd asked. Over the past few days he had relentlessly made his case. Her answer had not changed. "Please don't ask me again."

She tried to shut the door.

He wouldn't have it. Putting his foot inside the door, he forced it open. She stepped back, her mouth gaping open.

"I'm not going to hurt you." He assured her. "That's one thing you can always be certain of."

She chose to twist his words. Harley knew exactly what he meant. "And therein lies the problem. You know what I need. You've always known what I needed. But you can't give it to me."

Revel searched her face. He'd never understand why some people needed the bite of erotic pain. He just wasn't wired that way. Harper was. His mind raced back to the first time she'd confided this deep-seated craving to him. They had been young and he'd been idealistic. Looking back now, he hadn't handled it well. He was a man. It was his job to give his woman what she needed – to protect her, yes – but to fulfil her desires.

He had failed. And in his failure, he had pushed her away. It had not been his intention. Revel Lee Jones had never rejected Harper Summers. He would just as soon reject himself. But he had been surprised, he had shown that surprise and she had ran.

Her running had proved to be her downfall. Harper had fled his protection and sought out the affections of strangers, seeking for what she needed.

He took a deep breath and made his offer. "I can give you what need. I can be what you want."

A bitter laugh rose in Harper's throat. If only. "Don't make me laugh. This is what I asked you for before and you turned me away."

"I did not turn you away, I told you I didn't understand – that I didn't know how – that I was surprised, but I did not push you away." He was emphatic. "If you had given me time, I would have learned."

"My lifestyle is not something you learn, it's something you're born into. It's something you crave." Her voice rose, she was glad no one could hear their discussion. She'd been judged enough in her life, she didn't want to invite more.

She had backed herself into a corner. Revel took advantage, going to her and bracketing her in with his big body. "Give me a chance. I can't stand the thought of you being alone. You know I love you, I always have."

Words, beautiful words. Words she'd give the sun and the moon and the stars to hear and believe. And he meant them, she knew he did. But he didn't understand. "You think you do."

He crashed his lips against hers, not giving her time to say anything else. For a few precious moments, they kissed. He wordlessly offered her everything he had – his life, his body and his soul.

As much as Harper wanted to take what was offered, she couldn't. "No," she pushed on his chest. "I can't."

Revel bowed his head. "Why?"

"It's not right." I love you, she thought. "We're not right. We'll only end up hurting each other. I would disappoint you. I can't change."

With one powerful move, he hit the wall above her head, splintering the wood. She jumped. "Don't you understand," he bellowed in his pain. "I don't want you to change." He face contorted with pain. "I will change. I will be what you want. I will be what you need."

"I can't ask that of you." She looked at his beloved face. "I want you to go."

"Ask me anything. I'll give you all that I have, all that I am. But please don't ask me to walk away from you." He'd just found her again. Leaving her would kill him.

Harper forced herself to say the words which would take him away from her. Pain unlike anything she'd ever known ripped through her. And it wasn't the sensual pain she enjoyed. This was a soul-ripping agony and she never wanted to feel it again. "I don't want you, Revel. You do nothing for me. I need a man who'll give me what I need and you will never be able to do that."

Bowing his head, Revel felt her words slice through his heart like the sharp edge of a sword. "I see."

With a sinking heart, he turned from her. He walked away. Giving her what she asked for. To be parted from him.

***

El Duro Headquarters – Cantanea, Sonora, Mexico – Two weeks later

Esteban and Martina stood at the two way mirror watching Aron McCoy. He hadn't broken under the pressure. "You've tried everything from starving him to seducing him. I say we end his suffering."

"No." Martina offered no further explanation. She'd said everything she had to say days ago.

"What? Are you going to drug him again? We could give him some Devil's Breath, that would make him manageable. You could do whatever you wanted to with him then."

Martina didn't comment, but she had actually considered it. They had used scopolamine before. It was usually blown into the faces of the victims or put into their drinks. The victims became zombies, coherent, but with no free will whatsoever. Aron would be docile, perhaps even cooperative, but he would no longer be Aron or Austin, he wouldn't be the man she loved. It was his fire she admired. And Martina wasn't willing to put out that fire, she would almost rather snuff out his life.

"Have you become soft?" Esteban laughed. "I have seen you beat a female police officer to death with a two by four while her colleagues watched. Wasn't it you who had three traitors dismembered while still alive? Didn't you stuff Judge Escobar into a 55 gallon drum and set him on fire because he refused to take your bribe?"

"This is different." She watched Aron wipe his forehead on his bicep. He was so beautiful and she wanted him so much. Tonight, she was going to try one last ditch effort to win him over. "Give me a little time."

"You've had almost two weeks; he's not going to break. The man has an iron will."

"Diosa! Diosa!" Paco came running to get her. "Come, you must come!"

"What's wrong?" She turned to see what the problem could be.

"Your father and sister have been in a car wreck on the way to the airport."

***

Tebow Ranch

Jacob decided he had no choice but to tell Jessie what was going on. He had run himself to death between training with the men, overseeing the ranch and checking on BT and Jessie at the hospital. He spent most nights there sitting with his son so his wife could sleep. "I have something to confess." He'd told her the very best version of their plans, one that didn't include the machine guns, bombs and mercenaries. But his wife was no fool.

"Take care of yourself. You have a baby to think of."

"Yea, I have two." He held her close. "But I have to do this. He's my brother."

"Of course you do." She clung to him and cried.

Joseph had tried to lie to Cady, but he didn't get very far. "We're going on a hunting trip to…" Joseph thought quickly. "Colorado!" His magical wife raised one delicate eyebrow. How do you lie to a woman who can basically read your mind?

"A hunting trip to Colorado?" She stared him down. When he stared right back at her, she relented, kissed him and hugged him tight. "Please be careful. You are my world."

"I'll be home in time for the wedding, I promise."

At home, after they'd seen the men off, Avery and Cady looked at one another. "Where was Isaac going?" Cady asked.

"Wyoming with Joseph."

"Joseph went to Colorado with Isaac."

Skye didn't say anything and they quickly determined she was the weakest link – so they pounced. Libby was upstairs writing so the coast was clear. "Okay, Miss Blue," Avery grabbed her arm. "Spill."

"You might as well, I'm picking up some strong vibrations." Cady coerced her for information.

"Okay, okay, but you have to promise not to say anything to Libby or to any of the men if you talk to them."

They agreed.

Skye looked at them solemnly. "They've gone after Aron."

"What?"

"He's alive!"

"That's great!"

"Shhhhhh," she shushed them. "They're not telling Libby."

"Why?" Avery asked. "She would be over the moon."

"Do they want it to be a surprise?" Jessie asked.

"Maybe," Skye frowned. "I mean, yes, they want to surprise her." She looked down. "But it's also dangerous. Aron is being held captive by a Mexican drug cartel. Our men have gone down with guns and bombs and a helicopter to break him out."

"Good God!" Avery had to sit down.

"They'll be okay," Cady sat primly, calmly with her hands folded. "We have to have faith."

"I agree," Skye said, but she was nervous as well. "I saw that woman who's holding Aron prisoner. She's one cold looking bitch."

Avery covered her mouth, she wanted to laugh, but it wasn't funny. "A woman?"

"Yes, did you know there are women drug lords?" Skye led them to the kitchen. "Let's make some hot chocolate." She knew they were going to worry themselves to death, they might as well do it over something sweet.

"Wouldn't that make them drug ladies?" Avery grabbed Cady's hand, seeking what comfort she could.

"Listen to me, girls." Cady took control. "Everything will be fine. Our men are McCoy's. They're a special breed. The best thing we can do is keep busy and get ready for Christmas. They'll be home before we know it."

Avery eyed her soon to be sister-in-law. "Do you *know* this?"

"Yes." Cady said calmly and prayed she was right.

Upstairs, Libby worked on her project. She'd finished the scrapbook; it had turned into a legacy of love. Now, she was writing their story. Wiping a tear, she wrote about the time they'd gone skinny dipping in the pond and the perch had nibbled on her toes. Yesterday she'd related the night they'd first made love after she'd swam in the stock tank. This morning she had laughed about the time Molly threw her and Aron had gotten so mad. "I can't forget about the bar fight with Sabrina or our wedding."

Wait.

Libby put the pen down. She realized that she was thinking of Aron in the past tense. A trembling began in her knees and worked its way up to her hands. "When did this happen?" She couldn't let herself give up. Standing up, she went out and stared out the window at a moon so big it seemed to cover half the sky. "Please, please God. I need him. Send him back to me."

La Dura Headquarters – Sonora Mexico.

Aron stared out the window at a moon so big it seemed to cover the sky. "Please, please God. Help me. I don't want to die without remembering her face." He had been chained up so long his arms were numb.

Earlier, something had happened; he had heard an uproar in the hall. Martina had screamed. Honestly, he hadn't thought her capable of remorse over anything. What she could have been suffering over so, he had no idea. How much longer she would let him live was another mystery. There was no way she was going to let him go. These thoughts were torturing him, so when the door opened and he looked up to see her standing there – he was shocked.

The look on her face was different. She walked in slowly. Moving gracefully, she came to within a couple of feet from where he was tied. He saw she was wearing a silk robe, slowly she began to unbutton it. And she began to speak. "Tonight, I realized something. I've been wrong. My father and my sister were almost killed tonight."

"I'm sorry." He was. He liked Tomas and Alessandra. "They are too good for the likes of you."

She lowered her eyes. "My priorities have been different."

Aron could see she was naked beneath the robe. Then she slid it off her shoulders and let it fall to the ground. Her body was graceful, sensual and perfectly formed. Leaving him absolutely cold. "Cover yourself."

She was not deterred. Coming to him, she moved a hand down his chest, tracing his muscles. He knew he had to smell, regular baths had not been part of his torture regime. But she acted as if she did not notice. "If you will have me," she offered. "I will leave El Duro. We can start anew, somewhere else." Stepping closer, she kissed him on the chest.

Aron felt as if an icepick was being thrust into his heart. "No."

"Please." She moved her hand down to cup his cock, trying to coax it to life. She molded it and massaged it.

Aron gritted his teeth, he wasn't made of stone. But he refused to respond. He didn't want to respond. "No."

"For you, Aron. For you, I will change. For you I will become like other women. Like your wife."

She looked into his eyes and he looked back. "You could never be like my wife. I know you've stolen my memories of her, but I know I would never choose anyone like you. I don't want you, Martina. I wouldn't have you and all your money tied up in a neat little bow." She stepped back, withdrawing her hand as if she'd been burned. "If that's what you're keeping me far, you might as well kill me."

***

Operation Aron

Two planes and a helicopter winged their way from Texas to Mexico. They belonged to Chancellor Industries. Inside were friends who were willing to place their own lives on the line to bring one of their own home. Harley LeBlanc was one of those friends. She sat drawing a diagram.

"Do you have your plan finalized, cher?" Her husband sat beside her. Beau had stepped up to the challenge, furnishing enough firepower to take down a small country. He'd also worked tirelessly with the McCoys to make sure they all felt comfortable handling the weapons.

"Yes, I do. Jet and I have this part covered." She lifted her eyes and smiled at her new friend. He was an intimidating looking man. Of course, during her time in the Navy she had met her share of tattoo-covered muscle men.

Everyone knew their place. Everyone knew their role. There were some more dangerous jobs than others. Aron's brothers had demanded to be on the front line. "Has anyone talked to Brock, again? Do we have any idea how many men will be at the hacienda?" Joseph asked. He'd been keeping up with everything, but he was getting married in a few days, so his thinking was fragmented.

"We're still waiting. There's been a set-back. He says the old man and the sister were in a car accident. Brock has been at her side and he also had a run-in with Martina. Apparently she's decided she doesn't approve of Alessandra's low-class boyfriend." Jacob stated. "His words not mine."

"What time do we arrive?" Isaac was nervous, fidgeting in his seat. He wasn't scared, he just wanted this over with and for them all to be back at Tebow – Aron with them and this whole nightmare to be nothing but a bad dream.

"In half an hour," Roscoe answered. "We've sent everything to Cisco, and if our timing works out, they'll be arriving right about the time we're through. Clean up crew, I guess you could call it."

Joseph couldn't help but ask. "How are they going to feel about a group of Americans coming into their country and waging war?"

"Well," Roscoe laughed. "I don't know. This could turn into an international incident. They ought to be grateful, though. We're doing their job for them. The info Brock gave us is enough to shut down El Duro and their suppliers."

"Good," Noah nodded. "No use letting Aron's information go to waste." He looked out the window at the wispy clouds passing by. "I wonder if he's remembered more."

"I don't know." Micah put his food tray aside. "I do think you ought to be the one to approach him when we find him. At least he'll recognize your face and you can explain things. We don't want to have to fight him once we turn him loose."

"I wonder what they've done to him?" Bowie didn't want to alarm anyone, but he was familiar with the cold, sadistic practices of the drug cartels. Frankly, the fact that he'd survived this long was testament that he meant something to the Delgado woman.

"I'm afraid to see." Jacob spoke lowly, echoing the same sentiment everyone else was feeling. "I've got a doctor alerted back home, in case any of us or Aron is injured. I've also contacted a neurobiologist in case his memory is still fouled up from the drugs or the operation. His name is Scott Walker, he comes highly recommended."

"Good idea." Kyle agreed. "I want us to get together after all of this is over and celebrate. When we were training and working together, I realized we all have a great deal in common, a lot more than just our mutual love for Aron."

"I like that," Bowie smiled. "If we can pull this off, it's going to be a helluva Christmas."

Nerves were tense and there wasn't a lot of conversation when they landed and began to get ready for the planned assault. Vance had arranged for their transportation. Getting away after it was over was going to be as dangerous and tricky as the attack, they'd just have to make sure they damaged them enough to make their exit possible. "All right. It's time."

Before leaving the airport, they loaded up in three black SUV's, everyone armed. Beau had made sure they all wore bulletproof vests and Kevlar clothes. It wouldn't keep them from getting shot, but it would even the odds a fraction. Harley held her bomb in her lap, she was ready to hook it up and watch the fireworks display. Patrick and his team, would storm the gate. Revel would lead the charge. They had it timed out so the distraction of one assault would camouflage the next. As soon as the west wall was blown and Kyle's team had moved in, Tyson would lower the brothers and Bowie down by helicopter to storm the house and rescue Aron.

Jacob hoped to high heaven they hadn't missed anything.

The weather was warm as they made their way through the streets of Cantanea. Destry and Patrick rode at the windows, their rifles at the ready, just in case they were fired upon. Stray dogs ran across the road, kids played in the ditches as they passed. Life seemed to be going on as normal, but all were aware that every eye watched them closely as they went by.

"What do these people think about a drug lord in their neighborhood?" Jaxson asked. When he'd been down before, he had just gone to the airport and the ranch, not venturing out into the countryside.

"I suppose they're used to it, much like gang activity in the states, plus so many of them make their living one way or another off the cartel. I'm sure their presence stimulates the economy." Noah mused.

"That's debatable." Bowie commented. "Down here, it's either cooperate or die. In the last six or so years, the authorities estimate over a hundred thousand people have been killed in the drug wars. Mass graves have been uncovered, added together - over twenty-four thousand people have just been thrown away like garbage. Dismembered body parts are found in the streets or rotting in barrels of acid. They find dead bodies hanging from bridges, journalists are killed, women are raped – the drug war takes no prisoners."

"You can bet your ass someone has let them know we're here. I think we stick out like a sore thumb." Isaac's pessimistic streak was letting itself be known.

"Let's take them down." Jacob had been touched by Bowie's speech. "Rescuing Aron is my main objective, but anything we can do to alleviate the suffering of these people is just icing on the cake."

"We're getting close." Beau, who was driving the other vehicle, spoke through the headset. They were all wearing combat helmets, outfitted with state of the art audio and communication equipment. "Remember, we're parking next to the warehouse on the south side of the wall." Vance had taken video and photos of the surrounding area. The hacienda itself was an estate covering twelve acres, surrounded by a twelve foot stone wall with barb wire running across the top. The gate was electronic, but Saxon had found a way to override the signal, so the guards were in for a surprise.

The plan was to rush the gate, then five minutes later, blow the wall. As soon as they were engaging the cartel's mercenaries at the front and at the site of the explosion, Tyson would land the helicopter near the house and another team would join the fray.

After Brock sent the blueprints, Patrick and Kyle had studied them, finding the path of least resistance to get to Aron. Alessandra had furnished Brock with a description of where he was being held, so they knew the best door to enter and the directions to take them to the basement.

Esteban and Martina were deviants; they had a reputation for cold, vindictive torture. The room where he was being housed was six by nine foot. For most of the time, he had either been chained to the ceiling or to the wall. He hadn't been allowed to lie down, but a few hours every three days. Martina had sought to break his will by depriving him of rest, food and hope. Jacob only hoped she hadn't succeeded.

Chapter Twelve

When they pulled into the warehouse parking lot, Vance waited for them. He directed the SUV's to be parked inside one of the unloading bays where they would be out of site. Cananea was a mining town, but the industry had fallen victim to the drug trade as had everything else. So, the warehouses were vacant and a good place to mask their movements. They could use the building as cover until they came to the wall.

Jacob had decided to conduct their raid late in the evening, he felt they would be better able to create a surprise attack under the cover of night. He'd also chosen the dark of the moon. Each team member was also equipped with night vision goggles, the best money could buy, so they were prepared.

"Move out." The moment Kyle gave the signal, the troops began to move. They had rehearsed this, repeatedly. Everyone knew their function and knew whose back they covered. Patrick was communicating with Tyson and the helicopter was in place and ready to fly. Stealthily, they moved through the alley, guns cocked and ready. As one, they clung to the shadows, walking quietly – no one speaking. Once Team 1 was at the gate, there was the whispered command. "Override." Saxon, operating inside the SUV with a satellite hook-up, hacked their controls and the gate clicked. Immediately an alarm sounded – but they had expected this. The rushing of booted feet on concrete was heard between the sharp blasts of the siren. "Fire!"

Kyle, Destry, Micah and Tennessee stormed the gate, firing round after round into the startled surprised group who came to defend it. El Duro was well-trained, but unused to having to battle an enemy on home turf. Usually they were the aggressors, being attacked in the middle of the night by a group of whooping, rampaging Texans was a shock.

The sharp retort of rifle fire cracked through the night. Groans of men, riddled by bullets punctuated the night air. "Left,

Left, ten o'clock, ten o'clock!" Roscoe was part of Team 1 and he barked out orders, trying to protect their flank.

"Behind you!" Micah yelled as troops came at them from the street. What the hell? "They've got damn reinforcements. This is a surprise."

"I've got them." Jayco sat back on his heel with an automatic machine gun and cut the newcomers down with a constant stream of firepower.

"Good man." Kyle praised him. "Look to the right. More!"

"God, how many are there?" They fired in all directions, having to be careful not to take out one of their own. "How much more time we got till Harley blows?"

Beau's voice came over the headset speaker. "Forty-five seconds."

"Can't come soon enough, we're drawing them all."

"Just keep shooting," Tennessee ground out. "The more we can take down here, the better."

"Ten, nine, eight," they could hear the countdown.

"These bastards don't know who they're dealing with." Jayco spat out.

All of a sudden a huge explosion shook the ground. El Duro soldiers who had been defending the gate were pulled off to check the breach in the wall. Harley had been well out of harm's way, Beau had seen to that. And even though she was former Navy, he didn't intend for her to fight today. She and Jet had set up the bomb, detonated it and then she'd sought shelter. But Beau walked through the wall blasting. Hawke was with him, and when Beau gave the signal, he shot flash grenades onto the grounds which created more distractions, causing the soldiers near them to be blind and deaf long enough for the Texans to gain ground.

Jacob watched it all from the air. Mixed emotions were tearing him apart. Death was never acceptable to him. He'd insisted they all be trained in placing shots which would debilitate and not kill, but he knew that wasn't going to be possible most of the time. The men who would be shooting at them would be shooting to kill.

But he'd never been in war like some of these men, he had never looked into the face of someone as he took their life. Frankly, he was worried how everyone would handle it. As they flew over the compound, he could see men lying on the ground, see the flash of the gunfire, the peppery sparkle of bullets leaving the barrels of automatic weapons. He had to remind himself who these people were and what they were here for – Aron.

"Lord, protect our men." He prayed none of them would die today. Going in, they knew it was a possibility. They had discussed it. How in the world Jacob would ever repay his friends for this feat, he did not know.

"Okay, we're landing." Tyson barked. Jacob looked around at his brothers. Joseph, Isaac, and Noah. Joining them were Heath and Bowie Travis. All of them had solemn looks on their face, they knew this was it – what they had come for.

"Let's do it." As soon as the helicopter was hovering a few feet off the ground, they began to jump out, bending low and running for the side door. If all was working, Revel was covering them. He had been instructed to enter by the gate and make his way to the east side of the hacienda to be ready for the helicopter to land.

Pop, pop, pop. Screams and shouts filled the air. The smell of gunpowder and burning flesh seared his nostrils. "Hurry, hurry," he called. All six of them raced to the door as they heard the helicopter lift off. Tyson would take it out of the compound, Jacob hadn't wanted him to be a sitting duck. His orders were to return when given the signal. Just as expected, there were sentries at the door. Heath didn't even hesitate. "Saludos Muchacho." They fired at him and he fired back, clearing the way.

"Your Spanish accent is terrible." Isaac told him.

"Sorry," Heath laughed. "I'll try to do better next time." They entered the mansion, stopping to fight when they had to.

"Wonder where the big dogs are?" Joseph asked. "I'd like to get a pot shot at the leaders, myself."

"Hiding, I'm sure." Noah remarked. "Those types usually stay out of the heat."

"Not this time, gringo." A voice brought them all to a standstill. Jacob turned around to see a rotund man standing with a gun to Isaac's head.

"Let him go."

The man laughed. "Oh, sure. You come into my home, kill my people and ask me to let this man go. Why would you think I'd be so accommodating?"

"You're Esteban Rodrigo." Jacob sneered.

"Indeed, I am."

"Nice to meet you, Sir. We thank you for your kind hospitality." Behind Esteban, Revel came, holding a gun to the Mexican's head. A struggle broke out. Two more armed El Duro soldiers came barreling into the room and shots were fired.

A muffled groan sent chills down Jacob's spine. One of them was hit. When the gunfire stopped, it was Revel Lee on the floor. "Check him," he instructed Noah.

Noah was instantly on his knees, looking at the man who had come to ask him about Harper. "Where are you hit?"

"My thigh. If it didn't get my femoral artery, I'll live." He winced as Noah examined his wound.

"Damn, there's a lot of blood, but I think we can staunch it."

"Here try this," Joseph handed him a towel. "I found this in the bathroom over there."

"Hold this here." He motioned to Heath. "Stay with him, we'll be right back." Noah rose. "Just as soon as we get Aron."

"Bowie, guard them," Jacob pointed. "We can't leave these two unattended."

This wasn't the plan, but they'd have to improvise. Leaving the three of them behind, the brothers made their way deeper into the maze of halls and rooms. They went downstairs, distant cries and reports of automatic weapons still sounded from outside. "This is too easy." Joseph drawled.

"Yea, that's what I was thinking." Isaac whispered.

"It should be, right about – here." Noah rounded a corner and saw a steel door. "What have we got that can open this?"

"A little C-4." Isaac smiled.

"Do you know how to use that?"

"Hey, I practiced." They stood back while he put a small block of C-4 on the lock and set it off with a blaster cap. Turning their backs, they prayed the explosion would open the door.

Bam! It did. But when the smoke cleared and they saw what was in the room, their blood ran cold. Their brother hung limp, his arms over his head, his body bloody and striped. And standing next to him with a gun pointed at his heart was Martina Delgado. "You can't have him." She spoke calmly. "He's mine."

"You bitch," Joseph ground out the words. "Is that how you treat something that belongs to you?" The sight reminded him of abused animals, their sick owners using them for sport, just to see how much pain they could take.

"He didn't cooperate."

"It's over, Miss Delgado." Noah was afraid to move. She was cornered and desperate animals were deadly.

Jacob whispered. "Let me." He moved a slight step forward. "We've sent enough information to the District Attorney to close you down forever. You'll never see the light of day again."

She bristled. 'Swear to God', Isaac thought, she bristled. Taking one step toward them, she moved the barrel of her gun from Aron and aimed right at Jacob and pulled the trigger.

"No!" Aron yelled and in the same split second, he bucked forward, hitting her in the back and causing her to stumble. And when she did, the gun went up and she went down and Joseph and Isaac were on her, subduing her before she could pick up the gun.

"Aron." Noah walked up to his brother. "My God, what have they done to you?"

Aron lifted his head, his eyes all but swollen shut. Dried blood was crusted on dozens of welts which covered his head, neck and chest. "Are you my family?"

"Hell yeah!" Isaac answered. "Do you think we'd be risking our asses for you if we weren't?" The tenseness of the situation lessened as Joseph and Noah let out a small chuckle.

"Get him down. We've got to get out of here." Jacob had subdued Martina and put her in cuffs, attaching them to the table. "She's not going anywhere." A tirade of Spanish erupted from her mouth. She was cursing them, Aron, God and anybody else she could think of.

"Look at you," Joseph helped Aron down. "You look worse than when you did after Oklahoma stomped your ass in the Cotton Bowl."

"I don't remember," he said weakly. "Do ya'll see any water? I'm so thirsty."

"Hunt him some!" Jacob barked and Joseph took off, returning in a few minutes with a glass. "We've got to get out of here. The fighting is still going on outside."

"How did you do this?" Aron asked, leaning on Noah.

"We'll explain everything. I promise."

"I want to go home." His voice was weak, but his meaning was clear.

"That's what we came for, to take you home." The brothers looked at one another, smiled and got the hell out of Dodge.

* * *

On the way home

Getting out wasn't quite as easy as getting in. They managed to get Aron and Revel on the copter, but Revel was weak from blood loss. Jacob communicated with Kyle and Beau, telling them to retreat when they could, they had achieved their objective. "Tell me our status," he asked Roscoe.

"We're pulling out. We'll be back at the airport and in the air in a little over an hour. I can hear sirens now, I think the government is going to take advantage of our skirmish and finish the job. I'm telling Tyson to head out now. I want you all to head to Douglas, Arizona, it's just over the border and we can get Revel and Aron emergency treatment there."

"How are you holding up, buddy?" Noah bent down by Revel.

"I've had worse." He ground out, but his face was grey.

"Just hold on, we're only fifty miles away, won't take us but minutes."

The whirr of the blades was a comforting background noise as Jacob knelt down by Aron. "You do know we never gave up on you, right?"

Aron looked into a face very similar to his own, eyes the same color as his looked back at him. "I hoped." He smiled weakly. "What's your name?"

"Jacob, I'm the second oldest, you're the fossil." He laughed. "The retarded looking one is Joseph and hard-head over there is Noah. That's Isaac," he pointed at his brother who was tending to Revel, "you have to remember all the trouble he gave you."

"I will remember."

"Yes, you will," Jacob agreed. "Our wounded warrior is a good friend, Revel Jones, and Tyson Pate is flying this bird. You played ball with him at UT."

"There's five of us? Anymore?"

"Well, Nathan's at home, he's thirteen."

"Who named us, a preacher? We've all got old testament Bible names." Aron coughed.

Noah was worried. "How long since you ate?"

"I don't know," Aron confessed. He hurt all over. "Tell me more."

"Well, of course, there's Libby." Isaac said the name and they all looked at Aron. If anything could shake his memory, it would be Libby.

"Is she my wife?" He said the words reverently, with hope.

"Yes, she is," Jacob smiled. "And just as soon as we get on the plane toward home, I'll show you a picture of your lovely bride."

When they landed in Douglas, an ambulance escorted them to the hospital where Revel was admitted. He would have to have surgery to remove the bullet. Aron was examined and released, he was dehydrated and malnourished, but there was no internal damage. Tyson conferred with the others by phone and verified they were all stateside and doing well. Jacob took the time to talk to each one individually and thank them. Arrangements were made to get together as soon after Christmas as everyone could manage. Patrick would be coming to escort Revel back to Lafayette, but in the meantime, Noah sat by his bedside and asked. "Is there anyone I can call. Harper, perhaps?"

"How did you know I found her?"

Noah chuckled. "I didn't, but by the look on your face, I knew you were going to turn the world upside down looking for her."

"Well, I found her, but there's no need to call her. She wouldn't come."

"You sound pretty certain about that."

"Yea, I am." Revel looked at Noah. "Sometimes dreams don't come true. She's hurting and I would give anything if she'd let me help her. Of course, I'm in no shape to help anyone right now."

"You'll be fine." Noah assured him. "The bullet didn't hit anything major, the doc will fix you up."

"That's right, you saved my life, and I won't forget it." Isaac spoke from the door.

"We all thank you," Noah stood. "Tyson is going to stay with you until Patrick arrives later on tonight. We're going to get Aron home. Jacob has chartered us a plane back to Kerrville."

"Be careful, and thanks for letting me in on the action, I wouldn't have missed it."

Revel was too weak to shake hands, but Noah saluted him. "This won't be the last time our paths cross, we'll be in touch." As Noah walked away, he knew he had made a friend for life.

The flight back home was a happy one. Aron was feeling better. He had eaten a hamburger and a portable IV was hooked up to his arm, feeding glucose into his veins to hydrate him. The nurse had given them instructions on how to switch out the bags. Joseph had laughed and said he'd done the same thing for several cows, he knew the drill. As soon as they were in the air, the brothers grew quiet, wondering how best to handle the situation.

Aron didn't wait, he handled it himself. "You've got to realize something," he began with a sigh. "I'm flying blind here. My mind is pretty messed up. I don't even know what all they've given me. Martina said I'd remembered everything and she couldn't allow that, so she had some chemist feed me a dose of some crap that wiped out my memory. I don't know if it's temporary or permanent."

"Don't worry, we'll get you checked out. I've got an appointment all set up." Jacob wanted to ease Aron's mind. "And we'll tell you everything. Hopefully something will wake up your memory."

"What do you remember?" Isaac asked. "Anything?"

Aron paused, as if considering how to answer. "I have impressions. A sense of belonging, I knew you all existed, I knew I had a home and a family, I just couldn't grasp the reality of it. Everything was a foggy dream."

"Do you remember Tebow or Mama and Daddy?" Joseph asked, drawing closer.

"Tebow's our home?"

"Yea, it's our ranch. We've got a good size spread south of Austin near Kerrville. We raise Longhorns, Beefmasters and a lot of hell." Isaac laughed.

"Our parents?" Aron has suspicions, because they hadn't really mentioned them.

Noah hung his head. "God, there's so much I want to tell you. I've missed you so." Aron touched his shoulder in comfort. "Mama and Daddy are gone. They've been gone for years." With sadness, they told Aron how their parents had died and how Aron had made sure the family stayed together. "It was you, Aron. You made our family possible," Noah summed it up. Later he would tell him about the adoption and when Aron's memory came back, he wanted to know everything his daddy had ever said about his birth.

"How about my wife?" They all grew quiet.

Finally, Isaac spoke. "You are so loved and so damn lucky." Just that quick, the flood gates opened and they began telling him about Libby – the funny things, the messes she would get into, how much she loved Nathan. And that she was pregnant.

"I want to see her." He whispered.

Jacob was the first to realize he was asking for a photo. They all pulled out their phones and started sharing. "This is Libby." He handed him the phone. "She was giving Lady a bath."

Aron stared at the image. Long dark hair, a smile that would light up the world, loving eyes and a killer body. "I'm a lucky man." He kept looking, struggling to hear a voice, see a glimmer of a memory. "She's beautiful."

"Yes, and she loves you so much. This whole thing has nearly killed her."

Aron accepted phone after phone and he gazed at photo after photo. "She's pregnant."

"Yea, you're going to be a father."

With a hoarse voice, Aron answered. "Martina said I was, but I thought she was just adding to my heartache."

"Yea, you don't know how much you wanted these babies. With Libby being sick…" Isaac elbowed Joseph and he hushed, abruptly.

"What?" Aron caught the word. He sat up straighter. "Sick?"

"She's not anymore." Jacob was quick to add. "Libby beat leukemia."

"God," Aron looked into the distance. "I feel so helpless. You don't know how much I just want to scream and beat my head against the wall – make myself remember." He looked back down at Libby. "How could I forget someone like her?"

"You'll remember, Aron." Joseph tried to comfort him. "We've all been so blessed." He began to tell him about Cady and what all they'd been through. "I'm going to be a father, too."

"More babies?" Aron smiled.

"I'm a father now," Jacob said proudly. "Little Bowie Travis McCoy should arrive at Tebow right after you do." He told Aron about the surgery and how Jessie had been a surrogate mother and the battle they'd gone through to get her out of the clutches of Kevin McCay. "As soon as we land, I'm headed to the hospital and if the doctor has BT's release papers ready, I'm bringing him home."

"Some of this sounds a bit familiar," Aron admitted with a laugh. "Either that or I'm recalling episodes from that TV show Dallas. Sounds like our family is full of drama."

"You remember Dallas?" Isaac thought that was a good sign.

"Yes, I remembered how to ride and that I knew ranching. Martina let slip that I had remembered I was from Texas and at one point I knew where home was and all of you. She made me think she was going to come after all of you and she probably would have if you hadn't got to her first."

They took turns telling him about their lives. Noah spoke of Skye and Isaac told him about Avery and Hardbodies. When Joseph told him about being paralyzed, Aron pulled him in for a hug. "How did we survive all of this?" He asked with emotion.

"We're McCoy." Isaac said. "We can survive anything."

"Tell me what happened to me." He was trying so hard to piece it all together. "Tell me what you know of the accident. How did this come about?" Aron touched his head.

"You and Libby were on your honeymoon in the Caymans." Jacob explained. "You hate the water."

"That I remember." Aron laughed.

"Nothing would do Libby but that you go on snorkeling together. But when Libby came up, you didn't." Jacob shook his head; all of it had been so hard.

"It was a nightmare," Joseph picked up the story. "We didn't know if Jaws had eaten you or if you'd been swept out to sea."

"You thought I was dead." Aron looked at them.

"No," Noah assured him. "Libby never gave up and we have turned the whole damn southern hemisphere on its ear looking for you. There have been massive searches, not only in the water, but on the islands and in Mexico. All we'd found to hold on to was your wedding ring."

Aron look down. "How did that get off?"

"Well, if I had my guess, I'd say Martina." Joseph snarled.

"Yea, probably." Isaac agreed. "We even had DNA tests run on a piece of your dive suit we found – shredded with remnants of blood and bone on it."

"Dang," Aron frowned. "The first thing I remember was being at Los Banos. Tomas was good to me. Martina was all hands," he shook his head. "She told me we were engaged to be married."

"Did you?" Joseph hesitated.

"Did I what?" He looked at his brothers, their question finally dawning on him. "Did I sleep with her?" He looked affronted. "Hell, no. My mind might not be a hundred percent, but my instincts were damn good. That woman didn't do a thing for me."

"I'm not surprised. Since you've met Libby, there could be no one else. You fell in love with her at first sight."

"Yea," Joseph laughed. "I well remember the day she came to stay with us. The look on your face when your first saw her was priceless. Plus, she made you brownies. You always were a sucker for chocolate."

The pilot informed them they were approaching the Kerrville airport. "Well, here we are. Home sweet home." Jacob looked at Aron. "Are you ready for this?"

"I've been ready for this for a long time." He stood up. "How do I look?"

"Like shit," Joseph laughed. "But don't worry, Libby's going to love you anyway."

"Does she know I'm coming?"

"Nope, we didn't tell her. We wanted you to surprise her."

As they got ready to disembark, Aron had one more question. "What do I tell her about my memory? That's going to hurt her."

He looked from brother to brother. Finally, Jacob answered. "That's your call, but neither choice is going to be a piece of cake.

She's been holding on by a thread, praying ceaselessly for your return. But finding out you don't remember her – I don't know how she'll handle that."

"Shit." His heart ached for his wife.

"One thing I do know though," Jacob stopped him with a hand on his arm. "You're being alive is going to be the most important thing. Libby loves you. She'll work through this; all you have to do is love her back."

The ramifications of what Jacob said sank home. Aron looked at her photo one more time. "I don't think that will be a problem."

* * *

Tebow Ranch

"Libby! Can you check those cookies in the oven?" Cady was all a dither. She'd heard from Joseph and knew what was going down.

"Yes, I've got them." She called, wiping a bit of flour off her pooching tummy.

"How's your book coming?" Avery leaned on the counter munching on a celery stick.

"Good," Libby smiled. "Sure did bring back a lot of memories. But when Aron reads it, it will be worth it." She sighed. The idea that he'd be home for Christmas was beginning to seem impossible. Did everyone think she was crazy?

"I'm sure it will." Avery met Cady's eyes over Libby's shoulder. She was in the know also.

"How are we ever going to get this all done?" She looked around the kitchen. "The tree is decorated. The presents are wrapped. The baking is done." Then a look of horror came into her eyes. "Punch, what about the wedding punch?"

Cady came and hugged her. "This wedding is going to be a family affair. We don't need punch." She kissed her soon to be sister. "I want to marry Joseph. I want to be a part of this family. None of the extras are important." She had thought about putting off the ceremony, considering, but she just couldn't. "When I get his ring on my finger, I'll be the happiest woman in the world."

Libby's face fell. "I know the feeling."

"Stop it," Cady said. "Smile. This is the season of miracles."

"I know," Tears were in her voice. "It's just so hard."

It took all Cady had not to say anything, but she had promised.

"Libby!" Nathan called. "Lady wants a stocking. Everyone has one but her."

Libby laughed, "Well, how about one of Aron's socks? He wouldn't mind."

A commotion at the front door drew their attention. "Do you think that's Jacob and Jessie bringing the baby home?" She threw off the apron. "I have a cake made and the nursery is ready."

"Calm down, breathe." Avery held her shoulders. "It could be Skye, she went to the store to pick up some last minute items." Truthfully, Skye had gone to the airport to pick up the guys, but that was something she couldn't say.

A shout from the other room caused them all to pause. "Oh my God!" Nathan yelled at the top of his lungs.

"What's wrong with him?" Libby asked. She started for the living room, but a voice – a familiar voice froze her in her tracks.

She put a hand over her heart. Tears welled up and started spilling down her cheeks. She took one step and then two. Avery opened the door, her eyes twinkling. "I think Santa just dropped off a great big present."

"Aron," she whispered. She held her breath as she walked up to the door. There was several people in the living room – hugging. Nathan, Joseph, Isaac, Noah, Skye – and then they moved back.

And she saw him. Her knees almost gave way. "Aron."

He turned. Their eyes met. He was thinner, there were rough red marks on his face and neck – but he was the most beautiful sight in the whole world to her. "Aron!" She ran. She couldn't have held back if her life depended on it. "My Aron!" She flew across the room, arms open wide and he caught her.

Time stopped.

She was in his arms. He was breathing. His heart was beating against her chest. "You're alive. I knew you were. I never gave up. Not for a moment."

"Libby." He whispered. "I'm home." He winced at the pressure she was putting on the places where his skin was bruised and raw. But there was no way he was going to tell her. He'd suffer all day long for the privilege of holding Libby.

"Yes, you are my darling." She looked up into his dear face. "I missed you so much." She went up on tiptoe and placed her lips against his.

Aron was knocked for a loop. They were alone, he hadn't even seen the others leave. But his family had given him and his wife some privacy. His wife. All of the horror and hopelessness, all of the nightmares and desperation seemed to dissipate as the reality that he belonged somewhere began to sink in.

And in his arms was an angel. Her sweet lips were touching his – gently, searching, learning. And he could no more have resisted her than he could have denied himself his next breath. Accepting her kiss, he returned it. Lips as soft velvet caressed his. She tasted like the sweetest honey, and her tongue teased him – lured his out to play. There was no hesitation here. She was welcoming him home and he would be a fool not to accept the invitation.

Emotions swelled and exploded in Libby's heart. She tightened her arms around his neck and hugged herself close to his big body. The familiar sensation of hard muscle against her softness – husband and wife – male and female – was enough to make her moan. "Aron, are you real?" Her breasts swelled, her nipples drawing tight.

"Yea, I'm real, baby." Aron wanted to cry. For her. For him. For what they'd lost. God, she didn't even know. How would he tell her? Should he tell her? Looking at her face, the joy in her eyes, Aron knew he had to tell her, he couldn't lie to her. But not just yet.

"Kiss me, please. Kiss me like you've missed me."

Her small request nearly floored him. His eyes devoured her face. "You're so beautiful." He put a hand on her belly. "My babies." He breathed with a smile.

"Yes, your babies." She covered his hand, interlacing their fingers; the naked happiness in her eyes took his breath away. Aron cupped her face in his hands. Slowly he lowered his mouth, allowing his lips to relearn the softness and shape of hers. Rich, smooth velvet. One smooth touch of his lips blossomed into a dozen drugging kisses. At the insistent rub of his mouth, teasing nibbles and tiny flicks of his tongue, Libby's lips parted with a soft sigh. His tongue slipped inside and her flavor burst in his mouth - sweet chocolate, sweet woman and sweet promise. He knew it had been an eternity since he'd kissed her this way, with need, with promise, with a renewal of commitment,

Aron slanted his head, kicking the kiss up from a slow get reacquainted touch to an aching hunger. For Libby. Only ever for her. A warm, intense reunion of tangling tongues, panting breaths and the powerful build into passion their hearts and bodies had been denied so long. In spite of the passion and the heat of yearning, he held himself back – this was too critical to rush. He had to tell her everything before he could lose himself in her softness. Aron forced himself to ease up – break the kiss.

But Libby would have none of it. "I missed you, Aron." She stood on tiptoe and pressed butterfly kisses from his jaw to his neck. "I dreamed of you."

"I dreamed of you, too." He knew he had.

"Who hurt you?" She gently touched the marks on his face and neck. Before he could answer, Joseph knocked on the door.

"Hey, you two," he stuck his head inside. "Can we come back in?"

"Oh, lordy." Libby fanned herself. "I forgot we weren't alone. They missed you as much as I did." Then it hit her like a ton of bricks. Putting her hand on her hip, she pinned him with a stare. "Where have you been?"

Isaac broke out in laughter. "It's gonna be a long night."

Chapter Thirteen

Aron let himself be led into the living room. He had a hard time taking it all in. Nothing was familiar, but it all felt right. He could feel the pull of the connection with his brothers, especially Nathan. When the young man had hugged him, an overwhelming sense of love had welled up like a fountain. Their ladies seem to take it all in stride. He looked from one to another, just enjoying the fact he was a part of something so beautiful. A family.

And Libby. He had a hard time keeping his eyes off of her. She belonged to him? What a treasure. Her every touch spoke love. She brought him a plate of food, then sat at his feet while he ate, handing him a glass of tea when he needed a drink. Not once did she cease to touch him somewhere as if she couldn't quite believe he was actually here.

After they'd finished their meal, he drew her into his lap. She had been patient. "Libby, I don't remember the accident that caused all of this." He spoke of their snorkeling trip and how he had been injured. "The next thing I knew I had been picked up on a yacht and told I was someone else. They weren't good people." He spoke slowly. "The Delgado's were part of a drug cartel and when my memory started to come back, they drugged me. I didn't know who I was or where I was. You have to realize, I would never have stayed away from you if I could help it."

Touching his face, she whispered. "I knew it had to be something like that, you'd never willingly leave me. Would you?"

"No." He shook his head. "I'm just thankful Jaxson saw me down there, recognized me and called Noah."

She looked at Noah, who came over to where they sat. "Why didn't you tell me?" Her look was hurt and a bit accusatory.

"I had to be sure. You'd been hurt enough."

She realized he was talking about the memorial from the Cattle Barron's Ball and the fact he had questioned where Aron was and why he hadn't come home. "I'm strong." She lifted her chin.

"Yes, you are." Aron agreed. "The people who took me in told me my name was Austin Wade. I worked at a ranch in northern Mexico. But soon I realized they were into more than just cattle. The rancher's brother-in-law and daughter were the head of a massive drug operation, responsible for millions of dollars of drug sales a day and countless deaths."

Libby drew in a harsh breath. "What did you do?" Oh, God. "I could have lost you so easily." She nestled down in his arms. "Nathan dreamed about you!"

"He did?" Aron didn't understand her meaning. "When my memory started coming back, they felt threated. And well they should have, because I started gathering information to use against them. When they realized that, they gave me something which erased my memories."

Libby froze. She was just about to ask a question when there was a car honking outside. Nathan ran to the window. "It's Jacob and Jessie. And BT!" Everyone got up. Aron kissed Libby and she walked slowly behind the group, deep in thought.

They all walked out on the porch to see the little family get out of the car. Jacob ran around to open the door for his wife and to unstrap the carrier. "Look who's here!" he announced. The whole family cheered at seeing the proud parents and the new baby who had had such a rough start to life.

Aron was filled with pride. Looking at each face, he knew he would remember. He wanted it all back – he wanted to know their habits, what expressions they used – their likes and dislikes. He wanted to know it all.

"Come in out of the cold," Cady opened the door and urged everyone back in.

Jessie took in the decorations. "Oh, it is so beautiful! Where are you going to stand for the ceremony?" She asked Cady.

"Next to me." Joseph teased.

Everyone took turns holding BT, but it was soon evident that Nathan had appointed himself as the baby's guardian.

The atmosphere in the room was celebratory. Libby had never heard so much laughter. The relief she felt was tempered with fear. Something was wrong. He had all but told her, but she couldn't bring herself to even think the thought, much less say it out loud.

An ache was centered in her chest. It was evident. The way everyone kept explaining everything. And the nicknames he always used to call her – they were missing. He looked the same. He sounded the same. He kissed the same. But he wasn't.

He didn't remember her.

Libby was devastated.

Then she was embarrassed.

It took a while, but Aron finally realized Libby wasn't near him, not like she had been. He looked around the room. She was standing as far away from him as she could get and still be in the same room. This wouldn't do. When he gazed at her, something familiar spoke to him. True, his mind was having trouble placing her, but his body responded with a heated ache. He had touched this woman, kissed her, made love to her. His heart remembered, even if his brain did not. And he wanted more.

"Excuse me," he told Joseph and Cady. Aron had just consented to be Joseph's best man at the wedding, which was only two days away. Christmas was only two days away. According to what they had told him, he had been gone since October the 17th, over two months. Two damn months of his life had been stolen and so had his memories. The time, he'd never get back. But he fully intended to remember, especially Libby. He was greedy. He wanted it all – every nuance, every image, every word they'd ever whispered, every secret they'd ever shared.

Aron moved across the room toward her.

Libby saw him coming. Her heart clenched in her chest. What was she going to do?

"Hey, why aren't you standing by me? Are you tired of me already?" He grinned.

"You don't know who I am. Do you?"

For a moment, he was taken aback. "Of course, I do. You're Libby McCoy, my wife."

She held her ground. "You don't remember me, do you?"

He was quiet for a moment. She closed her eyes as if she was in great pain, then she took off across the room and ran upstairs.

Everyone was quiet. They were all watching. Aron looked around at his family. "I'm so happy to be back. I don't have the words to tell you grateful I am that you cared enough about me to throw another Texas revolution. But I need to take care of my wife. Please, excuse me."

No one tried to stop him.

Aron went upstairs. Hell, he didn't even know which room was his. Looking around, he saw his bags sitting by one door. Surely she hadn't set them out? No, that was probably where Joseph or Isaac had put them when they'd come in from the airport. Going to the door, he tapped on it. "Libby?"

Silence.

"Libby?"

"What?" He heard her small voice.

"Can I come in?"

"It's your room."

"It's our room, isn't it?"

"Used to be." She was speaking into the pillow.

Aron stopped at the edge of the bed. The sight of the beautiful woman lying among the pillows, her heart-shaped behind turned up for his delectation, made it hard to keep his mind on the matter at hand. He was still a little weak, but he was a man. "Libby, talk to me."

"I don't know what to say."

At least she was honest. "I didn't choose for this to happen, you know."

She sprang from the bed. "God, I know that." She batted away tears from her spiked lashes. "I don't blame you, Aron." Hiccupping back a sob, she went to her knees in front of him. "I'm so glad you're alive. I promised God all sorts of outrageous things if he would just bring you back to me."

Aron sat down on the bed, drawing her into his lap. This was his world, right here in his arms. His wife and his children. One day he would remember their past, but he had no trouble at all seeing their future. "I want to remember. Don't think I don't."

Easing up out of his lap, she went up on her knees facing him. "This is almost a new beginning for you, I guess." She looked into his eyes, trying so hard to read his expression.

He didn't know what she was getting at. "What do you mean?"

"My faith was strong," she told him. "I don't think I want to wait till Christmas to give you this." She got on her knees and dug under the bed. "Pulling out a present, she gave it to him.

"What have you done?" He couldn't help but feel a little thrill. "I guess I like presents, I feel like a kid."

"Well, this isn't a game or anything, you'll have to wait for Christmas Day for those." She pointed to their entertainment center so he could see his array of video games and players.

Aron laughed. "Super! Do we play together?"

"Yea," she winked at him. "I beat you all the time." She didn't really, but for right now – he wouldn't know that.

"I bet." He winked at her. She was fun, his wife. He couldn't wait to find out more about her. Unwrapping the gift, he found an album. "What's this?"

"While you were gone, Noah had an identity crisis." He might as well know, he would find out eventually. "Noah is adopted. You have the same dad, but different mothers." He was looking at her sort of blankly. "I didn't know. No one knew but you and Jacob. The family more or less ignored it. Which was a good thing, until he accidentally stumbled on the truth." She could see this was not ringing any bells. "If you get your memory back, I'm sure you'll be able to shed some light on the situation, but apparently, Noah's mother was a woman your dad met on the rodeo circuit."

"Shit." He stared at the floor as if he were trying to conjure up answers.

"Anyway," she waved her hands. "While he was digging in the attic for answers, he came upon these boxes of papers and photos. I thought about making you an album of your life and family."

He opened it. "Wow," he breathed turning page after page.

She knew it was probably asking too much, but she began to hope something would ring a bell, or jar loose whatever was damming up his memories. Libby sat by him and pointed out people and times and places. "Yea, you won every award you can think of." His high school and college sports days were fully chronicled.

"That's Kyle Chancellor." He pointed at a teammate. "He helped get me out of that hellhole." He picked the book up closer. "The son-of-a-bitch won the Heisman?"

His incredulity made Libby laugh. Then there was his rodeo days and his sculpting awards. "Yes, you sculpt."

"No," he laughed. "Really?" Aron stared at the accolades and newspaper articles about his art career. "Who woulda thought?"

"You're very talented. And handsome. And smart." He thumbed on over until he came to pictures of the two of them. "Way out of my league."

There it was.

She had always wondered how in the world Liberty Belle Fontaine had won the heart of Aron McCoy. It had been a fluke. An aberration. A once in a lifetime miracle.

And there was no way she could expect it to happen again.

Aron's hand stilled. He lifted his head and looked at her. "Have you lost your mind?" She didn't answer. "I'm the one who's been tortured and starved and had the shit beat out of him." His words were harsh, but his heart was breaking. He didn't know what to do. "I know things don't make sense. Especially for me. I look in the mirror and don't know who I am half the time." He went to the door and pulled his bags in. Picking up the duffle, he took out the shaving kit. "When they found me, I was clasping this coin in my hand. I held it so hard that it cut a circle in my palm. See?" He held his hand out to show her.

Libby touched his hand. Just like the first time, she felt an arc of energy. "What you must have gone through." She kissed his hand. "I nearly died when you didn't come up out of that water."

Aron swallowed a lump in his throat. "If I could turn back time, I would. You don't know how often I've fought and struggled and agonized over not remembering you or our life." He took her hand. "But if you ever say that you're out of my league, again." He got right in her face, smiled, kissed her nose, then frowned again. "I'll spank your sweet ass."

Her eyes grew wide. "Gee," she laughed. "That almost sounds like the Aron I know."

"I am the Aron you know. I just need you to help me find myself." Holding up the coin, he showed it to her. "Best I can piece together, I found this while we were diving."

"Gold?" She took it from his hand.

"Yea, best I can tell, but that's not what makes it valuable." He touched her cheek. "Look at the image on it."

Libby stood up and went to the light. Amazed, she looked again. "It favors me?"

"Yes, it does. I held on to that coin. Even when I didn't know anything about home or you, I held on to that coin."

She smiled at him. "That makes me feel better."

"It should, shows that you were on my mind at some level."

"Hmmmm," she nestled against him.

"Don't hmmmm, me." He pulled her close, going back to the photos. Laughing, he pointed at one picture. "What are you doing here?" He found one of her racing across the pasture, looking back, and smiling.

"You're chasing me."

"Did I catch you?"

She rubbed her tummy.

"What do you think?"

He put the photo album down and went to his knees by the bed. Laying his head on her stomach, he said, "Tell me about them."

"Boys. Two boys." She hesitated, but couldn't stop herself, she ran her fingers through his hair. "They're due in a few months."

He kissed the swell. "What are we naming them?"

"Well, we hadn't picked out names, I was planning on talking about that on our honeymoon. But I like Colt and Case. When you think of some, I'd like to hear your suggestions."

"I like your choices." He turned his head sideways and Libby worried over the marks on his neck.

"You're tired. Why don't you take a shower and get in your bed."

"That sounds like a good idea." He rose and began to undo his clothes. She helped. When they got his shirt off, Libby gasped in horror. "Oh, my god." She looked at the scars and marks from the whip. "What kind of monster did this to you?"

"A crazy woman, Libby."

She stepped back in horror. "A woman?"

"Yes, that was the whole problem." He began to relate the tale. "I had met Martina Delgado years ago. And apparently she developed some kind of crush on me. When she found me floating in the water off Seven Mile Beach, she decided it was a sign. She lied to me, told me I was her fiancé."

Libby closed her eyes. Stop it, she told herself. Your prayers have been answered. Your husband is alive. This woman had nearly killed him. There was no place for jealousy in any of this. "Is she still alive?"

"Yea, Jacob handcuffed her to the table after she tried to kill us and I suppose the authorities have picked her up by now. I put together a tidy case against her. Why?"

"I am thinking about whipping her ass."

Aron barked his laughter. "Like the bar fight?"

She perked up. "You remember?"

His smile faded. "No, baby. The guys told me on the way back. They told me everything they could think of. Trying to acclimate me, I guess."

"Go take your shower, I'm going to go get some salve to put on your sores."

He thought about asking her to join him, but he couldn't find the words. What was the proper etiquette for amnesiac husbands?

Libby slipped downstairs. Thankfully, everyone had retired to their rooms. She was trembling – vacillating between elation and worry. Aron was back! He was alive! That was all that mattered. Checking in the guest bathroom, she found the ointment and returned upstairs. Just knowing her husband was in the shower, in their bedroom gave her an enormous feeling of well-being. She had to stay positive.

She also had to stay realistic.

Sitting on their bed, she waited. Listening. The water turned off. She closed her eyes. He was stepping out of the tub. Toweling off. God, he was a gorgeous man. "Whoops." She forgot to send him in some clothes. Digging in one of his drawers, she pulled out a comfortable t-shirt and some lounge pants.

The door opened. And out he walked in just a towel.

Lord have mercy.

"Here." She gave him the clothes. "I hope you sleep well." She went to him and went up on tiptoe, kissing his cheek. "You'll never know how thankful I am to have you home, alive and well." She started for the door.

"Where are you going?" He asked dryly.

"I'm going to sleep in the guest room."

"Why?"

"Because…." She stopped. "Well, because…"

"Because why?"

She put her hands on her hips. "You don't know who I am! I can't sleep with a stranger!"

"I'm not a stranger to you, Libby. I'm your husband."

"But I'm strange to you!" She fumed.

"Just a little," he teased. When she turned to go he said. "Get that sweet ass back here, Libby-pearl."

With mouth wide open, she whirled. "What did you call me?"

He looked at her blankly. "What?" He hadn't noticed.

"You called me Libby Pearl!" She flew to his side, very careful of his injuries. "That was a thing between us."

He still looked confused. "The nicknames!" She emphasized. "You always called me Libby-mine, Libilicious, Libtastic, Libby-boo." By the time she finished, they were both laughing.

"See, I told you, I'm still me." He pushed her hair behind her head. "Just give me a little time. I'll remember you, Libby. I promise. I'll remember us."

***

They didn't make love that night, but it wasn't because he didn't want to, he did. But it was just too soon. Aron could see it sticking out all over, he was gonna have to woo his Libby again. She loved him, he had no doubt on that score. But she had lost her confidence in their love and it was his job to give it back to her.

During the night, he bonded with her. Oh, she wasn't awake to know it. But he stayed up most of the night just looking at her and touching her. He traced the line of her arm, loving the smoothness. He stole tiny kisses from her neck. He smelled her sweet scent. And he relearned how she slept – on top of him. God, he loved that. While he'd been gone, he knew his nights were cold and lonely. Something was missing. And here it was, it was her. She used him as her security blanket, one arm across his middle, one leg across his. Sometimes her head was on his chest and sometimes it was on his arm. He didn't care. He loved it all.

Deep in the night, he lifted her sleep shirt and rubbed her back. One of the few times when she was on her back, he picked up the shirt and kissed her belly, letting his babies kick him in the cheek. She needed her rest, but he got something he needed to. He used those twilight hours to relearn his wife and what he found was beyond rubies.

In the early morning hours, he looked around their room. Their wedding portrait stood proudly on the dresser. He picked the photo album back up and finished looking at every picture. They had been together only a few months, married only one day when they had been parted. But as far as he could tell, they had packed a lifetime of living in that little space of time. Some of his sculptures set around the room. As he looked at them his fingers itched. Soon, he'd have to go outside and try his hand at it, see if the skill would resurface.

On the bedside table, he found a book by Sable Hunter. Who? Hmmm, he opened and read a few pages. "Damn," he grinned and read a few more. "My baby's been reading sexy stuff." Opening the drawer, he saw some massage lotion. Interesting. He took it out and smelled of it. Chocolate Cream.

"Aron." Libby whispered. "Aron, I love you. Come home." She whimpered.

He realized this was probably nothing new. His baby had missed him. She had cried for him. He nuzzled the side of her face. "Sweetheart, I'm home."

With a cry, she threw her arms around his neck. "You are, aren't you?"

"Yes, I am." He held her close, rubbing her back. "Don't you cry. Everything is going to be all right."

"I know." She whispered. "It was just a bad dream. I had a lot of them while you were gone."

"Lie on your tummy and let me give you a rubdown."

"What?" She pulled away a little bit. "We shouldn't."

"Why not? You're my wife, I'm your husband. We're in the privacy of our bedroom. Take off your top." He coaxed. Waiting, he held his breath.

When she finally eased the shirt off, she kept herself facing away from him. God, he wanted to look at her. Touch her. Lord, look at that. Libby's bare beautiful arms, smooth back – all naked for his enjoyment.

She lifted her head. Her eyes glancing back over her shoulder. "Aron, I'm –"

"Let me, please." He unscrewed the lid and took a dollop of the creamy liquid on his fingertips. "You'll enjoy this, I bet I'm good at it."

"You're good at everything," she grumbled.

"Really," he snorted. "Do tell."

He saw a blush rise in her skin. "I didn't mean that."

"You didn't?" He began to rub her shoulders. "I'm gonna start at your shoulders and then head south to… parts south."

"This is your rodeo, Cowboy."

"And don't you forget it." God, she was so soft. As soon as his hands touched the naked skin of her back, his cock went hard as a rock. "You're so warm. Sweet."

"Hmmm," he heard a little purr.

"So, am I?"

"What?" His hands were amazing. She wanted to writhe under his touch, but she forced herself not to react. She didn't want him to know the effect he was having on her.

"Am I good in bed?"

Libby was afraid to move. He would know. She began to tremble. He would know how much she wanted him. "You don't know?"

"No," Aron spoke softly. "How could I? I've lost my past."

"You don't remember Sabrina?"

"Who?" Aron frowned at the name.

"Arg!" Libby buried her head in the pillow. "Your former wife?"

"What!" Aron yelled.

"Shhh," Libby would have giggled had it not been so sad. "You were married before me, but she was a horrible, money-grubbing leech."

"Did you ever meet her?" This was sort of entertaining. He could tell she was jealous.

"That's who I beat up in the bar fight." She muttered under her breath.

"Oh, you doll." He wanted to ask more questions, and he would, right after he touched her some more. She was laid out in front of him like a sumptuous banquet, and he was a starving man. Lust began rising in him like a tidal wave. Working the oil into her skin, he loved the way she sighed and moaned. Promising himself he would use his tongue next time, Aron massaged her tense muscles, working his way down her back. Straddling her legs, he got down to the swell of her ass, then smiled when she began to arch up to meet his sensual strokes.

"Aron…"

Leaning over her, he asked again. "Am I good in bed?"

"Maybe."

He smiled against her neck, taking the time to pepper kisses all along the curve of her shoulder. "Don't torture me, Pretty Girl." He continued his mission of seduction, rubbing and mapping ever muscle, every bare curve. When he noticed she was clutching the sheet with white knuckled fingers, Aron knew he was getting to her – big time. His cock was throbbing with need, but he wanted her to beg him. He needed her to make the first move – he had this desperate need to know he was welcome. And wanted. Valuable.

"Please."

"Please, what?" Progress, they were making progress. When he'd lavish attention on one area, Aron would finish off with open-mouth kisses all over her silky flesh, before finding another spot to tease. When she began to raise her little bottom up and down, seeking him, he wanted to shout. And when he got a whiff of her arousal, Aron lost it.

"Please touch me."

"I was gonna die if I couldn't," he confessed. Here she was on her stomach, he couldn't even see her breasts or her womanhood – and she was still able to turn him inside out. "Raise your bottom." She complied. He slipped her panties off. "Now, spread your legs." Open, wide. "That's it." Aron dipped his fingers between her thighs and almost came himself when he felt how creamy and wet she was – for him. Taking the pads of his fingers, he swirled through her honey, stroking her slit, slipping a finger into her pussy"

"God, that feels so good."

Satisfaction filled him as she began to move, pushing back against his hand, grinding her vulva against his palm. "More?"

"I've craved your touch, yes, more!" She almost shouted and he chuckled. He rubbed her labia, played with her clit and pushed a finger in and out of her rhythmically.

"Faster? Harder?" Aron was lost in lust. "I want to be inside of you so much. Can I?"

Libby would never deny him. He was her life. Instead of answering, she rose on all fours and tilted her bottom up to him.

"Fuck," he whispered. Standing, he jerked off the lounge pants and rejoined her on the bed. Curling his hands around her hips, Aron angled her pelvis. "I want you so much, Libby. I dreamed about you. I didn't know your name or exactly what you looked like, but it was you." Taking his cock in hand, he rubbed the head up and down, dragging it through her sweet, thick cream. "You're so wet. You want me don't you?"

"God, yes." She whimpered.

"So, I'm good in bed?" He sought reassurance. Not everything he knew made sense. Instincts that had no memories to back them up made him feel helpless, but there was one bit of sure knowledge – this woman could make him burn for her. Aron had a ragged need to be inside of her. It had been too long.

"The best." She confessed. Reaching beneath her, he found her tits. They hung down like lush, ripe fruit. Aron groaned as he cupped them, weighing them, massaging them, rubbing the puffy little nipples. "I'm dying, Aron." She panted.

Keeping hold of one breast, he took the other hand and guided his big cock head to the small opening. Taking care, he began to work his way in, but when she moaned, he surrendered and thrust deep, all the way to the hilt – balls deep. He mounted her.

Libby cried out with joy. "You are home," she panted.

Hot. Wet. Tight. Hell, yeah. He was home. "Hold on, baby. This is going to be a wild ride." He rammed in, covering her, using her tits as sexy handholds. Thrusting over and over again, slamming in, pulling out, slamming in again – he rode her.

"Yes, yes, yes," she sang as he fucked her, sating a voracious hunger.

"God, this felt good." His heart pounded. His blood was on fire. Sweat ran down his face. Yea, he knew how to do this. Thank God, it was like riding a horse or a bike – he might not remember everything, but he remembered how to love this woman and how to please her.

More. More. Mine. Mine. He thrust hard, the tightening in his balls letting him know he was about to erupt. But he wasn't going alone. "Come for me, baby." He moved his hand down from her nipple to her clit. And as he thrust inside of her, he played her distended clit like an instrument. Soon her high keening and vise-like contractions milking his cock let him know a powerful orgasm was overtaking her. "Aron!" Libby gasped.

A powerful pulsing contraction rose up from his balls, as hot bursts of semen spurted from his dick. Wanting to own her, he caught the flesh of her neck between his teeth and nipped. Libby threw her head back and screamed as he sucked on her neck. Throbbing aftershocks caused their hips to keep bumping together, wanting to strain every last drop of ecstasy they could from the act. "My God," he moaned.

"Does that answer your question?" She purred.

"What question?" He pulled her to one side and they rolled to their backs in the bed.

"You're good in bed."

He was listening, but her breasts had just come into view and he was almost struck dumb. "You are the sexiest thing alive." Before she could protest, he began suckling at her nipples, rubbing them, tweaking them, nursing from her bounty.

"God, I'm glad you're home." She gave herself over to the rapture, knowing whatever the future held, she was ready for it. Aron was back and all was well with the world.

Chapter Fourteen

"How are things?" Skye asked in a hushed tone. Libby looked happy, but she wanted to know for sure.

"Good." She tried to keep the grin off her face, unsuccessfully. "Very good."

"So, it doesn't bother you that his memory isn't complete?"

Libby sighed. "Sure, it bothers me." She had been thinking a lot about it. "We, all of us, are the sum total of every second we've ever lived, everything we've ever experienced with all the people in our lives. This is our history, this collection of moments is who we are. Aron still has his personality, his abilities, his intelligence – what he's lost is me."

"And his family, don't forget that."

Libby hung her head. "Of course not, I want him to regain all he's lost. I'm trying not to be selfish. I just don't know what I'm going to do."

"What do you mean?" Skye asked as they got the grooms table set up for the wedding.

"I want to be fair to him, Skye." Even though they had incredible sex this morning, she was still having doubts.

"You're not making sense. Fair about what?" The napkins were to be laid out next, then the forks. There were only about a dozen guests coming, but the girls wanted everything to be perfect for Cady.

"What if he can't fall in love with me again?"

"That's just crazy." Jessie had walked up behind them, with Avery on her heels.

"What's crazy?"

Libby covered her eyes. She loved the women the brother's had brought into the family, but sometimes she thought things were simpler when it was just her and the boys.

"She doesn't think Aron will fall in love with her again." Skye was talking pretty loudly.

"You have a big mouth, girlfriend." Libby tried to put a finger over her lips.

"Oh, watch it, watch it," Avery cautioned. "That's how I got a microphone hung in my mouth. You know I wrote that scene into one of my books and some reviewer said how unrealistic it was, and I laughed – that was the only true incident in the whole book!"

Cady walked in, Miss Serenity. "What is all the uproar about? This is my wedding day, I will not tolerate any sort of unhappiness."

"It's me, I'm being a Debbie Downer." Libby hung her head.

"Cady, tell her everything is going to be all right." Jessie took Libby's hand. "Listen to Cady, she told me on the day of BT's surgery that he would be home by Christmas and so would Aron."

Libby widened her eyes at Jessie, then at Cady. "Is this true?"

"Yes, I had a dream. It wasn't my normal way of learning things."

"Do you know anything about me and Aron? Any insight?" She was feeling desperate.

Cady took her by the hands and led her to one side, sitting her down. "Do you trust me?"

"Of course," Libby looked at her friend. "You're like my guardian angel. I still remember the night you took my illness. Who knows if I would be alive today if you hadn't helped me?"

"Lord, don't put me on a pedestal," Cady admonished her. "The only kind of angel I am is one with a broken wing, but I can tell you this..." Libby was hanging on her very word. "The vision that's been coming to me lately is one that involves those two little boys of yours. I see them running on chubby legs over this ranch land. I see them climbing trees and swimming in the creek. And watching them are two people – one of them is you. You are their mother, their nurturer. But the other one, who watches over all of you with protective pride and much love is Aron McCoy. This family, your family, has a bright future together. There is nothing that we can't overcome."

Libby hugged her. "Okay, I believe you."

"If you believe anything, believe this. You don't have to worry about Aron falling in love with you."

"I don't?"

"No, he doesn't have to fall in love with you, he never stopped."

***

The wedding was simple, but perfect. Beau and Harley came. All of Cady's New Orleans relatives showed up and Aron had a glimmer of memory when he shook hands with Nannette Beaureguarde. She winked at him and told him they were two of a kind. He asked her what she meant and she said, "Too hard-headed to keep down." He found out later she'd suffered a stroke and had steadfastly refused to let it beat her.

Holiday decorations lent a festive air to the ceremony. The girls had decorated everything in one of Cady's favorite themes – camellias in the snow. Rich reds and soft pinks were everywhere. Each of the girls wore a rich red Christmasy sheath with a small bouquet of pink camellias. A fresh blanket of snow fell on the ground.

When Joseph and Cady recited their vows, there wasn't a dry eye in the house.

"I Joseph, take you, Cady to be my lawfully wedded wife." The Stallion had finally been roped and tied, but he had gone willingly. Nathan had been standing by the Christmas tree and when Joseph had kissed Cady, a tiny bell had rung on one of the angel ornaments. He just smiled.

"I now pronounce you, husband and wife." He'd never forget the day he had met Cady and seen the vision of the beautiful wings rising behind her. That was one of those things he didn't talk about – there were others, but now that Aron was home, hopefully that would change. He needed to talk to someone about Tina and only his older brother would do.

Libby had stood up with Cady, while Aron had served as Joseph's best man. The whole time the ceremony had been taking place, she hadn't been able to take her eyes off of him. Their own wedding was so fresh in her memory. If she were braver, she'd ask him to renew their vows and start over – a new honeymoon, untainted by disaster – a fresh start. But she wouldn't, he had been through so much. All she really wanted was for him to be happy.

"Where are they going on their honeymoon?" Aron asked.

"Not to the Caymans," she joked, but he didn't laugh. "I'm sorry. I didn't mean anything by that."

"I know," Aron whispered, leaning down and putting his forehead to hers. "It's just a very serious topic for me. I almost lost you. I almost lost myself."

"Actually, I don't know where they're going. I've been too disheartened to ask," she sighed, "till now." Their question was answered when Joseph announced that Kyle Chancellor and his team had given them tickets to Paris, all expenses paid. They weren't leaving until after New Year's, but they were excited.

Beau had word on Revel. He had gotten out of the hospital and gone home with Patrick and Savannah. The McCoy cousins had called to wish Joseph well and they were all planning on coming for a reunion just as soon as Aron gave them the word. He wanted to do it, but there were other things on his mind right now. His wife. "Tell me about our wedding." He pulled her back against him as they watched their family and friends enjoy themselves.

"We got married on October the 16th, the Sweetest Day." She had to explain the significance to him. "The night we were on our way to the hospital, when we thought my cancer was out of remission, you promised me I would get better and we'd get married that day – and we did."

"When my brothers told me about your cancer, it scared me so much." He kissed her temple. "I want to visit with your physician, just to hear for myself that you are still okay."

This surprised Libby. "You do?"

"You don't get it yet," he looked at her. "You and those babies are the most important thing to me – bar none."

The day wore on, and the wedding festivities wound down. When only the family was present, they opened Christmas presents, passing them around and throwing paper everywhere. Nathan got his Playstation 4, and a big surprise from Isaac, a small motorcycle. Aron frowned when he heard that, but he told Nathan if he confined his riding to the ranch roads for a while, it would be okay.

When it was Libby's turn, she handed Aron several gifts. He couldn't wait, tearing into the biggest one with relish. "A leather jacket!" He was thrilled, standing up and putting it on.

"There's more," she gave him a smaller package. And when he opened it, he was shocked. It was a book she had written. "It's not bound or anything, but maybe you'll enjoy it."

"I love it already. Anything you make for me is the most precious thing in the world. What's it about?" He ran his hand over the paper.

"It's the story of us." She told him. "I hope you like it."

"No doubt in my mind." He gave her a box. "Here open this."

"You bought me a gift!?" She was shocked. "When?"

He grinned. "Yesterday, while you were wrapping presents."

She opened the box. "A ring!" Amazement colored her voice with joy.

"An eternity ring." He put it on her finger. "Do you understand the significance, wife?" He asked pointedly.

"Yes," she thought she did. "Always and forever."

"Good girl."

***

"You need to see this doctor. He'll answer any questions you have." Jacob gave him Scott Walker's card. "I've already called him about you. I did that before we even went to Mexico after you. He's the best. If there's anything that can be done about your memory, he's the man for the job."

"All right. When's my appointment?" He had found Jacob rocking BT by the fireplace. Aron couldn't wait for the day he could use that old rocker for the same purpose. For just a split second, he saw the image of his mother in the chair, holding Nathan.

"Tomorrow"

"The day after Christmas? I'm impressed."

Jacob laughed. "You should be. I had to bribe him."

"I'm grateful," he stood up. "Well, I'm tired, I think I'll find my woman and head off to bed. It's been an exciting day."

"I agree. We've had too many of those lately, it seems."

Bidding his brother goodnight, he went to the kitchen to find Libby. Aron was so worried that she would never be fully able to accept his memory loss. He intended to do everything he could, daily, to make her feel comfortable and adored. But the stress she was under was taking its toll. When she'd casually mentioned earlier that she was having slight cramps, that had been the last straw. "Ready to go to bed?"

"Yes, please." She was standing at the kitchen counter, still in her bridesmaid's outfit. The slight swell of her tummy drew his eye.

"You're gorgeous, did you know that?"

She blushed. And yawned. "No, but I like to hear you say it."

"You're going to the doctor for me, aren't you?"

"Yes, I will. I'll call and try to get in tomorrow, if it will make you happy." Libby couldn't help but pause and just look at him. It was only a couple of days since he'd been home, but he was looking better – more rested. Now all she had to do was fatten him up. But even his leaner body took nothing away from his male perfection. Her husband was to die for. Taking his hand, they climbed the stairs.

"Good, I'll feel better if you do." As much as he wanted to, he didn't make love with her that night. Oh, they'd kissed and hugged and cuddled, but he wanted to make sure everything was okay. "If there's something wrong, we need to know. Those cramps make me nervous. I don't want to take any chances." He held her tight as they lay in the bed Christmas night. He stroked her hair, counting his blessings. "In fact, I'd like you to get a thorough check-up." What he feared most was her leukemia flaring up, and stress was one of those things that could potentially trigger all sorts of problems. If there was anything he could do to make her life less stressful, he was willing to do it.

What she didn't really understand was although he despaired over his memory loss, he was improving day by day. Building new memories, learning things about her and his family – he was repairing his life bit by bit. But he wanted to do more.

"I think I'm okay, Aron, but I'll call Doc Gibbs in the morning early." She nestled into his warm body. Remembering her conversation with Cady, she longed to assure him that all would be well. "Just think where we were this time last week. We need to be thankful."

"Oh, I am, believe me." He pulled her over on top of him. "Lie here, I need to feel your body against mine." She giggled and wiggled and he had to give his cock a serious talking to, to bring him under control. "I'm going to the doctor tomorrow, myself. Will you go with me? I might need you to hold my hand."

Her head popped up like a jack-in-the-box. "Of course I'll go with you. What kind of doctor?"

"A neurobiologist, Jacob wants me to get checked out and make sure there are no lasting side-effects from whatever drugs I was given."

Libby shivered, instantly feeling the weight of her selfishness. Placing her hand on his jaw, she stroked the precious rasp of his beard. "I just want you to be okay. That's all I want."

Sleep was not long coming and they rested peacefully in one another's arms.

***

Libby did as she promised. She called her doctor, a man who had known and treated her for years. He told her to come right on in. Aron's appointment wasn't until after lunch, so they decided to make a day of it. When they came downstairs the aroma of sausage and biscuits filled the air. Noah saw them. "Hey, come on in the kitchen. Grub's about ready."

"We don't have much time," she protested.

"Oh, we always have time for a biscuit." Aron's sincere appreciation for food made Libby smile.

"Alright." When they all gathered around the table, the laughing and talking was chaotic. Jessie had cooked and she made gravy to die for.

Pointing at Cady and Joseph, Isaac smirked. "Last night was your wedding night. What are you two doing up so early?"

Cady blushed and Joseph winked at her. "I always am 'up' early in the morning when Cady is around." He kissed her, then looked down the table at Jacob. "Actually, it was that little bruiser on Jacob's shoulder who woke me up. That boy has a set of lungs on him!"

Jessie set another pan of biscuits on the table. "If you think he was loud from where you were, you should have been in the same room with him."

Jacob patted his baby boy. "That's okay. You won't have to put up with us much longer. Jessie, BT and I will be moving into our own house before you know it."

"I don't know if I like that idea." Libby said. "Our being together is important."

Joseph laughed. "It is. And I want us to eat as many meals together and visit as much as possible. But can you imagine this house after your babies are born and ours?" He waved his fork around. "And who's to say how many more McCoy's there'll be as soon as Isaac and Noah get busy."

Everyone agreed the house wasn't quite big enough to house their burgeoning family. "But no one is to go far. Tebow is big enough for a dozen ranch houses." Libby was adamant.

"My little mother-hen." Aron patted her knee.

Libby stared at him, wondering if he knew he'd called her that many times. "Yes, that's me. I can't help it."

"What do you all think about calling everyone and arranging that party we talked about, to celebrate my great escape." Aron looked all around the table.

"I want to do that," Jacob said. "As soon as possible."

"Me, too," Aron agreed. "Let's split up the names and try to give everybody a call tonight. Libby and I have a couple of doctor appointments, but we'll be back before supper."

On the drive into Austin, Aron surveyed the countryside. "You know, it's strange. I didn't forget everything."

He immediately got her attention. She'd been sitting there thinking about taking down all the Christmas decorations before the party. "What do you mean?"

"Well, I could picture the Guadalupe and I knew everything I'd learned in school. It seems I didn't lose knowledge or personality traits, I just lost people and events. And when things started to come back, I knew I was from Texas and I could remember there was someone in my family who loved computers and one who hated shots, but I just couldn't grasp the details."

"Maybe the doctor can help explain that." She hoped so.

There first stop, with Doc Gibbs eased their mind. After examining Libby and doing some blood tests, he assured them that all was on course. "I don't see any cause for concern." He had been ecstatic to learn that Aron was home. "I saw you on the news.

You've attracted a lot of attention these last couple of months." Writing on her chart he kept talking. "The two of you have been through a lot, worry and fretting can put undue stress on Libby and the babies. So my advice is plenty of rest, lots of kisses and pampering."

"How about sex?"

Libby gasped at Aron's frankness.

"Oh, Libby knows how I feel about that. I'd catch her reading romance novels all the time. When her remission came, I told her to get out there in the world and make one of those books come true for herself." The old man patted Aron on the shoulder. "And she did. Do you remember telling me the difference between romance and erotic romance?"

"I do." Libby turned beet red.

He wrote on a pad with a flourish and tore off the page. Here's my prescription. "As much erotic romance as you can handle."

Aron grinned and pocketed the paper. "I'll see about filling this prescription personally."

When they left Doc Gibbs, Aron was in high spirits. "Let's get a hamburger at Kerbey Lane."

"You remember Kerbey Lane? That's good." Every little thing he could recollect seemed like a triumph. They had gone to the diner just off the Texas campus and enjoyed a meal. Libby couldn't help but notice how the college girls eyed him. She felt a little big and clumsy. Did he still find her attractive? Insecurities were the bane of her existence. If he had his memory, he would have the image of her when she was at her best to fall back on, but here she was swollen and pudgy and not nearly as beautiful as he was.

But to give the man credit, he didn't look at any of the coeds – not even once. He seemed to have eyes only for her. For that, Libby was grateful.

When they arrived at Dr. Walker's office, Aron didn't know what to expect. "Come on in Mr. McCoy." He was younger than Aron expected and seemed to smile at Libby a bit too wide for his tastes. "How are you feeling?" Before he could answer, the good doctor was pulling out a chair for Libby and asking her if she wanted coffee. A flare of jealousy swept over him.

"I'm feeling like I could whip a bear, or a doctor." He drawled.

Dr. Walker had laughed. "That has to be a good sign."

Libby listened as he asked Aron questions. She learned some things about his time away she hadn't known.

"I had intense headaches after the surgery. And night terrors." He shifted in his chair, a little embarrassed. "I'd dream about Libby, but I couldn't see her face. Some nights I'd wake up in a cold sweat and feel an overwhelming sense of panic."

She covered his hand with hers. Libby hadn't realized the full extent of his suffering. She ought to have known, her own time apart from him had been such a misery.

"I need to get my past back. It's important to us as a family."

Scott Walker studied the couple in front of him. "There is an experimental procedure we could try. But I have to tell you, it's dangerous."

Libby tensed, but Aron spoke up. "Tell me about it."

"It's invasive." The doctor set up. "We'd have to do brain surgery. The operation would entail opening up your skull, performing a craniotomy. We would push electrodes into the brain and stimulate the hypothalamus with electric shock. This has proven successful in causing patients to regain memories which have been lost."

"No!" Libby interjected with force. "No!" He was doing this for her. "I do not want Aron to have one more minute of pain or surgery or..." She got up and fled, tears running down her cheeks.

"Excuse me," Aron went after her, finding her already in the hall, staring out a window. "Hey, what's the matter, love?"

She turned in his arms. "I want you just the way you are. No more risks. No more pain."

"But what if I can remember?"

She put her hands on his shoulders and looked him in the eye. "I want you. What if something went wrong and you died or what if you lost more memory." She shook her head from side to side. "I don't need for you to remember me to be happy."

Aron understood. He kissed her. "Don't worry. I'm not going anywhere." He led her to the waiting room. "I'll be back. Let me have another word with the doc." When she looked alarmed, he promised. "No surgery."

When he returned to the examining room, he explained. "I don't think we want to go that far." Aron told Walker a little about their situation and Libby's condition. "So, whatever you can do for me, otherwise, I'll take it."

Walker thought for a minute. "If you can find out who the chemist was and what they gave you, maybe we could go from there."

"I like that idea." Aron stood. "Let me see what I can do."

***

Things seemed to get easier for them. Libby relaxed and let herself enjoy just being with Aron again. He placed a call to Brock, but had trouble getting through. They escaped to their room to rest and he entertained himself by reading the book she wrote.

Libby enjoyed watching him read. She could tell when he came to a risqué part, because his eyes would get big and he would shift on the bed. There were one or two things she had left out. At the time, they seemed too personal to share, even with a pad of paper. But there was enough detail there for him to get a sense of what their life had been like. "Did we really make love on my horse?"

"Yes," she grinned. "And you didn't even drop me."

He chunked the book on the end of the bed. "Wanna ride me now?"

"I want to do everything with you." She pushed him flat on the bed. Of course he let her do it. Aron was a mountain of a man next to his petite wife. "Do you know what I missed most of all?"

"My massive manhood?" He teased.

She appeared to be thinking. "Well, there's that." Then she grew serious. "But I really missed you in the bed with me, how you used to cuddle me all night. Like you couldn't stand to be without me for even a second."

"I've held you every night, darlin'. And not only since I've been back." He unbuttoned her shirt. "While I was gone, I ached for you. Maybe I didn't know your name or your face, but my soul did."

She slid the shirt off, and he unclasped her bra. "I hugged your pillow every night. It was the best loved goose down in the world."

"Well, I'm here now. And I want to play." He took her by the hands and flipped her, reversing positions, almost bouncing her off the bed. Libby squealed, elated to see him in such a good mood. In one smooth motion, he took her hands in his and held them above her head. "Keep them there."

"Oh, I like the sound of that." She watched his gorgeous face as he stuck the tip of his tongue to the corner of his mouth in concentration. "Do you know, before we were married, we started experimenting..."

He raised his eyebrows. "Oh, really? With what?"

"Hmmmm, I'm not sure I should tell you."

He goosed her a little. "You better."

"Well, I don't know if you remember about Isaac being a Dom and how upset it made Noah because of Harper."

Aron laughed. "What did you say? Dom? Isaac? Dang." He traced the tip of her nipple with his finger. "Tell me more."

She tried, but he kept kissing her – warm, supple lips drifting over hers in seductive, teasing kisses. "Well, uh – we decided to see if we could put a little bit of kink into our lovemaking."

"Oh, really?" Aron kissed the corner of her mouth and mapped the seam with the tip of his tongue. "And did it work?"

"Yes, Sir," she whispered huskily.

"Damn, I'm gonna love being married to you."

"You said that on our honeymoon." Libby parted her lips, inviting a deeper kiss.

"I plan on saying it often, just to let you know I appreciate you." He gently nipped her bottom lip, taking it between his and tugging. When she whimpered for him, he didn't just kiss her, he devoured her. His hands were everywhere – on her tits, shaping her belly, caressing her thighs. And all the time his cock was slapping against her middle while his tongue thrust in and out of her mouth in a full-blown sexual feast of a kiss.

Libby was literally squirming with need. She kept her hands where he'd told her to, but the rest of her body went into overdrive. She arched her back, thrusting her tits up toward him as his mouth traced a hot trail down her throat and straight to her breasts. "All the time I was reading that hot stuff you wrote, I was dreaming about your tits. Last night, I had a hard-on the whole time, just thinking about waking you up so I could get my mouth all over these." He looked at her through half-closed lids, the most wickedly sexual look he'd ever give her. "Did we do this a lot, Libby? Do you like me to suck your tits?"

Libby shook. "It's my favorite thing." She pushed them up, offering the quivering mounds. "I missed this so much."

"Tell me if I do it right." He bent to the task, licking and sucking at her right nipple. He played with her – not taking it in his mouth, just tormenting her with nibbles and laves. His hands weren't idle, they plumped them together, molding them – lifting them, using his thumbs to sweep across her tender flesh.

"I think you got it," she muttered. "Almost."

He snorted against her tit. "Let me try harder." Placing his mouth over the nipple, he sucked, hard. Libby groaned. He didn't slow down, but sucked with long, hard pulls, giving little stinging nips which caused the cream to flow unbidden from her pussy.

"Damn, McCoy." She moaned as he changed breasts and gave the other one equal attention. Raising up, he admired his handiwork.

"So, pretty, pink, swollen. Want more?"

"More," she bucked her whole body, almost displacing him.

"Hold on." Then he just threw himself into the task – suckling, massaging, licking, biting until she was so turned-on she came – right there – no stimulation to her clit or her vagina. Just his mouth on her breasts.

"God, Aron!" Her cries were a testament to his manhood, he felt like a damn conquering hero. Sliding down her body, he kissed a path past her navel and over her protruding tummy, his longish hair forming a curtain around his face. She couldn't take her eyes off of him. The sight of Aron McCoy going down on her was a thing of beauty.

"Open up." He sat back and let his eyes have a party. Stroking the inside of her creamy thighs, he lowered his head and went to work, using his tongue to tickle her clit. "You taste so good."

His praise made her juices flow and he lapped them up with abandon. She didn't know if he had been fantasizing or what, but Aron did things to her he'd never done before – biting her pussy lips, flicking out his tongue and tickling her clit before covering the whole area with his mouth and sucking hard. She couldn't last –

there was no way. Forgetting his directive, she gripped his hair and let the orgasm take her, her breath leaving her in a pulsing explosion of pure bliss.

He held her until she calmed, and then she smiled. "My turn."

"What did you have in mind, darlin?"

"One of your favorite things."

"I don't think I have to get my memory back to know what that is." She sat up in the bed and scooted to the edge.

"Stand in front of me so I can reach you good." He came to her, his cock reaching her a good three or four seconds before the rest of him did. "Damn, you're big."

"Do you like it?" He seemed to be seeking reassurance, and that she was glad to provide.

Taking her hands, she slid them up and rested them on his hips, pulling him a tad closer. "You have never failed to exceed my expectations, Aron. You please me no end. I love your cock."

Opening her mouth, she took as much as she could inside and just began sucking – letting her tongue massage the underside while she applied unbelievable suction to the head. The wetness and heat of Libby's mouth was unbelievable. He closed his eyes – reveling in the sensation. Nothing could be better. It was heaven. But he needed inside of her. He couldn't wait. "You get on top."

As he'd been before, he spread his big self out on the bed and Libby marveled at the playground he made. Taking her time, she got between his legs and proceeded to crawl up his body.

He watched her, "you look like a she-cat on the prowl."

"Yea, I'm after big-game. You." Straddling his hips, she leaned over and crashed her mouth down on his, proceeding to kiss him like there was no tomorrow. Everything went a little wild – they rubbed and touched, caressed and teased. Kisses – wet, hot kisses – were exchanged and bartered, traded for licks and nips. Aron and Libby were relearning one another's bodies, showing each other exactly what pleased them and how good it felt. "Put him in," she demanded.

Scooting back, she slid off his cock and it bounced up between them – hard and big – ready to impale her. She rose over him, took him in hand and sat down on him, taking him to the root. She sighed. "How does that feel?" She asked.

"So fuckin' good," he growled. "Now bounce. I wanna see your tits jiggle."

Libby laughed. She had so missed all of this. His raunchiness, his passion – she had missed him so bad. Now, here he was. In her bed. In her life. She decided at that moment to be happy with whatever the future would bring. "Give me your hands, cowboy." He did. She laced their fingers together and proceeded to ride him, sliding up and down his pole, grinding her pussy down so her clit could join in the fun. And when he came – when she watched the ecstasy on his face, Libby came. She came so hard she almost blacked out. And then she surrendered to him, relaxing in his arms, his cock still deep inside of her.

They slept. At peace.

Chapter Fifteen

"Phone." She handed him his cell.

Aron glanced at the caller. "It's Brock." Pulling her down beside him on the couch, Aron answered. "McCoy."

"Hello, Amigo. How are you?"

"Better than the last time we talked, that's for sure. How are things?"

"Better, as you say. Alessandra and Tomas are out of the hospital. Martina is behind bars and the El Duro Cartel is no more, thanks to you."

"Not just me, Brock. It was you and a whole passel of friends. I was at her mercy. If you hadn't called my brother, I might still be there."

"Ah, your family would have rescued you without me, they are an impressive bunch."

"That they are." Aron agreed. "I wanted to talk to you for two reasons. First, I'd like for you to tell me anything you or Alessandra knows about that chemist or the drugs they gave me. I'm working to put my life back together again."

Brock was quiet for a minute. "Well, hold on." Aron could hear muffled conversation. In a moment, he was back. "My girl says the chemist is a woman, a good woman who owed Martina a favor. Her name is Emily Gadwah and her number is..." Aron wrote it down.

"Thanks. I don't know if she can tell me anything that will help, but I have to try."

Libby rubbed her fingers over the back of his hand. His adamancy to regain his memory was as much for her, as him. She needed to make him understand, it didn't matter. Over the last few days, he'd proved to her that they could rebuild what they had.

"Second, I wanted to invite you all to Texas. I don't know what your plans are, but you're welcome here anytime. We're planning a party in a couple of days and if you could fly up and join us, we'd love to have you." He gave Brock the information and nodded his head, this always amused Libby. Aron always acted like the person he was talking to could see him – he would gesture and measure and say something was about this long and hold his fingers up. It made her smile.

As soon as the conversation was up, he kissed her quick. "I'm going to call Scott Walker and get this ball rolling."

***

All the arrangements had been made. Everyone was coming and Tebow was decked out in its finest. Aron had spent a lot of time riding around the ranch, looking at his cattle, checking out his horses. When he found the hunting cabin had burned to the ground, his heart had hurt. He'd read in Libby's book and knew it had belonged to his mother. Looking around the grounds, it seemed as if he could picture them running around as boys and him chasing Libby down the dock as she'd faithfully recorded.

Libby had taken over and made sure all the Christmas decorations were down, but she had turned around and transformed the place into a winter wonderland with zillions of little white lights and white poinsettias. His wife was a marvel. His whole family was fuckin' awesome. Aron McCoy was a lucky man.

A phone call from Scott Walker brought his nostalgic journey to a halt. The doc wanted him to come in for a consultation. Aron headed back to the house, but Libby was deep into party food preparations. People would begin arriving tonight and she wanted everything to be perfect. "I'm going in and see Scot Walker. He thinks he has information for me."

"Do you want me to stop this and go with you? Cause I can."

"I know, darlin." He kissed the end of her nose. "There's no need. I'll be right back and I'll tell you every word he says."

She wrapped her arms around his neck, making sure she didn't get her floury hands on his clean shirt. "Don't you go having no operation while you're over there." She admonished him. He grinned. But she persisted. "Let me explain. What we have now is good."

"You're right." He just wanted it to be the best it could be – for her.

The drive to Austin was a quiet one. He didn't even turn on the radio. Instead, he just let his mind wander. Sometimes he thought he was recalling things and then he'd have to admit it was because Libby or his brothers had told him something. Yet, he knew how to get around Austin, he could even picture running down the field at Texas Stadium under the direction of Mack Brown. He could recall how it felt to have an angry bull between his legs and when he'd taken the sculpting clay between his fingers, it wasn't hard to mold it into what he wanted it to be. Memories or instinct? He didn't know.

Sitting in front of Scott Walker, Aron was nervous. The man was smart, there was no doubt about it and he was popular with the women if all the photographs on the wall were any indication. Plus, just while he'd been in the waiting room, he'd seen four – count 'em – four stacked blondes sashay in and out. The man definitely had a type.

Aron chuckled. So did he – but he leaned more toward one curvy, brunette dynamo.

"All right. What's the verdict?"

Walker stood. "There's someone I want you meet." He went to an adjoining office and opened the door. "Emily?"

The moment the woman walked in, Aron knew who she was. He stiffened. This memory came slamming back hard and strong. "You drugged me." She might look harmless in her pink hair and purple sweat suit, but he knew different. She was brilliant and ruthless.

"You don't know the full story," she began. Aron resisted, but soon he began to listen. "Martina Delgado had me between a rock and a hard place. She saved my son, she didn't have to." Emily shook her head. "The Diosa was a contradiction. She could have someone killed with a snap of her fingers, true. But she also had a soft side, I saw that with you."

"Pardon me, if I don't agree. She reminded me of that story about the alligator who would give the frog a ride across the bayou, being nice, and when it got to the other side, it would eat him. That was his nature."

"You may be right, but there's something you don't know." She folded her hands in her lap. "I'm smarter than Martina. I did what she asked me to do, I erased your memories, but not permanently. I've told the doctor here what I used. It was a peptide called Zip that's being tested to permanently eradicate specific memories. I worked with a colleague on this and it works. I was able to get you to talk about your wife and your family, even the drug cartel, and after I gave you the injection – those memories were gone."

Aron closed his eyes in pain. "Permanent, huh?"

"Not exactly, I don't think." Aron jerked his head up. She continued. "I diluted the Zip and added two other drugs, as I explained to Dr. Walker. To the best of my calculations, your memory should start returning anytime. I hope."

"Are you sure?"

Emily shook her head. "There are no guarantees. This all is basically untested. But it was never my intent to harm you. In fact, I put my own life at risk to try and help you. If El Duro hadn't been taken down and news came to Martina that you had regained your memory, she would have had me killed." Emily smiled. "It's just her nature."

Aron sprung up, pacing back and forth across the room. He looked at Walker. "So, what are you telling me?"

Dr. Scott Walker smiled. "I'm telling you to go home and live your life. Your memories will most likely return on their own. But until then – you have to decide – is your past more important than your present and your future?"

***

When he returned to Tebow, Aron didn't get a chance to talk to Libby right away. People were already arriving. When he walked into the kitchen there were two women he didn't know – they looked familiar. He offered his hand. "I'm sorry, I'm Aron McCoy." They laughed.

"We're McCoy's too. My name is Pepper and this is my sister Ryder."

"Oh, Lord. I bet you're trouble." The two petite dark-haired girls laughed.

"We heard about your trouble and we're so glad you are back in one piece."

"Me, too." Footsteps coming through the dining room alerted him that their brothers were here in full force. He met Philip, who hadn't been able to go to Mexico due to his upcoming trial. Zane had briefed him on his cousin's trouble and he'd volunteered to do what he could to help as soon as he got his feet on the ground.

Kyle Chancellor and his team arrived and he began to wonder if they would have enough food. If their appetites all matched their size, they were in trouble. But when he looked over to what his Libby and the other's had laid out, he realized they were well acquainted with big men and their big appetites.

Beau and Harley had stayed in the area since the wedding; they'd been visiting friends in San Antonio. When they drove up, it seemed the party got started. No one could liven up a crowd like the Ragin' Cajun'. Joseph made a run to the airport, bringing in Patrick, Savannah, Philip Hawke and Jayco Johnson. Kane and Zane drove in with Lilibet and Presley. It wasn't long before music was playing and beer was flowing. The only ones who wouldn't be joining them were Roscoe, Vance and Revel. The PI's were on a case and Revel was still unable to travel because of his wound. Aron hadn't forgotten him though, and he had made sure his friend had everything he needed – no expense spared.

The group was in for a surprise when Brock Philips called from the airport and Joseph took off on another trip. When they pulled in, Libby had to force herself to be civil. She didn't know how she felt about Martina's family showing up at Tebow. She knew Aron had made it clear they had helped, but it was still hard.

Partying went on well into the night and Aron and Libby found their way onto the dance floor. He finally got the time to tell her what Scott Walker had said about his memory returning and until it did, they needed to decide what was important.

Libby had no problem doing that. "Let me tell you how I feel," she laid her head on his chest. "I want you. I want a future with you, Aron McCoy. The past doesn't matter nearly as much as what we have now. I ask you for today and all of your tomorrows – the yesterdays can take care of themselves."

His heart felt full. He looked around at his home and his family. Libby kissed him hard and ran to help take care of some minor crisis. His eyes followed her everywhere she went. She was so beautiful. Her smile would make the sun rise. It was obvious the other men appreciated her beauty too, because they seemed to hang on her every word. They laughed. They talked. In fact as he watched, he decided it was time to make sure everyone remembered exactly who that beautiful woman belonged to. Sauntering over to where she was – he gazed at his friends, his cousins and his brothers. Then he raised his hand. "Excuse me, I have something to say about my wife, Liberty Belle McCoy."

Everyone stopped. She stopped. They all looked at him.

Then he said one word.

An unmistakable word.

"Tag."

Libby's eyes widened. She began walking toward him – slowly. And as she did, it all came flooding back. He saw her rising like a siren from the stock tank, he heard her giggling as she begged him not to eat 'leon'. He remembered how it felt as he carried her in his arms to the hospital scared to death. He recalled making love to her in the hammock, holding back a laugh as she made friends with the other prisoners the night she went to jail for wrecking Shorty's bar. He saw her as she stood by Joseph when he was paralyzed, how she bent over Nathan when he learned to use the special computer programs to help with his dyslexia. He saw her walking down the aisle to him at their wedding. He even saw her wading into the deep the day their life fell apart.

"Do you remember?" Her voice was shaking.

He held out his hand. "I remember you, Libby. I remember falling in love with you. I remember asking you to marry me. I remember making love to you on our wedding night. In my heart, Libby, I didn't have to remember you, because I never forgot you for a moment. You are branded on my heart and on my soul forever."

Applause broke out as the McCoys and their friends celebrated the fact that Aron had finally come home.

230

EPILOGUE

"If you tell me to push one more time, I'm going to brain you with a frying pan!"

Aron wasn't laughing, honest to God, he wasn't. He was so happy his heart was about to burst. Colt McCoy had made his way into the world and Case wasn't far behind.

His beautiful Libby was brave and fearless. One moment she was facing down pain and the next she was casting tender looks at him and their baby.

"Here he comes!" The doctor gave them fair warning. When a lusty, strong baby cry rent the air, Aron McCoy shouted for joy.

"Yes, I love you!" He kissed his beautiful wife and gazed at the twin sons she had blessed him with. They had a life time ahead of them, a lifetime to make precious memories together. And he intended to enjoy every second of it.

Thinking back over all they'd been through, he lifted up his eyes to the heavens in gratitude. "Thank you. I wouldn't have missed this for the world."

Nathan's dream

ABOUT THE AUTHOR

Sable's hometown will always be New Orleans. She loves the culture of Louisiana and it permeates everything she does. Now, she lives in the big state of Texas and like most southern women, she loves to cook southern food - especially Cajun and Tex-Mex. She also loves to research the supernatural, but shhhh don't tell anyone.

Sable writes romance novels. She lives in New Orleans. She believes that her goal as a writer is to make her readers laugh with joy, cry in sympathy and fan themselves when they read the hot parts - ha!

The worlds she creates in her books are ones where right prevails, love conquers all and holding out for a hero is not an impossible dream.

Visit Sable:

Website: http://www.sablehunter.com

Facebook: https://www.facebook.com/authorsablehunter

Amazon: http://www.amazon.com/author/sablehunter

Hell Yeah! Series Reading Order
Cowboy Heat http://amzn.to/WhY6dw
Cowboy Heat Sweeter Version http://amzn.to/11fiBVQ

Hot on Her Trail http://amzn.to/U3zpT1
Hot on Her Trail Sweeter Version http://amzn.to/19m1WHf

Her Magic Touch http://amzn.to/11b1aw6
Her Magic Touch Sweeter Version http://amzn.to/1byKNL0

A Brown Eyed Handsome Man http://amzn.to/17zmNpY
A Brown Eyed Handsome Man Sweeter Version
http://amzn.to/15oW1k9

Badass http://amzn.to/UsrJJ4
Badass Sweeter Version http://amzn.to/16TqDNX

Burning Love http://amzn.to/15Z4Lyi
Burning Love Sweeter Version http://amzn.to/1iEzOV0

Forget Me Never http://amzn.to/U3PjwK
Forget Me Never Sweeter Version – Coming Soon

I'll See You in My Dreams http://amzn.to/11nsvpg
I'll See You in My Dreams Sweeter Version – Coming Soon

Finding Dandi http://amzn.to/12kK4Kh
Finding Dandi Sweeter Version – Coming Soon

Skye Blue http://amzn.to/1cixwWR
Skye Blue – Sweeter Version – Coming Soon

I'll Remember You
I'll Remember You -- Sweeter Version – Coming Soon

Thunderbird – Coming 2014

*Books in the Hell Yeah! Series are grouped by Hell Yeah!,
Hell Yeah! Cajun Style AND Hell Yeah! Equalizers

Cookbook
Sable Does It IN The Kitchen http://amzn.to/VAqFo4

Available from Secret Cravings Publishing
TROUBLE - Texas Heat I
My Aliyah - Heart In Chains - Texas Heat II
A Wishing Moon - Moon Magick I
Sweet Evangeline - Moon Magick II
Unchained Melody - Hill Country Heart I
Scarlet Fever – Hill Country Heart II

Bobby Does Dallas - Hill Country Heart
Five Hearts - Valentine Anthology - A Hot And Spicy Valentine

For more info on Sable's Up Coming Series El Camino Real
– Coming Out 2014
Check out Sable's Fan Page on Facebook
http://facebook.com/authorsablehunter

Made in the USA
San Bernardino, CA
24 December 2013